Dear Reader,

I am so excited about *A New Chapter*, the first book in the series Secrets of Mary's Bookshop. I loved writing this story and watching Mary's Bookshop come to life on the page. I wrote this book because I believe people should follow their dreams, and Mary's dream of opening a bookshop led to a wonderful new chapter in her life.

Like Mary, I recently relocated to help my husband follow his dream. After twenty-seven years of country life, my husband and I moved to the city, so he could begin a new career. It's been a big adjustment for both of us, but we're slowly settling in. We enjoy meeting new people and joined a new church family. I'm fortunate that my career allows me to work anywhere, so I didn't have to transition to a different job. But, boy, can I relate to Mary's new journey in life as she settles into the close-knit community of Ivy Bay and begins to make a new home there.

Mary and I have something else in common: We're learning and improving constantly. Mary realizes that she has some natural sleuthing skills, but as the story goes on, she learns how to refine those skills and, through every book, she'll be constantly refining. I felt the same way as I wrote. The more you write (and read!), the better a writer you'll be. The most important thing is to write the story that's in your heart. I loved learning to become a better writer as Mary grew to be a better sleuth. And, most of all, I hope you enjoy the ride!

Blessings to you,
Kristin Eckhardt

A New Chapter

SECRETS *of* MARY'S
BOOKSHOP

A New Chapter
Kristin Eckhardt

Guideposts
New York, New York

Secrets of Mary's Bookshop is a trademark of Guideposts.

Published by Guideposts
16 E. 34th St.
New York, NY 10016
Guideposts.org

Acknowledgments

Every attempt has been made to credit the sources of copyrighted material used in this book. If any such acknowledgment has been inadvertently omitted or miscredited, receipt of such information would be appreciated.

"From the Guideposts Archives" originally appeared in *Daily Guideposts 2009*. Copyright © 2008 by Guideposts. All rights reserved.

Cover and interior design by Müllerhaus
Typeset by Aptara

Printed and bound in the United States of America
10 9 8 7 6 5 4 3 2

A New Chapter

ONE

Mary Fisher opened her eyes and squinted against the light filtering in through the open window. The early morning sun reflected off the white wainscoting, and her bedroom was bright and cheerful, but something wasn't right.

She pushed herself up, rustling the crisp white sheets and throwing aside the chenille bedspread. She took her glasses from the wicker nightstand and slipped them on. Then she swung her legs over the side of the bed, slid her feet into her fuzzy slippers, and slowly straightened up.

"Gus?" she called. She glanced toward the dresser, craning her neck to see into the closet. The cat wasn't in the room. She padded out to the hall, her footsteps muffled by the soft slippers. "Where are you?"

Gus always slept at her feet. She couldn't remember a night he hadn't. At least not since John died. John had never allowed pets into the bedroom, but now that—

Mary took a deep breath. Tears welled in her eyes, and she rested her hand on the wall to steady herself. It would get easier. That's what everyone told her. Just give it time. Mary wasn't so sure, though. After a lifetime with him, she didn't think she could ever get used to waking up alone. She'd moved in with her older sister Betty when she'd relocated to Ivy Bay three weeks ago and was thankful to have her near. After another deep breath, she called out again.

"Gus!" She continued down the stairs and peeked into the living room. Betty had painted the walls a light gray, the color of the ocean when it washes ashore.

Gus wasn't there. She moved down the hall, walking toward the kitchen. He wasn't waiting by his food dish or pawing at the screen door. Where could he—

Then she spotted him, crouched down on the floor under the telephone, just as the phone began to ring. Mary marveled—Gus always seemed to be in the right place just as things were about to happen. The cat had a kind of sixth sense or something. Mary didn't actually believe in that stuff, but she couldn't deny Gus was always in the middle of the action. He quirked his ears up, pushed himself up, and gave a long, lazy stretch, arching his back.

Mary shook her head and grabbed the phone on the second ring.

"Mary?"

She recognized the voice immediately. Benjamin McArthur, Ivy Bay's chief of police, was a big man, but he had a kind voice, and he cared deeply for the people of his town. Mary had known him when they were both kids splashing in the waves, and she'd been pleased to reconnect with him after moving back last month.

"Chief McArthur, what's wrong?" She felt Gus rub against her legs, his soft gray fur soothing her heightened nerves.

"Could you come down to the shop?"

Mary could hear vague noises in the background—people talking and what sounded like a siren. "My shop?" An icy shiver ran down her spine. "Why?"

"I think you should come down here, Mary," he said gently.

She felt sweat bead on the back of her neck. There just couldn't be anything wrong with the shop, could there? She hadn't even opened for business yet.

"What happened, Chief?" She hoped he couldn't hear the pleading in her voice.

"You'll see when you get here, Mary. No use explaining things twice."

Mary stood still for a moment, trying to make sense of the conversation. Something was wrong with her bookshop. The store she'd put everything into.

"Okay. I'll be there as soon as I can," she said. She set the phone back in its cradle, scooped up Gus, who nuzzled against her shoulder and purred, and headed back to the bedroom.

As she made her way back down the hallway, she noticed that her sister's door was still closed. The phone hadn't awakened her or she'd be out here to question the early morning call. Betty often had trouble sleeping, so Mary didn't want to disturb her—not until she knew for certain that there was something to be disturbed about.

Her hands trembled as she dressed in her favorite khakis and a white turtleneck. She then put on a red cardigan. Only taking time to run a comb through her short, curly gray hair, she picked up her cat-carrying case and put Gus inside.

She carefully slung the bag over her shoulder, grabbed her bag and then walked back into the living room. She scribbled a quick note to Betty and left it on the hall table. Then she rushed out the door and onto the wide porch.

Mary paused on the first step. For the first time since she'd moved back to Ivy Bay, she didn't feel safe. She turned back, headed to the front door, and slipped her key into the lock, turning it until the dead bolt slid into place. Her car was parked on the driveway, but she walked past it. The bookshop was close. Driving would take as long as walking.

She hurried out past the white picket fence, turned down the cracked concrete sidewalk, and headed toward the village common. Between cottages edged with glorious climbing roses, she caught glimpses of the breathtaking blue of the bay.

She crossed a small stone footbridge, passing over a cranberry bog, which had been drained since its autumn flooding. Green vines grew thick along the bottom of the bog, and soon blossoms would burst forth, each guarding a berry. She often thought that the Lord had certainly saved a generous serving of beauty for Cape Cod. This morning, however, she didn't pay much attention to the view.

At the edge of the bog, Mary turned left onto Main Street, a wide boulevard in Ivy Bay. Her shop was about halfway down, and she craned her neck to see what was happening.

She flinched when she saw the small crowd gathered around a police car. Its flashing lights reflected in the windows of the neighboring shops. The bookstore looked like other cottages in the village, except for the wooden sign that hung over the door with the words *Mary's Mystery Bookshop*. The wooden storefront held a large, paned window, and there was a smaller window over the door. An elm tree stood in the grassy area between the street and the wide sidewalk, partially blocking her view of the shop.

A few neighbors called out to her, some wearing robes and slippers. Owen Cooper, the president of Ivy Bay Bank & Trust, stood in a green jogging suit, obviously out for an early morning run before the bank opened. Lori Stone, a local Realtor and the woman who had helped her buy the bookshop, was there too, with her miniature schnauzer Bitsy on a short leash.

What had happened to the shop? She didn't see any smoke, but maybe a fire had already been put out. As she got closer, she walked by the small crowd, and Susan Crosby, owner of the bakery next to Mary's shop, gave Mary a sympathetic pat on the arm as she passed. Normally, Mary would be delighting in the smell of baked goods coming from Sweet Susan's, but she barely noticed it as she smiled at the plump woman and continued toward her shop. She noticed a line of yellow police tape roping off the sidewalk in front of her store. Shards of glass littered the ground, reflecting the sun. Several of the panes of glass in the door were gone.

Chief McArthur met her at the entrance of the shop. His build almost filled the doorway. He was only a few years from retirement, and she was glad to have his experience now. He gave her a sympathetic smile as he ushered her inside the small bookshop.

"Mary, take a deep breath. It's going to look worse than it actually is." He stepped back to reveal the shop.

Broken glass dotted the wide pine floorboards in front of her, along the circular display table on which she planned to feature book specials and best sellers. The floor-to-ceiling bookcases that lined the walls hadn't been touched, but the shop had half a dozen freestanding bookcases, one of which was tilted, leaving a pile of dented hardcovers and creased paperbacks scattered on the floor. The braided rug near the children's section had been flipped aside, and half of it was now on the other side of the room, hung over the upended rocking chair.

Gus mewed sharply. With a mumbled apology, Mary set her bag on the floor, well away from the broken glass, and he darted out and started sniffing.

"What happened, Chief McArthur?" She ran her hand along the painted molding on the wall. At least the structure itself didn't appear to be damaged. Mary whispered a prayer of thanks that the intruder had come when no one was here. Yes, there was a mess, but things could be repaired or replaced. No one had been hurt. Gus moseyed around the corner, stopped and then pawed at the wall.

"Who would do this to my store?" she said, almost to herself.

The police chief gave a weary sigh. "Well, we had a couple of incidents of vandalism last night; some graffiti and that sort of thing. It was probably kids making trouble, since school let out for the summer." He surveyed the shop. "But can you tell me if anything was taken, Mary? That will help us figure out where to start."

Mary crouched down and picked up a book from the pile next to her. It was a cozy mystery by one of her favorite authors. She dusted it off and laid it down on a shelf. She drew back and shook her head.

"It will take me a while to make sense of all this. I'll have to look at my inventory records, to be sure." She bent down to pick up another book. The binding was cracked, as if it'd been stepped on. She gently set it back on the ground. Then she stepped around the pile of books and moved toward her gram's rocking chair, setting it carefully back into place. She ran her hands over the high crown-shaped back and scrolled arms, checking for damage, much like she used to do to her children after they'd taken a bad tumble.

After assuring herself that the rocker hadn't been damaged, she walked around the shop, switching on lights, peeking behind doors. The rolling ladder used to reach the top shelves was just where she'd left it the day before. She walked to the back reading area, where posters for story time were still propped on an overstuffed chair by the fieldstone hearth.

Then she noticed that the pine floorboards, usually hidden by the rug, had been swept clear of dust. Had the intruder tried to find something there? She tested each wide board with her foot. None of them had been loosened, and the original pegs hadn't been removed.

Mary took a deep breath as she went to the glass-fronted counter. In it, she had stocked valuable first-edition books, as well as displays showcasing Cape Cod and local authors. She smoothed one hand over the top of the satinwood case, surprised that it didn't seem to have been opened.

She turned to the chief and shrugged. "Nothing seems to be missing."

"How about from the till?"

"There's no money in it yet." She pulled her key ring out of her handbag. The key chain hanging from it banged against the drawer as she twisted a key in the lock. A quick glance into the neat drawer was all she needed. "As far as I can tell, everything's just where it should be."

"Well, that's good." Chief McArthur tipped his hat. "I'm sorry you have to deal with this mess, Mary, but I'll do what I can to find the vandals who caused it."

"Thank you," she said with a grateful smile. She headed toward a narrow closet to grab a broom and dustpan. "I'd better start cleaning up."

Gus started meowing as he continued his way around the shop.

The police chief moved to straighten the tilted bookcase. More books cascaded to the floor. He continued to maneuver the case but didn't have much luck straightening it. "I'm not sure if I'm making this better or worse," he said ruefully.

Mary chuckled and moved to help him. Together, they straightened the case. They had begun picking up the fallen books, when Gus let out an indignant yowl.

"Gus!" Mary shook her head. "Not right now, okay?"

He rubbed his face against the edge of a short satinwood bookcase near the front window and looked up at Mary expectantly.

"What is it?" she asked him as she walked toward the bookcase. Something crunched under her shoes. She stopped and lifted her shoe, surprised to see tiny shards of glass embedded in the sole. The broken window was on the other side of the shop, so where had this glass come from?

"Come here, buddy," she said, bending down to scoop Gus into her arms. "Are you okay?" She carefully checked each of his paws as Chief McArthur approached her. Somehow, Gus had avoided the tiny slivers of glass on the floor. Mary held him tightly in her arms, and he seemed content with her protection. She looked up at the front window and saw that it was untouched.

"What broke?" he looked around and then moved the short but heavy bookcase out from the wall a few feet, revealing larger shards of glass behind it.

Mary bent down to examine the broken glass, wondering, too, how it had gotten there.

"Careful," he said as he picked up some of the larger shards.

She looked up at the light coral wall in front of her and slowly rose to her feet. "Wait," she said, furrowing her brow. "There was a picture there." She pointed to the bare nail head protruding from the wall. "I hung it here just three days ago."

"Oh? What kind of picture?"

"It was an old photograph of the shop in an eight-by-ten-inch antique frame," Mary told him. "I found it stashed in a box in the cellar." She stared down at the broken glass and put a hand on her hip. "The intruder must have taken it off the wall and dropped it. That would explain the glass, anyway."

"Was it valuable?"

"Just to me and my family," she said, perplexed. "It was a photograph of the front of this building, taken about fifty years ago when my uncle owned it. Nothing particularly special, really."

"That's strange," he mused, rubbing the back of his neck. "Nothing was taken from those other two establishments that were vandalized. Why take something from you?"

She ran her eyes over the empty wall again, her heart beating faster. "Why would someone break in just to steal a dusty old photograph?"

TWO

◆◆◆

Mary and Chief McArthur had cleaned up the broken glass and examined the entire layout of the shop and had found nothing else missing. In the spirit of thoroughness, the police chief suggested they search the cellar. Mary was no fan of the basement, but she agreed that since she had found the photograph down there, there was good enough reason to take a look.

"I'll go first," he said with a teasing smile, clearly sensing Mary's trepidation.

They moved toward the cellar door. "Be careful," Mary said. "The stairs are not in the best shape."

Mary opened the door to the cellar, the hinges creaking. She reached over to flip on the light switch. "Let me grab a flashlight. It's pretty dark down there."

Chief McArthur waited while she retrieved a flashlight from the back room and then he led the way down the stairs. She left the door open behind her as she began to descend the steep staircase. The wood railing was smooth under her palm after two centuries of use.

"A few of these steps are loose," Mary warned, "and the second one from the bottom is the worst. I need to have Kip come back and reinforce them for me." Kip Hastings was the local handyman she hired to paint the shop shortly after she signed the mortgage. "Maybe he can fix the window at the same time."

The police chief hesitated before the second step from the bottom and then set one foot on it, the board wobbling under his weight. "It's loose, all right." He steadied himself and continued down the stairs. When he reached the bottom, he turned around to lend Mary a hand.

"Thanks," she said as she climbed down the last two steps.

One bare lightbulb glowed in the center of the room. Mary used the flashlight to illuminate the dark corners and recesses of the cellar. Some of the bricks in the cellar walls were loose, the mortar having fallen out years ago. A few even lay on the ground, leaving rectangular holes in the wall.

When she first saw the fallen bricks, she'd checked with the real-estate inspector before signing the mortgage to be sure the foundation of the building was solid. He'd assured her that the building was in superb condition, and that a few downed bricks were simply par for the course in an old building like hers. Overall, the place had been very well maintained over the years, considering the number of changes it had undergone.

She'd done careful research about the building and discovered it was over two hundred years old, built by a master craftsman of that era named Nathaniel Hardy. It had gone through several owners, beginning with a local apothecary and including her uncle George Nelson, who had run an auction house here in the 1950s. More recently, it had housed the county clerk's office and a law firm.

Mary had so many wonderful childhood memories of visiting the auction house with her cousin Jean, who was Uncle George's only daughter and one of her close friends. Those memories, along with the subtle proportions and architectural details of the historic building had made her fall in love with the place. She hadn't hesitated for a moment to sign the purchase papers. The place was perfect.

She and John had dreamed about opening their own business for years, and they'd decided a mystery bookshop would be the perfect enterprise to blend their talents. She'd handle the mystery books, and he'd handle the finances. During his short illness, John had enjoyed talking about their future bookshop and had insisted on giving her helpful tips about the financial side. More than anything, he'd wanted her to fulfill their dream after he was gone. And Mary had done just that—feeling as if he were with her every step of the way. A flutter of excitement rushed through her, even in the musty basement. She couldn't *wait* for the grand opening. She had scheduled for the shop to open in late June, just before tourist season typically began to gather steam.

"Does anything look different to you?" Chief McArthur asked, bringing Mary back to the present.

Some of the mortar crunched under her feet as she walked over the floor. "Not that I can tell. I don't see anything that wasn't here before." There were a few pieces of old furniture scattered throughout the cellar, including an armoire standing in the corner.

She pointed the flashlight beam toward the armoire. "That's where I found the box. It was filled with mostly junk—old cables and stuff. But if I hadn't dug through it, I never would have found the two framed pictures."

He turned to face her. "Two?"

She nodded. "There was a photograph of the back of the shop too. The frame was cracked, so I didn't hang it up." The picture had been less interesting than the one she had hung; there were no people in it, just a weedy backyard. She still intended to hang it, for sentimental value. But she also hadn't been in any real hurry to fix the cracked frame.

"Where is it?"

"I took it back to Betty's house—I mean, our house— planning to glue the frame back together, but I haven't gotten around to it yet." She still had to remind herself occasionally that she was living in her sister's house now too. The thought made Mary smile despite her present circumstance.

Chief McArthur walked the length of the cellar. "I don't see anything suspicious, and there doesn't seem to be much worth stealing." He turned toward the furniture. "Unless those are valuable antiques?"

Mary chuckled. "Not according to my sister. She's an antiques lover, and she said these pieces would be more valuable as firewood."

He laughed and then waved her ahead of him toward the stairs, following her as she ascended. After they returned to the main floor and shut the basement door behind them, Mary asked the chief about the next steps.

"I'm going to make a report, and you should file a claim with your insurance company. I'll be happy to send them a copy of the report, if they want one."

"What will the report say?" she asked.

"That some kids were making mischief around town. It isn't the first time," he said with a heavy sigh, "and probably won't be the last."

"And the picture?"

He shrugged. "Who knows why they took it? Kids do some pretty silly things." He surveyed the bookshop once more. "You should probably give Kip a call about temporarily boarding up that window and fixing the stairs. And please call me if you find anything else missing or have any questions."

"Thank you, Chief. I will." She walked to the door with him. "When can I take down the yellow tape?"

He opened the door. "I'll take it down after I clean up the glass on the sidewalk."

Mary stepped over the threshold. "Oh, it's okay. I can sweep that up."

He pulled a pair of sunglasses out of his shirt pocket. "Hey, it's the least I can do after this not-so-friendly welcome to Ivy Bay. I don't want you having second thoughts about moving back here."

She smiled. "I spent every summer here when I was a girl, remember? This was my second home, and now it's my first. It will take more than a broken window to drive me away."

"You never were one to run away." He chuckled. "I remember the time you stood up to Billy Donahue after he made fun of your grandma. I really thought you were going to deck him."

"I never got the chance," Mary replied with a wistful smile. "Gram might have been blind, but she still had two good ears and a mighty good aim. Poor Billy didn't know what hit him when she whacked her white cane across his behind."

The police chief snorted. "I've never seen a kid run so fast in my life. I'm still not sure who scared him more, you or your grandma."

Mary laughed. "I don't know, but he never bothered either of us again."

Chief McArthur grinned and then looked at his watch. "Glad to have you back, Mary." He donned his sunglasses and headed for his police car. "Cynthia is looking forward to seeing you again." Mary smiled. She'd always liked Benjamin's sister. "And my wife can't wait until your shop opens. She's a big reader."

"I so look forward to finally meeting her." Mary watched from the doorway as Chief McArthur retrieved a collapsible broom from his trunk and expanded the handle before sweeping up the glass on the sidewalk. He made quick work of it, took down the yellow tape, and waved to her as he got into his squad car and drove away.

Mary returned to her shop, closing the door behind her. Gus wove around her ankles until she bent down to pick him up.

She carried him to the antique shop counter with a glass display case that had come with the building. It was about six feet long and the back of the counter was full of small drawers and cubbyholes, except for a wide opening for her legs when she sat. Mary sat in one of the two comfortable, full-backed, and bar-height swivel chairs behind the counter. Although she was the only one working in the shop as of now, she assumed that someday she would need to hire an employee. The thought of such success gave her a stirring of excitement.

She booted up the desktop computer, which sat atop the counter on the opposite side of the antique cash register that Mary had bought the moment she set eyes on it.

She turned back to the computer. The question of why someone had stolen her photo gnawed at her. She tapped her fingers on the counter, when a thought occurred to her. She had scanned a copy of the photo onto her computer before hanging it on the wall. She knew the frames were fragile, so she had kept the frame intact as she scanned the photo. She worried there would be a glare from the glass, but thanks to good scanning software, the pictures turned out fairly clear on her computer.

She had wanted both photos on her computer so she could e-mail them to her cousin Jean. Uncle George had sold his business in 1960, and Mary knew her cousin would appreciate the photos, especially since Uncle George, Jean's father, was in one of them. Jean lived in Chicago, and the last time Mary had seen her was at Uncle George's funeral, only four months ago. Mary had e-mailed the photos to Jean with a note that said: "His legacy lives on. I will be hanging these in the shop. Love, Mary." Thinking of her uncle put a smile on her face and made her ever curious, and rather irritated, that someone had stolen that photo. She opened the computer files of the two pictures and selected the image of the stolen photograph, before turning on the printer. The police chief had suggested that perhaps the vandals had stolen the photo for no reason. But Mary couldn't understand that. Sure, kids will be kids. But what could they have possibly wanted with an old photograph of her shop? It didn't add up.

Had someone broken in specifically to steal that photograph? Nothing else had been taken, after all. It didn't make sense, but Mary had a hard time consenting to the idea that this break-in was a random act of vandalism. She hit the Print button. Maybe if she studied the photo, she could figure out a reason why someone would take it.

As the printer whirred into action, Mary pulled her cell phone out of her bag. The number for her handyman Kip was still in her phone, so she dialed it while the printer began to spit out the page.

The phone rang several times before diverting the call to Kip's voice mail. "Hey, you've reached Kip Hastings," the voice said in a thick New England accent. "I'm not available right now, but leave a message, and I'll get back to you soon."

"Hi, Kip, this is Mary Fisher. I'm hoping you can help me with a few repairs at the shop, including a broken window and some creaky stairs. Could you give me a call as soon as you can? Thanks, Kip."

Mary ended the call and set aside the phone. She looked over toward the wall where the photo had been stolen, and when she did, she noticed a small shimmer on the floorboard. A shard of glass remained.

The miniature broom and dustpan still leaned against the wall. Mary swept the small piece and did yet another search of the floor to make sure there were no more shards.

"He leadeth me, O blessed thought," Mary sang softly as she searched. "O words of heavenly comfort fraught. Whate'er I do, where'er I be, still 'tis God's hand that leadeth me."

The words of the hymn gave her comfort after the unsettling way she'd started the day. Mary loved to sing but couldn't carry much of a tune, so she saved her songs for the times when she was alone. When Mary was satisfied that there was no more glass on the floor, she put the dustpan away and began to sing the refrain. "He leadeth me, He leadeth me, by His own hand He leadeth me; His faithful follower I would be, for by His hand He leadeth me."

There were still a few piles of books on the floor, so Mary moved to pick them up. She had spent the past several weeks buying mystery books for the store, both new and used. It had been one of the more enjoyable experiences in her memory. She loved the classics, especially books by Agatha Christie and Dorothy Sayers, but she also loved to find new voices in the wide scope of the mystery genre. She'd attended estate sales and searched online for rare books that she knew mystery readers would seek out. And she'd purchased books from private sellers—people who loved books but needed to thin their bookshelves. She'd also met with sales representatives from big New York publishers and smaller, independent houses. They showed her their catalogs and helped her place orders for their upcoming books.

She placed the books on the counter in front of her and began checking them for tears or other damage. A few had loose bindings, so she set them aside to repair later. The rest seemed in good shape, other than a few bent pages.

When she picked up a copy of Agatha Christie's *The Secret Adversary*, one of her all-time favorites, she cracked it open, telling herself she'd only read the first couple of pages before getting back to work.

She was in the middle of the second chapter when the front door chimed and her sister walked inside.

At sixty-four, Betty had classic features that had worn well through the years. Her hair was the same honey blonde it had been four decades ago, when Edward Emerson had fallen in love with her. Edward had come from old money and his family had dedicated themselves to honing Betty into a "proper" Emerson. Mary loved and appreciated her sister's refinement, but sometimes Mary missed the good old Bets she knew still lived somewhere inside her polished sister; the Betty who had once made a homemade mud bath for them by filling a large hole in the ground with water from the hose. It was the first and only mud bath that either one of them had ever taken, and Mary still smiled at the memory of her teenage sister covered in mud from head to toe.

There wasn't a speck of mud on Betty now as she walked toward Mary. The white slacks she wore accentuated her slender figure, and the short-sleeved cashmere sweater matched the blue of her eyes.

"What happened?" Betty asked. "How did the door window break?"

Mary set down the book and wiped her brow with her forearm. "Someone broke in here last night."

"What?" Betty's mouth gaped. "Are you serious?"

"I'm afraid so. The police chief's phone call woke me up this morning. You must not have heard it."

Betty shook her head. "I slept really well—a blessed change."

Betty had been diagnosed with rheumatoid arthritis two years ago and sometimes struggled to sleep during flare-ups. She was never one to complain and didn't let the condition slow her down too much, but there were times Mary could see her sister was hurting.

"I can't believe it. In Ivy Bay of all places...." Betty looked around the shop. "So what did they take?"

"Well, that's the good news," Mary said. "Nothing techni- cally valuable was taken, just that photograph of the shop I had hanging on the wall."

Betty turned toward the empty wall, her long silence con- veying her disbelief. Finally, she spoke. "Really? How strange."

"I know. I have a display case full of valuable first editions and a brand-new computer at the front counter, but all they took was that old picture." Mary moved toward the counter. "Chief McArthur thinks it was just some kids goofing off. Apparently, there were a couple of other incidents last night, some graffiti on shopwindows and that sort of thing, but no- body else had a broken window or anything stolen."

"So he doesn't know who did it?"

"No, but he leans toward assuming it was just another case of vandalism." Mary moved toward the printer and re- trieved the photo she'd printed earlier. "I guess I'm not so sure. I did happen to scan the photo the other day, so at least I have a copy of it." She set the picture on the counter between them. "I keep trying to imagine why someone would want to steal this. Any thoughts?"

Betty fingered the string of pearls around her neck as she leaned closer to study the faded black-and-white photo of their uncle George standing at the storefront.

"I don't think so. But who is that woman?" Betty pointed to the woman standing next to Uncle George in the photo- graph. Mary had wondered the same thing when she initially saw the picture but figured it was probably one of the patrons of the auction house. "She's definitely not Aunt Phyllis."

"I know. I assumed it was one of Uncle George's clients." Mary studied the couple standing in the shade of the elm tree in front of the shop. Uncle George wore a gray flannel suit, the fedora hat on his head cocked at a rakish angle. The woman next to him was leaning one hand on a car parked in front of the shop and smiling up at Uncle George. She wore a knee-length swing dress and a pair of cat's-eye glasses. A child's bicycle leaned against the front of the brick building. The year 1957 had been scrawled in ink on the bottom-right corner of the photograph, and the building was undeniably the same one she and Betty stood in now. Mary looked again at the woman. At second glance, she had to admit that the pair seemed more comfortable than professional.

Mary looked at her sister. "You don't think she and Uncle George were—"

"Oh goodness, no," Betty exclaimed, though Mary noticed the slightest hint of doubt shadowing her expression. "No use even thinking such a thing. He and Aunt Phyllis were devoted to each other until the day she died—that's always been clear to us. Besides, people who have affairs don't usually pose for a picture together in public."

"Good point. Maybe Jean knows who she is. I suppose I could e-mail her and ask." Jean had replied to Mary's original e-mail with the pictures with a simple, "Thanks so much." But she had given no detailed explanation of the picture, and Mary hadn't asked for one. Mary had simply assumed that the picture captured an innocuous moment in time. Was there any reason to doubt that now?

"Jean will be in town next week," Betty reminded Mary. "She'll be working to get Uncle George's house ready to put on the market."

When their uncle passed away four months ago, after a long battle with heart disease, Mary had stayed at Betty's house for the funeral. That trip was the first time Mary had told her sister that she was thinking about moving to Ivy Bay and opening a bookshop. Betty had been thrilled and immediately began helping her formulate a plan.

Mary couldn't think of a more perfect place than Ivy Bay for Mary's Mystery Bookshop. It was here, during the summers she and Betty spent with their grandparents, that Mary had discovered wonderful stories by authors like Agatha Christie and Rex Stout. Every evening, her blind Gram would sit in her rocker and ask Mary to read mystery novels out loud to her. Mary was only twelve years old the first time she met Miss Marple; now she felt like an old friend.

Mary absentmindedly looked over the shop, her gaze settling on the rocking chair. "They tipped over Gram's rocker," Mary said to Betty, walking over to it, "but I don't think there's any damage."

A look of concern crossed Betty's face as she followed Mary to the chair. "I hope not. That thing is far too precious. Heavens, Gram used to rock us to sleep in it."

"And read us countless stories before she lost her sight," Mary added, caressing the scrolled arm of the rocker. "We wanted it in the bookshop to honor her, but not if there's a chance something could happen to it."

"Believe me, Mary, things like this just don't happen that often in Ivy Bay. Maybe the police chief is right—it's just some kids making trouble." Betty sat in the chair and rocked back and forth. "I think Gram would want her rocker in your bookshop. She'd be so proud of you."

Mary smiled, touched by Betty's words. "Maybe I should dig out her white cane in case those kids come back. She knew how to keep the naughty ones in line."

Betty laughed as she stood. "That she did."

Mary's stomach rumbled and she realized she hadn't eaten breakfast yet. She glanced at the wall clock, surprised to see that it was almost eleven o'clock. "How about lunch? My treat."

"I'd love to," Betty replied, "but Eleanor invited me to lunch with her today. We're going to the Chadwick Inn. You're welcome to join us."

Mary hesitated when she heard the name of Betty's sister-in-law. She appreciated the invitation but assumed that Mrs. Eleanor Emerson Blakely wouldn't appreciate Mary as a last-minute tagalong, especially at a place like the Chadwick Inn. It was one of the nicest restaurants in town and catered to wealthy residents and tourists alike. "Thanks, but I think I'll just grab a sandwich and bring it back here. I don't want to leave the shop unattended for long until the window is boarded over."

"Of course," Betty said. "Give me a call if you need anything."

"Thanks, I will." Mary walked back to the counter to check on Gus, who was curled up asleep in her chair. Certain he'd be fine, she picked up her handbag and followed Betty out of the shop. "I'll see you at home later."

"Okay," Betty said, turning left toward the Chadwick Inn while Mary turned right.

She started down the sidewalk toward the Tea Shoppe, a quaint little store two doors down that sold a wide selection of teas and included a small café. As she moved past the shady elm in front of her shop, the glare of the June sun blinded her for a moment, and she collided with a man headed in the opposite direction.

"*Ohhhh!*" Mary cried out in surprise, struggling to keep her balance.

"Whoa, there," the man said, reaching out to steady her. Strong hands gently grasped her shoulders as she found her footing once more.

She looked up at the man. He was about her age, with silver hair and sea-green eyes. "I'm so sorry. I…" Her voice trailed off. He looked so familiar.

"Mary Nelson!" A dimple flashed in his cheek as he smiled down at her. "I heard you were back in town."

Her heart skipped a beat. "Henry?"

THREE

enry Woodrow." Mary stared at him. "I hoped I would run into you."

"You probably weren't expecting it to be literal," he said wryly, dropping his hands from her shoulders and taking a step back. "Are you all right?"

"Yes, I'm fine," she said with a smile. Growing up, Henry had been one of her closest friends in Ivy Bay. She hadn't seen him since the last summer she spent with her grandparents before going off to nursing school. It seemed like a lifetime ago. It *was* a lifetime ago. "How are you, Henry?"

"Good, thanks," he replied. "I hear you're opening a new bookstore in town."

She nodded. "Yes, I'm so excited. It's called Mary's Mystery Bookshop, and I'll be selling new and used mystery books. My grand opening is in a couple of weeks. I hope you and your wife will come."

He hesitated. "I'll be there, but Misty..." He cleared his throat. "I lost Misty two years ago."

"Oh, Henry, I'm so sorry." Mary reached out to touch his arm. "I know how much it hurts." She took a deep breath, her own pain still fresh. "I lost my husband John this past year."

He took her hand and patted it, and an awkward silence settled between them as Mary's hand fell away. The silence lengthened as she struggled to find something to say. She and Henry used to be so comfortable with each other, talking and laughing all the time. They'd spent their teenage years going sailing and attending clambakes and taking in the weekly movie at the drive-in theater. He had even spent time with John, when they first started dating.

"I was just headed to the Tea Shoppe to pick up a sandwich," Mary said, finally breaking the silence.

"That sounds like a good idea. Do you mind if I walk with you?"

"Please do."

He fell into step beside her as she continued her way down the sidewalk. She looked across the street to the Black & White Diner. The popular restaurant, which had been around since Mary was a girl, was a staple on Main Street. Mary could smell the bacon from here and was tempted to suggest grabbing lunch there. She knew that the head waitress, Nicole Hancock, of the family who'd owned the diner for generations, would be ready for her with a cup of hot coffee. But she had already gotten the Tea Shoppe's delicious tuna sandwich stuck in her mind, so she continued heading that way.

When they arrived at the Tea Shoppe, Henry reached out to open the door for her. As they walked inside, Mary inhaled the fragrant scents emanating from the jars of spiced teas. Lace curtains fluttered at the open windows, and an antique china cabinet on the wall opposite the door featured a colorful array of teapots and matching cups. The store owner, Sophie Mershon, was occupied with a customer at the front counter. Thirty-year-old Sophie was tall and lithe, with a long blonde braid that hung almost to her waist. She'd danced with a Boston ballet company before moving to Ivy Bay to open the Tea Shoppe. Sophie smiled at them and held up one finger to signal that she'd be with them soon.

The café was nestled in the far corner of the shop. There were a few small mission-style tables with matching chairs scattered over the wide plank floor. A teacup-shaped chalkboard hung above the counter advertising the special quiche of the day.

Mary walked over to the refrigerated cooler that held several premade deli sandwiches and salads, and was surprised to find she wasn't as hungry as before.

Henry opened one of the sliding glass doors, grabbed a ham and cheese sandwich, and then turned to her. "What will you have?"

"I'll have the tuna fish sandwich, please," she said, figuring she could share it with Gus since they'd probably be at the shop until Kip could board up the window. She'd use that time to go through her inventory and make certain nothing else was missing.

Henry handed her the plastic-wrapped sandwich and stared at her for a long moment. "Is there something bothering you, Mary?"

She met his gaze, disarmed by the kindness in his green eyes. "Well...it's just..." Mary couldn't see any reason not to share the story with Henry. "Someone broke into my shop last night. They smashed the window on the front door and caused a bit of a mess. I'm afraid it's still got me a little rattled."

He frowned. "I can see why. Do you have any idea who did it?"

She shook her head. "The police chief believes it's probably the same kids who spray painted graffiti on a couple of the other shopwindows last night."

"But you don't?" he asked softly.

"I guess I'm not sure. It just seems so strange." She looked down at the sandwich in her hand, realizing she'd been gripping it too tightly. Loosening her grasp, she met Henry's gaze once more. She hesitated but then felt reassured that although many years had passed, she still trusted Henry implicitly. "They stole an old photograph off the wall. I'm still trying to figure out why. And they broke the window; they didn't spray paint graffiti on it. So it seems like a very different type of incident."

His brow crinkled. "Has the window been fixed yet?"

"Not yet. I've got a call into my handyman. I'm hoping to hear from him soon."

He moved toward the front counter. "Then I'm sure you want to get back to your shop."

Mary reached into her handbag for her billfold, but by the time she pulled it out, Henry was already paying for both sandwiches.

"My treat," he said before she could protest.

———

They walked back to her shop together, and Henry surveyed the broken window. "What a shame," he said. "Ivy Bay is such a safe town. It's a bit rattling when something like this happens."

Mary expressed her agreement as she opened the door. "They could have cut themselves on the glass, but there's no sign of injury anywhere." She turned around to see Henry standing in the threshold, his gaze slowly moving around the shop. A smile began to form.

"This is a beautiful place, Mary," he said at last with a New England accent that wasn't as thick as some, but distinct enough to make Mary feel right at home. "You've done an amazing job with it. Last time I was in here, it was the county clerk's office, and it looked nothing like this. A total transformation."

She felt herself blushing slightly as she followed his gaze, trying to see the shop through his eyes. Sunbeams danced through the windows on the west side of the shop, giving the satinwood bookshelves a warm, golden glow. The walls were the color of light coral and gave a softness to the room that contrasted nicely with the handcrafted white window frames and crown moldings.

Betty had helped her shop for the decorative throw pillows that now sat nestled in the two overstuffed chairs near the fieldstone hearth. The pillows incorporated the colors of the sea—turquoise, green, blue, and teal—in a lovely abstract design.

But the rows upon rows of books that neatly lined the bookshelves, just waiting to be read, were what Mary cherished most in the store.

The only thing that seemed out of place was her Gram's rocker. She loved the rich walnut finish of the rocker and the deep box-seat leather cushion that made it so comfortable. She'd set it near a window to take advantage of the natural light, but something wasn't quite right. Maybe she needed to get some flowering plants or something to make the reading area cozier.

Gus appeared at her feet and looked up at the sandwich in her hand, his nose twitching. She looked over at Henry, realizing she'd gotten lost in her thoughts. "I'm sorry, Henry. I tend to think too much."

He just smiled. Then he looked down at the cat. "And who's this little guy?"

"This is Gus," she said with a warm smile. "And I think he's ready for lunch." She gestured toward the front counter. "Do you have time to sit down and eat with me?"

He checked his watch. "I guess I've got a few minutes. I was on my way to the bank when we bumped into each other. I'm scheduled to give a charter fishing trip on my boat this afternoon and was trying to run a few errands first."

"Please have a seat. I'll be right back." Mary set her bag and sandwich on the table, and then hurried into the small back room. She'd furnished it with the floral love seat from her home in Boston, along with a dorm-style refrigerator and a microwave oven that sat on a small table. The corner sink with the mirrored medicine cabinet above it was already there when she moved in.

She retrieved two water bottles from the refrigerator and grabbed a small bowl, wishing her beverage station was ready. She planned to serve complimentary tea and coffee to her patrons, but she hadn't stocked it yet.

When she returned, Henry was already seated at one of the chairs behind the counter and was unwrapping his sandwich. She felt a twinge of delight that he had already made himself comfortable. It was exactly what she had hoped for the shop, a place where people could feel at home.

Gus sat patiently in the other chair staring at the wrapped tuna sandwich in front of him.

Mary set the water bottles on the counter, quickly opened her sandwich and scraped half the tuna into the bowl. Gus moved to the floor where he waited for his lunch before she even had time to set the bowl down.

Henry chuckled. "Looks like he's as hungry as I am."

Mary settled into her chair and picked up her sandwich. "So tell me more about your business."

"Well, once in a while, I charter fishing trips," Henry said as he unscrewed the cap from his water bottle.

The word *charter* sounded more like "chah-teh."

"But most of the time, I supply fish for local restaurants and shops." He took a swig from the water bottle. "How about you? What did you do before you came to Ivy Bay?"

Mary still couldn't believe it had been so long. "Well, for the last thirty-some years, I was a librarian in Boston. And I loved every minute of it."

His brow crinkled. "I thought you were going to be a nurse?"

She chuckled. "That's right. I had almost forgotten about that. I attended a year of nursing school, but then my son Jack came along, and I wanted to be home with the kids, at least during their early years. The next thing I knew, I had Elizabeth too. By the time they were in school, I'd decided to become a librarian instead of a nurse."

Mary took a bite of her sandwich and chewed thoughtfully. "For me, there's no bigger thrill than helping someone develop a lifelong passion for reading."

He looked around him. "And now you're continuing that mission."

"I hope so." She set down her half-eaten sandwich. "Now what about you? Did you and Misty have children?"

"Twin girls—Karen and Kimberly," he said proudly. "They're both married now. Karen lives in Richmond and works as a CPA, and Kim is in Boston trying to keep up with my two grandsons. I try to visit them as often as I can."

"I've got three precious grandchildren myself," Mary said. "Daisy, Emma, and Luke. Daisy is Jack's daughter and they're in Chicago, where Jack works as a pediatrician, so I don't get to see her as much as I'd like, but Lizzie's family is in a suburb of Boston."

Henry finished off the last of his sandwich. "Maybe they can spend the summer with you sometime, like you and Betty used to do with your grandparents."

"Now that's a great idea," Mary said. "And how is Annie?" she asked, referring to his cousin who had played with them as children.

"She good. She lives in Wellfleet now. She has a grown daughter."

"I always liked her," Mary said.

Henry nodded and then crumpled up the plastic wrap on the counter in front of him and stood up. "I'd better get going. Duty calls. It was nice seeing you again, Mary."

She rose to her feet and patted his shoulder. "You too, Henry."

Henry walked toward the door, his gaze focused on the window once more. "If your handyman doesn't come through today, give me a call." He fished a business card out of his shirt pocket and handed it to her. "I can come over and board that window up myself, if you need me to." He straightened his shoulders in a pretend show of machismo. "I pride myself on being handy."

"Well, that's good to know, Henry. Although you may regret telling me, because I may just need your help once in a while," she said with a playful grin.

"That's the idea," he said, growing slightly serious.

She tried to ignore the flushed feeling that came over her as she took the card from him. She met his gaze again. "Thanks for lunch, Henry. It's *so* nice to see you."

He walked out the door. "You take care, Mary."

Mary walked over to the west window and watched him cross Meeting House Road on his way to Ivy Bay Bank & Trust, which sat right across the street from her shop. Then she glanced down at the card he'd given her. It read Woodrow Fishery in bright blue letters across the top and included his telephone number, e-mail address, and the name of his boat, *Misty Horizon*.

Mary walked over to her bag and tucked the card inside. Then she looked at Gus, who was now sitting in her chair looking at her half-eaten sandwich. She laughed. "Okay, you can have the rest. But then we have to get to work."

———

Later that afternoon, Mary watched Kip test the small plywood board he'd placed over the broken window. Mary guessed that Kip was in his early thirties, with his average build and short, curly brown hair.

"That should do it, Mrs. Fisher," he said, stepping back from the window. "It's tight enough to keep rain or anything else from getting in here until we get the glass replaced. I called the glazier on my way over, and the earliest he can be here is Friday, if that works for you."

"Sure," Mary replied. "And thanks again for getting here so quickly."

"Oh, it's really no problem," Kip said sincerely. He had such a sweet demeanor it was almost as if he had all the time in the world. His calm, almost bashful attitude was certainly a nice trait to have in a handyman.

She breathed in a familiar scent and wondered if he used the same aftershave her husband had always worn. "Back in Boston, we'd have to wait days, sometimes even weeks, for a handyman to put us on his schedule."

"Well, I knew that this was an emergency," Kip said sympathetically, "so I moved you to the top of my list." He looked around the bookshop. "I guess it's good that the damage was only minimal."

"Well, that's true. Although there was more damage than just the window. I'm hoping you can help repair those things too." Mary pointed out the bookcase that had been tilted during the intrusion. She'd picked up the books that had fallen out of it and stacked them in piles around the shop. "I've also got a couple of steps leading down the cellar that need reinforcing. Any chance you can take on these projects before my grand opening in a couple of weeks?"

"I'm happy to help. The more jobs the better, anyway," he said. "I just got engaged and, well, money's a little tight right now. I'm happy to do whatever I can for you."

"Oh, Kip, congratulations! What's her name? Is she from Ivy Bay?" Mary stopped the questions before more flowed.

It was amazing how she, like so many women she knew, turned into practically a schoolgirl at the mention of young love.

He gave a small laugh. "Yes, she lives just north of Main Street, where I'll be living after we get married. Her name is Heather Wade and she's a dental assistant."

"Oh, that's wonderful. Have you set a date?"

"We're thinking maybe sometime around Christmas, although she's worried that won't be enough time to plan everything and figure out how to put two households together."

"I know what that's like," Mary said sympathetically. It had been a bit tough to combine households with her sister. They were still working out the kinks even weeks after the move.

Kip checked his watch and then moved toward the door. "I've got to run. Why don't you make me a list of everything you want done, and give me a call when you're ready for me to begin."

"Sounds great. Thanks again, Kip," Mary said.

Gus padded over as Kip said good-bye. "See ya later, little fella." The bell above the door chimed on Kip's way out.

"We'll be done here soon," Mary promised the cat, retrieving the inventory list she'd set aside when Kip had arrived.

After her lunch with Henry, she'd spent the afternoon checking each book on the shelves against the list. To her relief, all of them were accounted for.

There were still several boxes of new books stacked in the back room that needed to be stamped, cataloged, and shelved, but the seals on the boxes were still intact, so she knew no one had tampered with them.

A yawn escaped her as she placed the inventory list on the counter. She glanced at the clock, realizing she'd been at the shop for almost ten hours. Chief McArthur's phone call seemed like it had happened days ago instead of only this morning. She made a note on a Post-it to write a list of needed repairs for Kip next time she came to the store. She was too beat to think of it all now.

"It's time to go back home," she said out loud, pleased at the sound of calling Betty's house her home. Gus bounded over to her, and she lifted him up and placed him inside his bag. She slung it over her shoulder, picked up her handbag and then double-checked the back door to make sure it was securely locked.

As she returned to the front of the store, her gaze moved to the board over the door window. She was so grateful for Kip and Henry, both of whom had been willing to come to her aid to board up the broken window. But she still didn't understand *why* someone had broken it.

"Thank You, Lord," she prayed softly, "for giving me helping hands in my time of need. Please help me to make sense of all this. Amen."

FOUR

The next morning, Mary sat on the blue-and-white-striped damask sofa in the living room, basking in the warmth of the sun shining in through the arched Palladian windows. Gus lay beside her, his tail twitching whenever he heard a bird chirping outside.

The living room looked out over the wide finger of water flowing into the marsh that divided the house from the beach. Grasses sprouted on the dunes, and the golden sands welcomed the soft waves. Mary loved to sit with Betty in this room, where they could look out at the sea. At nights, she loved to read, to think, to pray, and to remember.

She'd done a lot of thinking last night, even taking a moonlit walk on the beach as she tried to figure out why someone would break into her shop and steal that photo. The copy she'd printed out now sat on the table next to her. She picked it up, studying the picture once more. The image looked innocent enough, but there was something about it that gnawed at her.

Gus leaped off the sofa and onto the floor, curling himself around her feet. She reached over to brush away a few gray cat hairs he'd left behind on the sofa. Betty didn't like cat hair on the furniture. In fact, she'd been clear that she didn't really like having a cat living in her house, but she'd accepted Gus on Mary's promise that he was a perfect gentleman. So far, he'd been just that.

Betty had decorated the two-story, Federal-style house herself, from top to bottom. The living room walls were painted a light, calming gray and accented with white wood-work and corner-block medallions. All her furniture was in the Federal style, from the curved-back sofa to the antique wing chairs and the candlestick end tables.

When Mary moved in, her own furniture had looked so plain in comparison that she'd decided to sell most of it rather than ask Betty to make room for it. The only thing Mary had insisted on keeping was Gus. He'd quickly made himself right at home, although he seemed to sense when Betty was near and never let her find him on the furniture.

Mary glanced over her shoulder to see Betty walk into the living room.

"Oh, hi, you're still here," Betty said, smiling at Mary. "I thought you'd left for the shop already."

"Not yet." Mary set the picture in her lap. "I had some trouble sleeping last night, so I'm getting a late start this morning."

"I figured as much since you were still out on your walk when I went to bed." Betty sat down in the wing chair op-posite her. "I noticed that you forgot to activate the security system when you came back in."

Mary winced. "Oh, I'm sorry. Honestly, I just keep for-getting about it."

"Don't feel bad," Betty said, waving off the apology. "You'll get the hang of it soon enough. When Edward first

installed it, I'd forget about it too. I felt that it was so unnec-
essary, but Edward was always very protective of me. Now it's
just part of my bedtime routine."

A routine Mary had altered with her walk on the beach
last night. The security system was only activated at night.
Ivy Bay was as safe a town as they came, but people were still
people. Some of whom, as evidenced by the break-in, were
worse than others.

"So what are your plans for the day?" Mary asked.

Betty leaned forward, her hands clasped together on her
knees. "The first thing on my list is a trip to the library. Did I
tell you that Eleanor asked me to join her book club?"

"No." Mary cocked her head to one side. "You don't
sound very excited about it."

Betty sighed. "I'm just not sure we have the same tastes in
books. I'm sure you know what I mean since you met them
the other day."

Eleanor and her fellow book club members had come for
a tour of her bookshop a few days ago. They were a small,
exclusive group of four women, all in their late sixties to
midseventies, and some of them seemed less than impressed
by the selection of books Mary had to offer. Betty's sister-in-
law had introduced each one precisely, taking special note
of their clearly prestigious backgrounds. There was Virginia
Livingston, a descendant of one of the founding families of
Ivy Bay; Frances Curran, a retired literature professor from
Dartmouth College; and Madeline Dinsdale, a prominent
local artist. Eleanor was the head of Ivy Bay's Chamber of
Commerce, and Mary suspected it was important to her to be
closely associated with the neighborhood elite.

"They seem to prefer books that confuse readers rather than entertain them," Betty continued and then chuckled. "They confuse *me*, anyway, but I figured I should give it a chance. They are interested in mysteries, after all," she added with a wink. Then she nodded toward the printout on Mary's lap. "So have you learned anything else from that picture?"

Mary smiled. "I should have it memorized by now, shouldn't I?" She stared down at it for a long moment. Then she tapped one finger on the bicycle in the photo, suddenly pinpointing what had been gnawing at her. "I think this is the bike that I used to borrow from Toad."

Betty covered her mouth, unable to contain her laughter. "Oh my goodness, I can't believe you still call him that!"

"I guess he'll always be Toad Milton to me," Mary said fondly. The Milton family had lived next door to their grandparents in Ivy Bay. Toad, whose real name was Todd, had fit squarely in between the two sisters, being a year younger than Betty and a year older than Mary. He and Mary used to play marbles together, although he'd always preferred Betty's company. He'd often tried to get rid of Mary by offering to let her ride his bike, a candy-apple-red Schwinn Phantom with a horn mounted on the handlebars. "Does Toad still live in Ivy Bay?"

"Yep," Betty said. "That's why it's funny for me to hear you call him Toad. *Todd* is an important member of the community!" Betty chuckled. "He and his wife run a bed-and-breakfast called the Beacon Inn. It's on Colonial Road." Betty walked over and sat next to Mary. She took a look at the photo. "Are you sure that's his bike?"

"Not 100 percent, but the frame looks the same and it has whitewall tires, just like Toad's bike had. And the horn is in the same spot on the handlebars."

"It never ceases to amaze me how you always remember the tiniest of details."

Mary shrugged. "Well, I didn't remember this until just a few seconds ago. I loved riding that bike."

"I suppose it's possible it is the same one."

Mary looked up at her. "I wonder if Toad might have any thoughts about the photograph. Maybe by some chance he took the picture. Or perhaps he'd know who the woman in the photograph is. He was always hanging around the auction house in those days."

"Who knows what he might remember," Betty said in agreement.

Mary folded the photocopy and slid it into the bag at her feet. Then she scooped up Gus and placed him inside as well, ready to start her day, first by visiting her old friend. "I mean, what else do I have to go on? And anyway, if nothing else, I'll renew an old acquaintance."

Betty walked with her to the front door. "Just remember not to call him Toad. He was never very fond of that nickname."

"You got it," Mary said as she headed outside.

Daisies and tulips splashed a bright palette across the yard and a line of rhododendrons separated Betty's house from their nearest neighbor, Sherry Walinski.

Sherry stood on her lawn watering the flowers in front of her house. She was a tall, slender woman with green eyes and red hair styled in a cute pixie cut. Mary had met her once and learned that Sherry worked as a secretary at the high school and was a single mother to two teenage boys. According to Betty, her husband had walked out on her not too long ago, but Sherry's deep faith and cheerful demeanor carried her through the tough times.

Mary walked over to the rhododendrons to greet her.

"Hello there, Mary," Sherry called out. "Isn't it a gorgeous day?"

"It's beautiful. How are Nate and Tyler?"

"They're good, from what I hear. They're spending a few weeks with their father." She turned off the hose. "I miss them, but it's nice to have a little time to myself. I'm really looking forward to my summer vacation."

"Hasn't it started already?"

"It's started for the kids and the teachers," Sherry explained, "but the principal and I keep working for another several weeks after school's over. It gives us time to make sure all the graduating seniors have what they need for college and gives the annual staff time to put the finishing touches on the yearbook."

Mary nodded. "My daughter worked on the yearbook staff when she was in school. It kept her hopping."

Sherry began rolling up the hose. "How about you? Does your shop open soon?"

"My grand opening is in two weeks." Just saying the words made Mary feel almost electric with anticipation. "I hope you can stop by."

"I'm planning on it. I can't wait to see it." Sherry glanced at her wristwatch. "Oops, I'd better get to work if I don't want to be late. Nice to see you, Mary."

"You too, Sherry." Mary walked over to her silver Impala sitting in the driveway and carefully set the bag inside before climbing in. She pulled out of the driveway and headed toward Colonial Road, wondering if Toad—er, Todd—would think she was silly for asking him about the bicycle in the picture.

Mary crested a small hill and saw a historic inn located just ahead. A hand-painted signpost on the front lawn read Beacon Inn. She parked the car along the curb, grabbed the photocopy out of her handbag and cracked the window for Gus before climbing out.

The inn was a large two-story white house with dark green shutters adorning the windows. A lush bed of sunny yellow daylilies bordered both sides of a cobblestone walkway that led to the wide front porch. She could smell cinnamon and the savory aroma of bacon before she even knocked on the door.

A few moments later, the door opened and a stocky, barrel-chested man stood on the other side. His hair was gray now instead of brown, and he wore a Hawaiian shirt and a pair of knee-length khaki shorts instead of bib overalls, but it was the wide-set, slightly bulging gray eyes that made Mary instantly recognize her childhood playmate.

"Hello, Todd," she said with a smile. "Remember me?" She playfully put her arms out as if presenting herself.

He stared for a long moment. Then his eyes widened, and a smile spread across his face. "Mary Nelson! I heard you were moving to Ivy Bay to open some kind of store. Welcome back!"

She gave Todd a warm hug and then stood back. "Yep, that's right. I moved back three weeks ago and have been busy preparing to open my new mystery bookshop. Betty and I were just talking about you this morning, so I decided to stop by and say hello."

"I'm so glad you did." He opened the door wider. "Please come in. We finished serving breakfast about an hour ago, so most of the guests are out and about. I wish you could meet my wife Bev, but she left a few minutes ago to go to the market."

"Oh, I'm sorry I missed her," she said, walking inside. "I'm on my way to the shop, so I won't take up too much of your time."

He led her into a parlor with a tin ceiling and a fireplace so high and deep that she could easily fit her five-foot-one-inch frame inside the square opening. Antique furnishings filled the rest of the room, adorned with plush velvet uphol-stery in rich jewel tones.

"Oh, Todd, this is lovely," she said, admiring the detailed woodwork around the beveled glass windows.

He beamed. "Thank you. We've done a lot of work to the place. It was built in 1760, and we've been able to restore a lot of the original woodwork and architecture."

She took a seat on a sapphire-blue settee. "It's so beautiful."

"Thanks. We love it. The best part is that we've got plenty of room when the kids come to visit. We have two boys and a girl, and they've each got kids themselves, so it's quite a houseful when we all get together."

"That sounds wonderful. I have two children and three grandchildren as well. They're sure fun, aren't they?"

He grinned. "Fun, but not as fun as we were. Video games and the like." He looked nostalgic. "Boy, you took some of my best marbles, didn't you?"

She laughed. "My, that was a long time ago. But it doesn't always seem that way, does it?"

"It sure doesn't. Some days I wish we could go back to that simpler time."

"Me too," Mary said, before fishing the photocopy from her pocket. "Speaking of the good old days, I have something I wanted to ask you about." She tentatively showed the picture to him and waited a moment while he studied it.

"Well, look at that…my old bike," he said. Then he looked up at her with another wave of nostalgia crossing his face. "Where'd this come from?"

"Pretty cool, isn't it? I found it in my shop, which is the same building my uncle George used to own."

"Of course," he said, still gazing at the photo. "And there's your uncle. But who's the woman?"

Mary swallowed a sigh of disappointment. "You don't recognize her? I was hoping you might be able to tell me."

He slowly shook his head. "She doesn't look familiar, but like we said, that was a long time ago. My memory's not as sharp as it used to be." Then he looked up at Mary. "What's this about, anyway?"

Mary hesitated, torn between telling her old friend everything and keeping some of the details to herself. At last, she said, "Well, I found the original of this old photograph in my shop and started wondering about it. I didn't recognize the woman either, but I was hoping you might."

He handed the photocopy back to her. "I wish I could help, Mary. The only thought I have is that she'd have to be in her seventies by now, if she's still around."

Mary agreed. "You're right. I wonder if she's still in Ivy Bay and how she knew my uncle."

He grinned. "You sound like a detective in those mystery novels we used to read."

"*Used* to read?" she said, laughing. She supposed it did seem a little curious, coming here and asking about a strange woman in a photograph. Technically, she supposed she should leave that work to the experts in the police department. But with Chief McArthur's conjecture that it was just a random incident, she knew she couldn't rely on them to sniff around about this relatively insignificant photograph.

Mary rose to her feet. "Well, Toa—, I mean, Todd, it sure was nice seeing you again." She was glad she corrected her near mistake of calling him Toad, but the wry smile on his face showed that he'd been expecting it.

"You too, Mary. Feel free to come by anytime."

"Will do. And please do bring your wife to my shop sometime so I can meet her. I'm having a grand opening soon."

She walked to the door. On her way out, she noticed a beautiful rustic wall sconce mounted by the front door. "What a gorgeous sconce," she said.

He looked at her with a curiously proud smile. "You want to know the best part about it? This'll really satisfy the mystery lover in you," he said conspiratorially, leaning in and talking slightly more quietly. "The sconce doubles as a security camera." He pointed to the sconce. "See that little silver bead at the bottom of the brass lamp?"

Mary couldn't help but smile at Todd's enthusiasm over technology, so she played along, moving in for a closer look. "That's it? It's so tiny."

Todd nodded proudly. "Exactly. It gives a wide-angle view of the front porch."

She smiled up at him, but she was thinking of her own break-in. "Do you worry about safety?"

He shrugged. "Not really. With so many people coming and going, I like the added security."

"Well, I don't blame you one bit," Mary said. She wished she'd had a security camera at her shop so she could simply see who broke in, but it certainly wasn't worth what she assumed would be a rather hefty expense. Surely this kind of thing wouldn't happen repeatedly.

Todd's cell phone rang, which gave them both an excuse to part ways. "I should take this, but I'll see you again soon, Mary."

"I'll look forward to it."

Todd took the call, and Mary walked back to her car. She placed the photocopy back into her bag. It had been nice seeing Toad again and catching up on his life, but she was a little disappointed that he couldn't identify the woman in the photograph. Although what did she expect? Maybe it was just one of those mysteries that would never be solved.

FIVE

Mary arrived at the bookshop just as a delivery truck appeared at her door.

"Good morning," the young man in the brown uniform said. "I've got three packages for you."

"Wonderful," Mary exclaimed as she unlocked the door.

He walked in behind her, carrying one of the boxes. "Where do you want me to put these?"

"Could you set them on the counter?" Mary asked.

"Sure thing." He placed the box on the counter. Then he approached her with a clipboard. "I just need your signature, ma'am."

"Please call me Mary," she said, taking the clipboard from him and signing her name. "I have a feeling we'll be seeing a lot of each other if this is your regular route."

He grinned. "It is, starting this week. I'm Joe, by the way."

She smiled as she handed him the clipboard. "It's nice to meet you, Joe. Thank you so much for carrying these boxes inside for me."

"Hey, I'm glad to do it." He walked out and then brought in two more boxes. "You have a nice day," he said, giving her a final wave as he headed for the door.

"You too," she called after him.

Then she turned to the unopened boxes. The address labels told her they were from an online bookstore, and Mary was sure these were more books she'd ordered a week ago. Each time she received a shipment of books for her shop, it felt like Christmas morning.

Mary opened the first box, peeking inside to see the glossy covers of some of her favorite mysteries. There were books by Elizabeth Peters, Raymond Chandler, and Lilian Jackson Braun, along with a handful of Encyclopedia Brown books.

She began lifting them out of the box and setting them on the counter. Gus leaped up on the marble top and began pawing at the Lilian Jackson Braun books.

"Are those your favorite?" Mary asked him. Braun was known for her series of "The Cat Who..." mystery novels, and Mary enjoyed the exploits of the two Siamese cats in the series, Koko and Yum-Yum.

Mary began humming a favorite hymn as she set the rest of the books on the counter. She arranged them in alphabetical order by author and then placed them behind the counter to catalog later.

She disposed of the boxes and used a soft dust cloth to wipe the fine cardboard fibers off the marble counter. Then Mary moved to the nearest bookshelf and began dusting the satinwood shelves until they shone, finding it more a pleasure than a chore.

"Thank You, Lord," she said out loud, "for giving me work that I love and the means to make my dream come true. May this work be a blessing to everyone who enters my shop. Amen."

As the morning wore on, Mary kept looking at the empty space on the wall where the photograph had hung and she wondered if the vandals had been caught yet. Even if she never recovered the photograph, she still wanted to know why they took it.

Soon her curiosity got the best of her. She grabbed her bag and headed for the door, ready to find out if Chief McArthur had any new information. "You stay here, Gus. I'll be back soon."

The police station was located just off Main Street in a modern, white concrete-block building that stood out like a weed in a flower garden among the more historic colonial and Victorian-style buildings that surrounded it.

When Mary walked inside, she found the interior of the building a little cozier, with its sage-green walls and wide-plank floor. The wooden desks and chairs in the small reception area were thick and sturdy but bore the scars of heavy, prolonged use.

"I'm Mary Fisher," she told the young, crew-cut deputy seated at the front desk. His name was Bobby Wadell, according to the name tag pinned to his shirt. "Is Chief McArthur here?"

The man nodded without looking up from his computer screen. "He's in a meeting right now, but he should be finished soon, if you'd like to wait."

"Thank you, I will." Mary selected a chair near the door and fished *The Secret Adversary* from her bag. The story was set in post–World War I England and featured a young, adventurous couple named Tommy and Tuppence who unknowingly stumble upon a mystery.

Mary opened the book with a contented sigh, even while surrounded by the quiet buzz of the police station. She loved how, in the Tommy and Tuppence mysteries, Agatha Christie had aged them in real time. The fictional detective duo were in their early twenties in the 1922 release of *The Secret Adversary* and in their seventies when the last story featuring the couple, *Postern of Fate*, was released in 1973.

One of the things she enjoyed most about mystery novels was guessing what the characters were going to do next and seeing if she could solve the crime before the protagonist did. Even though she'd read all of Agatha Christie's books several times, Mary often found a new clue each time she reread a story. It had taught her an important lesson about looking at something more than once if you really wanted to get the full picture.

She'd even started a mystery novel of her own years ago, but it still sat in a drawer in her desk in her bedroom, less than half finished. No matter how hard she tried, her fledgling story just didn't seem to measure up to the classic mysteries she enjoyed so much.

She began to read where she'd left off. Too soon, she heard her name being called.

"Mrs. Fisher?" Deputy Wadell said. "Chief McArthur will see you now."

"Thank you." Mary closed the book, stuck it back into her bag and walked to the police chief's office.

The door was open, and the chief was seated behind a black steel desk with a walnut top. He pushed his chair back and stood up when he saw her enter; the beige shirt of his uniform was neatly pressed and the silver badge pinned to it gleamed in the sunlight streaming through the window.

"Hello, Mary." He motioned to the chair opposite his desk. "Please have a seat."

"Hello, Chief McArthur. I hope this isn't a bad time." She sat down, noticing the neat pile of folders stacked on his desk. "I just wanted to check in and see if you've discovered anything new about the break-in at my bookshop."

He leaned back in his chair. "Well, I talked to Phil Custer. She's a photographer who owns the Frame Shop."

"She?" Mary said, wondering if she'd misunderstood him.

The police chief smiled. "Her full name is Philippa, but she goes by Phil. Anyway, it seems Phil was out on Little Neck Beach just before dawn yesterday taking some pictures when she saw a couple of boys running around with cans of spray paint. They fled when they saw her."

Mary leaned forward, intrigued by this new information. "Did she recognize them?"

He shook his head. "I'm afraid not. Phil didn't think they were from around here. She said they were a couple of runts, probably around twelve or thirteen."

"I see." She sat back, disappointed. "So what happens now?"

He shrugged. "There's not much else I can do, I'm afraid. Not unless somebody can identify them or they confess." He reached for a sheet of paper on his desk and handed it to her. "I did finish the police report for your insurance company, if that helps."

"It does." Mary took the report from him. "Thank you for getting it done so quickly." She'd have to pay a small deductible, but at least the majority of the repair costs would be covered by her property insurance. She briefly skimmed through the report, noting that he'd listed vandalism as the reason for the damage. The report seemed so nice and tidy, yet she still had so many questions.

He rose from his desk. "Thanks for stopping in, Mary. I'm sure you won't have any more trouble. Those boys are probably vacationing here with their families, and I'm sure they got spooked when Phil spotted them with those spray paint cans."

"I hope you're right," she said, rising out of her chair.

The questions that nagged at Mary didn't seem to bother the police chief as he ushered her to the door.

Mary turned around to face him in the open doorway. "Oh, there is one more thing I wanted to ask you."

"Yes?"

"You said there were other incidents of vandalism the same night as mine," Mary began. "Can you tell me where they happened?"

"Sure," he said. Mary knew he had to be discreet and selective about what he told to whom, so she appreciated his willingness to share with her. "The Gallery was hit, and so was the new county clerk's office."

Mary's heart quickened. The county clerk's office had moved from her building to a new location shortly before she moved in. Could there be a connection? She smiled up at the police chief. "Thanks again."

Mary walked out of the station into the warm sunshine. She strolled along the sidewalk, taking the long way around to her shop. She wanted to enjoy the outdoor weather for as long as possible before she headed back inside.

As she rounded the corner, she saw a couple across the street with two little girls, all of them emerging from Bailey's Ice Cream Shop with waffle cones in their hands. They were smiling and laughing, enjoying the beautiful day. The sight put a smile on her face.

She continued down Main Street, her spirits lifting by the step, past her shop and around the corner. The county clerk's office and the Gallery were in adjacent buildings located on Meeting House Road about a block from Mary's bookshop.

Mary entered the clerk's office first and was struck by the musty odor of centuries-old public records and archives that were packed in file cabinets and cupboards around the cramped office. Even though the office had recently relocated, the place looked and smelled as though it had been there for years. Behind the cluttered counter sat Bea Winslow, the clerk who had notarized the documents transferring ownership of Mary's bookshop from its previous owner, attorney Paul Becker. Bea was a tiny woman about seventy years old. She had short, closely trimmed silver hair and reading glasses she wore perched on the end of her nose.

"Hello there, Mary!" Bea said, hopping out of her chair. "Nice to see you again. How's the new bookshop coming along?"

"Hi, Bea." Mary smiled and leaned her forearms on the counter. "It's so much fun putting my shop together that it doesn't even feel like work. I hope that feeling lasts for a while."

"I'm sure it will," Bea said. "Your face lights up when you talk about it."

"I truly can't wait," Mary said, feeling almost giddy.

"So what brings you here today?" Bea asked.

"Well, I heard that someone vandalized your office and I wanted to compare notes with you," Mary explained. "I'm afraid they broke a window in my store."

Bea grimaced. "I know—I saw it boarded up. I guess I got lucky that the kids only doused my window with spray paint."

Mary turned toward the shiny windowpane. "It looks like you've done a great job of cleaning it all off."

"I did. It just took some paint thinner, a razor blade, and a lot of elbow grease," Bea said, flexing the muscle in her right arm.

Mary smiled at Bea's display of strength. She loved the woman's exuberance. "Was there any other damage to your office?"

Bea shook her head. "No, just the spray paint. They wrote, 'Teachers stink' and 'We love summer vacay.'"

"Things kids would write," Mary noted. "I hear the Gallery was vandalized too," she added.

Bea nodded. "It was, although there was only a long, thin streak of hot-pink paint across the window. The Gallery has a motion light that probably came on when the boys started spraying. It must have scared them off."

A motion light would be cheaper than a security system, Mary thought to herself. Although, if the intruders weren't afraid of making noise by breaking her front window, she wasn't sure a light would have stopped them.

A smile touched the corners of Bea's mouth. "I told the police chief that I could provide plenty of community service if he ever caught the young punks. There are boxes of files in the storeroom dating back over a hundred years that need to be sorted and reorganized. That would keep them too busy to play graffiti artists."

"Now that's a great idea," Mary said, knowing the kids would probably benefit from Bea's positive influence. "And a much more productive use of their time."

Bea looked sympathetically at Mary. "Don't worry, honey, this was an anomaly. It's just too bad that you got the worst of it."

Mary nodded, wishing she could brush off the incident so easily. The fact that someone had entered her shop bothered her, but what troubled her more was that they stole such a personal photograph. What could they possibly have wanted with it? She reasoned again that perhaps it was just a casualty of the kids' carelessness—but why would they take the photo with them? Wouldn't it just be deadweight?

Mary chatted a little longer with Bea and then walked to the Gallery next door. Ivy Bay was popular with artists, and this art gallery was home to several quality works of art. Now that it was tourist season, the Gallery had extended its hours and was open from midmorning until dusk. A tiny, melodic chime sounded as she opened the door. The Gallery was housed in an old Victorian that had been completely remodeled inside.

"I'll be right there," a man's voice called out from above.

Mary looked up to see a dapper, elderly gentleman begin to descend the open wooden staircase that led to the main floor. He wore a black suit with a white dress shirt and a burnt-orange tie. As he came closer, she could see a sculpted, silver mustache above his thin upper lip.

"I'm Mason Willoughby." The man folded his hands in front of him as he approached her. "Welcome to the Gallery."

"Thank you," she said warmly. "I'm Mary Fisher. I just moved to Ivy Bay a few weeks ago."

"Ah," he said, with a slight nod. "If you're looking for art pieces for your new home, I'll be happy to help you."

"Actually, I'm not shopping today." She looked around the gallery. "Although you do have some beautiful paintings."

"Then what can I do for you, Mrs. Fisher?"

"Please call me Mary." She smiled. "I'm opening a book-shop on the corner of Main Street and Meeting House Road, so we're neighbors. I wanted to stop in and say hello."

"Hello," he said.

She waited for him to continue, but he just stared at her. Mary cleared her throat. "I'm afraid we have something else in common as well. We were both hit by vandals."

For the first time since she'd entered his shop, a smile crossed Mason Willoughby's mouth. "Some say vandal; some say street artist."

She was intrigued by his comment. "I wouldn't exactly call my broken shopwindow a work of art."

"Well, I do think those kids were more interested in mak-ing mischief than art. Although sometimes it's possible to do both." He waved her toward a spot in the gallery. "Here, let me show you a piece we just got in last week. It's by a young artist who grew up on the streets of New York, and you can see a gritty determination in his work that is really quite unusual."

The eccentric Mason might not be good at small talk, but his face lit up when he talked about art. For the next several minutes, he showed her paintings and sculptures and woven textiles. Each piece had a story behind it, and he had a way of telling a story that enthralled her.

"Have you ever thought about writing?" she asked him. "I'll bet you could come up with a great art-related mystery."

He smiled. "I'm flattered, Mary, but I prefer to tell my stories with a paintbrush."

"Oh," she said. "Can I see one of your paintings?"

"They're not here," he said, clearing his throat. "I don't want to display them until they're perfect in my eyes, no matter how long it takes."

Mary thought about the unfinished manuscript in her desk drawer and realized that she and Mason had something in common. "Well, thank you so much for the tour. I really enjoyed it."

"You're welcome."

Mary walked out the door, the chime tinkling behind her. As she headed back to her shop, she thought about the tour Mason had just given her. The price tags on some of those paintings had been five figures. If the vandals were going to steal something, a painting worth thousands of dollars made more sense than an old photograph that had nothing but sentimental value. Perhaps that could mean that the police chief's theory was true; that the vandals who had broken her window were just kids looking to make mischief. If theft was their main agenda, surely they would have stolen from the Gallery. Yet again, Mary thought, the difference between the incidents at the county clerk's office and the Gallery and the one at her shop continued to seem bigger.

Mary unlocked the door to her shop and walked inside. Gus was sleeping on the leather cushion of her Gram's rocking chair. He cracked open one eye, staring at her for a long moment before closing it again.

She yawned, wishing she could take a nap too, but she had work to do. She decided to try and get some distance from the mysterious theft, so she spent the rest of the afternoon cataloging new books into her computer before placing them on a bookshelf. The software she used allowed her to search her inventory by title, author, or ISBN number. By the time she'd finished going through three boxes of new books, it was after six o'clock.

Mary shut down her computer and turned the lights off before picking up Gus and heading out the front door. She turned around to lock it, aware of someone passing behind her. Mary looked up to see a young girl approaching the corner. After a quick glance in both directions, the girl skipped away across Meeting House Road toward Ivy Bay Bank & Trust on the other side of the street. Mary watched until she was sure the girl had gotten safely to the other side, but then something else caught her eye.

Mary trailed after the girl, her heart beating faster. As she crossed the street, she noticed the girl had walked past the bank to a bench where she tapped on the shoulder of an older woman. The two of them laughed together as they made their way across the street toward the Ivy Bay Public Library.

Mary wasn't focused on the girl, as she turned her attention to the brick building in front of her, or more specifically, to the square antique brass plate attached to the bank. Like many of the buildings in Ivy Bay, the brass plate showed the year the building had been established. In this case, that year was 1893. But it wasn't the year on the brass plate that had caught her attention. It was the small silver bead right below it.

She'd just found a hidden camera.

Mary turned around to see the west side of her shop. According to Toad, his surveillance camera provided a wide-angle view. If the bank's camera did the same, she might finally be able to see exactly who had broken into her bookshop.

SIX

Mary couldn't wait to get home. She was exhausted after another long day, and she was anxious to share her new lead with Betty. She didn't have any more clues than she'd had this morning, but she was optimistic.

She climbed into her car and set her handbag and Gus's carrying case on the seat beside her. The bank was closed, but as soon as it opened tomorrow morning, she'd be at their door to ask for the surveillance recording from the night of her break-in. She hoped they'd comply.

As she pulled away from the curb, she thought about stopping by the police station to tell Chief McArthur about the security camera but then thought better of it.

"He's probably already gone for the night," she said out loud, ostensibly to Gus. "Besides, the recording might not show anything. I don't want to bother him until I have something to share."

A few minutes later, she pulled into the driveway in front of her new home. As the sun began to set, the sight of Betty's house, light green with dark green shutters, brought Mary joy. She once again reminded herself that she lived here now and wasn't just visiting. Despite recent events, she couldn't help but think, *This is the good life.*

She said a brief prayer of thanks and then climbed out of the car. When she reached the front door, it opened before her fingers even touched the doorknob.

"Mary!"

Mary gaped at her cousin Jean, surprised to see her standing on the other side of the doorway. She was even more surprised to see that Jean looked exactly the same as she had four months ago, at Uncle George's funeral. She had on the same gray suit and sapphire pendant necklace, and her brown eyes were red-rimmed, as if she'd been crying. As Jean held the door open for Mary, she could see a crumpled tissue tucked into her cousin's hand.

"Jean." Mary walked inside and gave her a big hug. "This is a wonderful surprise. I thought you weren't coming until next week." Mary wrapped her arm around Jean's shoulders. "Is everything okay?"

"I was able to leave work earlier than I expected." Jean took a step back and dabbed at one eye with her tissue. "It's strange how Dad's death seems to be affecting me more now than when it first happened. I can't explain it."

Mary gave Jean a squeeze. She knew firsthand that the grief process didn't always make sense. For the first two months after her husband's death, she kept buying his favorite breakfast cereal every time she went to the grocery store. It had taken three months more before she finally convinced herself to donate the unopened cereal boxes to the local food pantry.

Betty appeared in the living room with a tray holding a pitcher of lemonade and three glasses. "Oh, good, you're home," Betty said to Mary. "I wondered what was keeping you."

Mary wanted to tell her about finding the hidden camera, but with Jean standing beside her on the verge of tears, this didn't seem like the right time. "I'm sorry I'm late. I was cataloging some books and lost track of the time."

Gus chose that moment to leap from the bag on her shoulder. He landed on the floor and sniffed at the rug.

Jean smiled with watery eyes. "I never thought I'd see a cat in this house."

"Me neither," Betty murmured with a playful roll of her eyes as she set the tray on the coffee table. She poured three glasses from the pitcher.

"Do you two remember Aunt Lucille?" Jean asked as she took a seat in a wing chair. "She must have had a hundred cats living in that tiny house of hers."

Mary sat down on the sofa and accepted a glass of lemonade from her sister. "I think it was closer to thirty, but that's still a lot of cats."

"Her house was surprisingly clean, though, even with all those cats. And it didn't smell at all." Betty handed a glass to Jean before joining Mary on the sofa.

"I made the mistake of wearing a navy-blue dress there once for a family dinner," Jean said, her tears drying up. "It was a brand-new dress from Dora's Dress Shop on Main Street, and by the time I left Aunt Lucille's, it was covered with cat hair."

Mary smiled at the story. She loved how the three of them shared so many wonderful memories of their family. In moments like these, Jean felt almost like a sister. "So, Jean, when did you arrive?"

"This afternoon," Jean said. "And the first thing I did was stop at Bailey's Ice Cream Shop. I couldn't believe it when

I saw that black walnut ice cream was their special for the week." Her eyes grew misty. "That was always Dad's favorite, so I ordered a small cone in his honor."

"He did love ice cream," Betty mused. "I remember he always used to offer me a bowl when I came to visit."

Jean's mouth curved into a smile. "Mom used to warn him that so much ice cream wasn't healthy, but he said a man had to have some vices." She grew quiet for a long moment. "I really miss him."

Mary's heart went out to her cousin, who looked so much like Aunt Phyllis. Jean was average height, with stick-straight brown hair and naturally rosy cheeks. The gray suit she wore was a little snug at the waist, and a pair of thick ankles peeked out between the hem of her gray slacks and her sensible black shoes. At sixty-one, Jean worked as a bookkeeper at an accounting firm in Chicago. Her husband David was a dentist.

"So how's your family?" Betty asked. "Did David come with you?"

"Oh no." Jean took a sip of her lemonade. "He's got so many patients that he can barely fit them all into his schedule. I didn't even ask him to come because I know he could never leave his practice for that long."

"How long will you be here?" Betty asked.

"At least a month to clean out Dad's house. I'd like to put together a family scrapbook too, as long as I'm digging through old memorabilia. A month will give me time to do that and to putter around Cape Cod."

"I'm glad to hear it," Mary said, looking forward to spending time with her. "And how's D.J.?" she asked, speaking of

Jean's only child. "Is he ready to start his senior year of college this fall?"

Jean shook her head. "He's decided that college isn't for him." She set her glass on the coffee table, and Mary could see a hint of parental disapproval in her face. "You know, he's always been so smart. They never challenged him enough in school, and he was bored to death in college." She smiled resolutely. "Bill Gates quit college too, and look how he turned out." Jean turned to Mary. "And I'm guessing you've been keeping busy too, with the opening of your shop."

Gus sat on the floor by Mary's feet, looking among the three of them as if he were engaged in the conversation.

"You can say that again. The grand opening is coming up soon," Mary told her. "I'm hoping to have all my ducks in a row." She smiled. "I'd love for you to be there too, now that you're in town."

"And our church is having an ice-cream social on Sunday afternoon," Betty added. "We'd love to have you join us for the worship service and the ice-cream social."

"That sounds lovely. I'll be there." Jean drained the last of her lemonade and then rose to her feet. She looked ever so slightly uplifted. "Well, I'd better get going if I want to get any work done at Dad's house before it gets too late. I've hardly been here a day, and my social calendar is already filling up!"

"Oh, won't you stay for supper?" Betty asked. "It's nothing special, just crab salad, but there's plenty for all of us."

"Oh yes, please stay," Mary urged her cousin. "We've barely had a chance to catch up."

"Thanks, both of you; that's so nice. But I'm going to take a rain check. I'm really eager to get started."

"Of course." Betty walked over and gave her a hug. "You stop by anytime. And please let us know if you need help with the house."

"I will," Jean promised, as she and Mary embraced. "It's wonderful to see you both again."

Mary and Betty walked her to the door and said their good-byes.

As she watched Jean walk to her blue rental car, Mary sent up a silent prayer. *Dear Lord, please watch over Jean and give her the comfort and strength she needs during this difficult time.*

After Jean drove away, Betty turned to her sister. "She seems pretty fragile, doesn't she?"

Mary nodded. "She and her dad were so close. I'm sure she misses seeing him in that big old house."

"I know I do," Betty said wistfully. Then she tilted her head to one side. "Now what's going on with you?"

"What do you mean?" Mary asked, surprised by the question.

Betty arched a brow. "I mean, something's up. I could tell as soon as I saw you."

Mary disliked the fact that Betty could read her so easily. On the other hand, she couldn't wait to tell her the news. "You're right; something is up. I found a hidden camera on the exterior of the bank building and it's pointed at my store."

Betty sank down in a chair. "So you might be able to see who broke in?"

Mary nodded, too excited to sit down. "Maybe. The bank was already closed when I saw the camera, so I won't know for sure until tomorrow."

"What about Toad? Did he know anything about the picture?"

"Oh, now you're calling him Toad too, huh?" Mary said playfully.

"Guilty as charged," Betty replied. "So? Did *Todd* have any insight?"

"Unfortunately, no, but it was great seeing him again. Although, because Todd had told me that a wall sconce on his porch doubled as a security camera, I was then able to spot the tiny camera at the bank."

"Wow," Betty said. "You're turning into a regular Nancy Drew, aren't you? You're well on your way to solving this case."

"I hope so," Mary replied as she started gathering the empty glasses and setting them on the tray. "I just can't seem to get any relevant information. But I suppose that camera could help move things along. Maybe the police chief will be able to identify the vandals in the video, if we can see anything at all, and if he has their pictures. I'd sure like to get the original photograph back. Not to mention an explanation for why they stole it in the first place."

"And then you can finally put all of this unpleasantness behind you and just concentrate on your bookshop." Betty rose to her feet and headed to the kitchen. "For now, let's celebrate the latest development in your 'case' by eating dinner out on the deck."

"That sounds wonderful." Mary picked up the tray and followed her sister. Betty's encouragement was just what Mary needed. And Betty was right. Mary did want to know who had broken into her shop, but she also couldn't deny that it'd been surprisingly fun, talking to people about the incident and trying to figure out what happened. It was as if she were living out a mystery novel, and despite the strange circumstances, she was thoroughly enjoying the adventure.

———

On Thursday morning, Mary stood outside Ivy Bay Bank & Trust, waiting for an employee to unlock the doors. She checked her watch, noting that she still had five minutes until it opened. A wooden bench sat on the sidewalk next to the front of the bank, so she took a seat, not wanting to look too eager. She felt a little ridiculous showing up so early, but she could barely sleep last night imagining what she'd see on the security camera recording.

She looked down the street and saw a trio of gray-haired men open the door of the Black & White Diner and walk inside. Betty had told her that Edward had gone there for coffee and conversation every morning after he retired, and Mary felt a moment of loss for her brother-in-law.

She looked toward the Chadwick Inn and saw a young couple emerge, carrying a picnic basket and a matching pair of yellow towels. Mary assumed they were headed for the beach and smiled at them as they passed by. It didn't seem that long ago since she and John had gone on a picnic together.

Now Edward and John were both gone. "There is a time for everything," she murmured, reciting the passage she'd memorized from the third chapter of Ecclesiastes. She continued the passage in her head. *And a season for every activity under the heavens: a time to be born and a time to die, a time to*

plant and a time to uproot, a time to kill and a time to heal, a
time to tear down and a time to build, a time to weep and a time
to laugh, a time to mourn and a time to dance.

She closed her eyes for a long moment, wondering if she'd
ever feel like dancing again. Then she heard a key turning in
a lock and opened them again.

The bank was open.

Mary stood up and walked inside, wondering about the
best way to approach this. She assumed the bank didn't have
people routinely asking them for their surveillance record-
ings. In fact, it was quite possible they wouldn't be happy that
she'd detected one of their hidden cameras.

"Good morning, Mrs. Fisher. May I help you?" Sandra
Rink asked as Mary approached the teller window. Sandra
was in her early twenties, and the tiny gap between her two
front teeth gave her an endearing smile.

"Hello, Sandra," Mary greeted her. "I was wondering if I
could speak to Steve," she said, referring to the man who had
helped her open both a personal and business bank account
when she'd first moved to Ivy Bay.

Sandra smiled. "Of course. Please have a seat, and I'll let
him know you're here."

Mary walked over to the small seating area in the center of
the bank. There were eight leather chairs around a low, square
table, two chairs on each side. She sat down and glanced
at the magazines on the black granite table, finding none that
caught her interest.

A few minutes later, the door to Steve's office opened and
he walked toward her, a wide smile on his face. "Good morning, Mary. How are you?"

"I'm just fine, thank you," she replied, rising to her feet. "I do have a question for you, and I'll try not to take up too much of your time."

"My time is all yours," he said, escorting her into his office. He was dressed in an olive-green suit with a black tie and walked with a slight limp. The first time she met him, he told her that he'd been in a bad motorcycle accident and had been blessed to walk away from it relatively unscathed. Then he'd added that his limp was a daily reminder that he'd been given a second chance.

Now, as Mary took the chair opposite his desk, she hoped that she could convince him to give her a chance to look at that surveillance recording.

Steve rounded his desk and sat down. "What can I do for you today?"

She took a deep breath. "I couldn't help but notice that you have a surveillance camera on the east side of the building."

"You couldn't help but notice? That's some eagle eye you've got there…." He looked a little surprised but not at all irritated, which instantly disarmed Mary.

She let out a small laugh. "Oh, the only reason I noticed it is because a friend recently pointed out a similar camera to me. Otherwise, I'm sure I wouldn't have seen it," she said.

"That's good to know," he said. "And do me a favor and keep the camera quiet."

"Will do," she said with a smile. "But I wondered if I could see some recent footage."

"And I suppose I should ask why you'd like to see the recording," Steve said, leaning forward in his chair.

"Yes, of course. Well, you see"—she knew she seemed a little crazy so she tried to sound as pragmatic as she could— "your hidden security camera is facing the west side of my shop, which as you know was broken into the other day. I'm hoping the recording might show who broke in."

He looked thoughtful as he rolled his chair a few inches away from his desk. "I can see how that might be helpful."

Mary pressed on at his encouragement. "Might your surveillance recording go back that far?"

He gave a slow nod. "It does. It's on a seventy-two-hour loop, so"—he looked at his watch—"it's eight forty-five on Thursday morning, which means it would go back until eight thirty on Monday morning."

"Oh, that's perfect." Mary tried not to sound too excited.

"All right." He rose from the chair. "You wait right here, and I'll see what I can do."

Mary sat in his office for almost ten minutes. The longer she sat there, the more she feared that someone was balking at releasing the recording. At the fifteen-minute mark, she was about to stand up and see if she could disarm anyone who might be worried, but just at that moment, she saw Steve headed in her direction.

"Sorry it took so long," he said, holding up a blue DVD case. "Our surveillance system is a type of specialized computer. It has a hard drive, and we are able to burn the recording onto a DVD, but it takes a while. And then we had to watch it before we could give it out." He handed her the DVD case.

"Thank you so much," she said.

"No problem. I hope you find what you're looking for."

"I hope so too. Thanks again, Steve."

She wasted no time making her way back to her bookshop. She let Gus out of his carrying case, and he immediately began to prance around. She loved how used to the shop he was becoming.

"Look what I've got," she announced, waving the DVD case in the air as she made her way to the computer.

Gus followed her there, leaping up onto the corner of the counter to watch her.

Mary turned on the computer and waited for it to boot up. Then she opened the DVD case and carefully removed the DVD, not wanting to scratch the surface. She sat down and activated the button on her computer that opened the DVD drive. The small tray slid out. Then she set the DVD in place and pushed the tray back in.

The computer made a soft whirring noise. A moment later, a picture came up on the screen. The image showed the sidewalk along the east front of the bank as well as Meeting House Road and the west side of her building. There was a digital counter at the bottom of the screen that showed the date and time as Monday morning at nine o'clock. Mary watched it for a few minutes and then realized it would take hours to watch the color recording in real time.

She moved the mouse on the screen to the fast-forward button and pushed the slowest speed. This allowed her to see everything that happened, but the time moved much more quickly. The window had been broken sometime after dark, but she wanted to see if anything unusual had happened before then.

She sped past Monday afternoon and into the evening. Eight o'clock, nine o'clock, ten o'clock....

At exactly 10:03 PM on Monday, Mary stopped the DVD.

SEVEN

❖◆❖

M ary gaped at the frozen image on the screen.
It was Jean.

But that was impossible! This recording was from Monday evening, and Jean hadn't arrived in Ivy Bay until yesterday. Mary checked the date on the bottom of the screen again, just to be sure, but it clearly showed the date to be Monday.

Mary leaned closer, wondering if she could possibly be mistaken. The camera had captured Jean's profile as she stood at the corner. The angle of the camera made the picture a little distorted, but she could see Jean's features clearly. She had the same straight brown hair, the same silhouette, and she wore the apricot lace cardigan that Aunt Phyllis had made for her years ago. A large tote bag hung from one shoulder.

"What's going on?" Mary said out loud, trying to make sense of it. Was it possible she'd misunderstood what day her cousin had arrived in Ivy Bay? She didn't think so, but why would Jean lie?

She pushed the Play button on the screen, almost afraid to see what would happen next. She watched Jean hesitate at the corner, her gaze on Mary's bookshop across the street. A few moments later, Jean crossed the street, turned and then headed south on the sidewalk, toward the back of the bookshop, until she was out of the camera's view.

Mary sat back in her chair and breathed a deep sigh. Jean was the last person Mary expected to see on the recording. There was no image of her actually breaking in, but why else would she have been there?

She let the surveillance DVD run in real time, wondering if she'd see Jean again. Twenty minutes passed, then thirty. A few people Mary recognized from around town passed the bank, and groups of tourists wandered by, licking ice-cream cones and laughing, but there was no sign of her cousin. The sunlight faded as dusk set in. At 10:37 PM, a figure appeared on the same sidewalk where she'd last seen Jean, only this person was headed in the opposite direction. The figure wore a bulky, black hooded sweatshirt, black pants, and black gloves. The black hood was pulled down low over the person's forehead, concealing the face. The gait was steady and even, but Mary couldn't tell if it was a man or a woman. Perhaps this was the person who had broken in? Was this person associated with Jean?

The height of the individual was hard to gauge due to the camera angle, but the shape was neither thin nor heavy. The figure slowed, stopping at a west window along the side of the shop and cupping both hands around his eyes as he—or she—peered in the bookshop window. Mary watched the figure stand there for a long moment. Then the figure backed away from the window and continued down the sidewalk and around the corner that led to her storefront, disappearing from the camera's view. Mary couldn't see if the person's next act was to break her front window, but it seemed likely.

Mary leaned back in her chair, hitting the Fast-forward button again. But the hooded figure never appeared again, and neither did Jean. No one else passed by her shop that night—at least no one who had been caught by the camera. If they'd come from the east, down Main Street, to break into the shop, they might have avoided detection.

But she didn't think it was someone else. It would be too much of a coincidence for *three* people, let alone two, to scope out her bookshop on a random Monday night. The hooded figure, and maybe even Jean—although Mary didn't want to believe it—was looking for something and had broken in to take it. But why?

Something puzzled her. She got out of her chair and headed for the door. She stepped outside and headed around the corner to the same window the hooded figure on the recording had peered through.

Now she did the same, cupping her hands around her eyes and pressing her face against the cool glass. From this angle, she could see the front door of the shop, four long rows of bookshelves, the hearth in the back and the two chairs beside it, the closed cellar door, and just a glimpse of her Gram's rocker and the braided rug.

But just as she expected, there was one thing she couldn't see—the place where the framed photograph had hung on the wall. It was on an opposite wall, making it impossible to see from this angle.

Mary stepped back from the window, imagining herself as the intruder. Perhaps he'd been looking to see if anyone was inside the shop, having already planned to break in. Maybe he'd even "cased the joint" as they wrote in mystery novels, before he'd broken in. Or, strangest of all, had the intruder been *looking* for the photograph?

Up until this moment, she'd had a hard time believing that someone had stolen the photograph intentionally. She realized that all this time she had *wanted* it to be a random act of vandalism, because she just couldn't wrap her mind around the idea that someone would want that old photograph. But she couldn't deny it any longer. There must be something in that picture that had motivated someone to break in to her bookshop. And she was going to figure out what it was.

She was just about to return to her computer when a car horn sounded behind her. For an instant, her blood ran cold.

EIGHT

———◆◆◆———

Mary turned around, only to see Henry seated in the driver's seat of a vintage blue-and-white convertible, the sun beaming down on him through the windshield. Mary laughed nervously at herself. By the intensity of her reaction, she wondered if she was a little *too* caught up in this mystery. Even in the light of day, she had been spooked.

She walked over to Henry as he stepped out of the car, her heart still beating faster than normal. "Henry, hello! So nice to see you again," she said, focused on slowing her breathing.

"Hey, Mary. How's everything going?" He nodded toward the door. "I see your window's been boarded up."

"Yep. The glazier is supposed to come tomorrow. I'm looking forward to having it fixed." Mary looked at the convertible. "You're still driving this old car? It looks amazing!"

He laughed. "Well, it's the same model, but my old Chevy retired to the junkyard decades ago. A friend of mine restored this one, and when I saw it, I had to have it." He caressed the shiny chrome edge of the windshield. "It's a 1953 Bel Air and it's in mint condition. I have fun taking it to local car shows."

"It's beautiful."

"Thanks," he said as he opened the back door. "I brought some books for you." He pulled out a large cardboard box.

"They belonged to Misty, and I'm sure she would have liked you to have them. You don't have to take them, of course, but I thought there might be some good ones in here."

"Henry, that's so sweet of you. I'd love to take a look at them." She walked to the door, her head still spinning because of what she'd seen on that recording. She cleared the way for Henry to carry the box inside. He set it on the counter and opened the top flaps.

Mary reached inside for the top book. "Nancy Drew." It was one of the older, original volumes bound in blue cloth. They had stopped binding them like this decades ago when they switched to the familiar yellow covers of the modern editions. "This is an antique."

Henry smiled. "My wife loved Nancy Drew books when she was younger and never got rid of them. There are quite a few more in the box."

"Wonderful. I have a few in stock already, but not this volume. And I've been wanting to add more young-adult mysteries to my collection." Mary pulled out more books, impressed by their condition. "It looks like you and your wife took great care of your books."

"Misty took good care of everything she loved." He paused for a moment and then sifted through the box for a book. "Have you ever read *The Secret of the Old Clock*? That's a good one. There's also *The Sign of the Twisted Candles*."

"Of course I've read them. Every true mystery fan— at least of the female variety—has read Nancy Drew. She's legendary!"

"Oh, of course," he said with a chuckle as he handed her both books.

"These are wonderful," Mary said as she looked at several other books in the box. "I'd like to buy all of them."

His brow furrowed. "Buy? Oh no, no, no. I'm giving them to you."

"Oh, Henry." Mary smiled warmly, grateful for his generosity. "I appreciate it, but this is a business. These books are worth money, and you deserve some of it."

She recognized the stubborn tilt of his chin before he even replied. Funny how there were some things you didn't forget, no matter how many years had passed.

"These are a gift." He pushed the box toward her. "Consider it your housewarming...or maybe it should be your bookshop-warming gift to welcome you back to Ivy Bay. Okay? Case closed."

Mary couldn't refuse such a gracious gesture. "Thank you, Henry. You couldn't have given me a finer gift."

Henry glanced at the boarded window. "It's certainly a nicer one than the intruder left you, huh?"

"I'll say." She hesitated, too intrigued by this latest development to keep it to herself any longer. "Actually, I think I may have the intruder on a recording."

He arched a brow. "Really? How?"

"I noticed that the bank has a hidden camera pointed at my store. I got the DVD and although it doesn't show the front of the building, I did see someone looking through the window that night." She'd seen her cousin too, but there was no need to mention that. Jean couldn't be involved in this, Mary told herself, not her loving cousin Jean. It must have been a coincidence.

He looked impressed, and Mary felt a twinge of pride at her newly discovered investigatory talents. "Who did you see?" he asked.

She sighed. "That's the hard part. I can't tell." Then she looked up at him. "Actually, would you mind taking a look to see if you catch something that I may have missed?"

"Not at all. I'd love to help."

She led him to the desk, and he sat down in front of the computer. Then she carefully reset the DVD to play at the 10:37 mark on Monday night. "That's him—or her."

Henry stared at the screen, watching as the hooded figure peered inside the bookshop. "Whoever it is didn't want to be identified; that much is clear."

"Exactly. And another thing is for sure—this was not done by two preteen boys randomly vandalizing the town."

He nodded and then glanced up at her. "Have you shown this to the police chief?"

"Not yet." Mary didn't want to involve him again until she had something more, especially since Jean appeared on the disk. The last thing her grieving cousin needed was the police chief questioning her about that night. Besides, he had already written the incident report and moved on to other things. "The intruder didn't actually steal anything of value, just that old photograph. So it's a personal mission of mine. I simply can't see any reason the intruder would have broken in except to steal the photograph directly, yet I can't imagine what anyone would want with the picture. It must have to do with something *in* the photo."

"May I see the photo?" Henry asked.

"Of course." Mary was glad to have a sounding board in Henry. She drew the photo out of her bag. "It's getting pretty wrinkled. Give me a moment and I'll print out another copy."

Henry moved aside to give her full access to the computer. She moved the cursor over the screen, ready to click the Print button when a thought stopped her.

"Hold on a minute," she said. "Why don't we enlarge it on the screen?"

"That's a great idea," Henry said. "Actually, do you have any photo-editing software? We may be able to zoom in closer and see more detailed images if you do."

Mary had just recently bought the computer and wasn't sure of half the software on it. "Be my guest!" she said and stood up, waving for him to take her place on the chair.

Henry sat down in the chair and clicked around. "Aha, here we go." He double-clicked on an icon and waited while the program loaded. Finally, the application opened, and Henry pulled up the photograph.

"Let's try this. I'll break up the photo into four sections," he said, moving the mouse once more, "and enlarge and enhance it so we can see the fine details."

She watched him work, much too aware of the strong ripple of muscles on his forearms that came from piloting a fishing boat. Mary cleared her throat and focused her attention back on the screen.

"Here we go," he said, clicking another icon on the screen. "Ready to print."

It took four pages of letter-size paper to print the entire picture. She removed the pages from the printer tray, the paper still warm as she set them on the counter and matched the edges of the four pages together.

Gus padded over to the counter and sat down to watch as Henry moved beside her.

The enlargement revealed details Mary hadn't noticed before—like the small white poodle crossing the street and the framed painting of a lighthouse in the auction-house window. She had no idea whether any of these additional details would actually be helpful to her, but they certainly couldn't hurt.

"Notice anything new?" he asked.

She continued to study the printouts. Uncle George and the woman stood beside each other, next to the car's front bumper. Then something caught her eye. She tapped on the center of the photo. "Looks like the woman is holding a book behind her back—you can see part of it in the gap between her and my uncle." Even though the photo was enlarged, she still couldn't make out any words on the apparently leather-bound book. "Can you read the title?"

"No, I can't." Henry leaned closer to the enlarged photo and squinted. "But that's a nice car in front of your store. Looks like a Cadillac Eldorado Brougham. It must have been brand-new because that model came out in 1957. It was pretty pricey in those days."

Mary turned her attention to the car, realizing it was the only automobile in the photograph that was parked directly in front of the shop. Only the front half of the car appeared in the photo, and the white letters and numbers on the dark license plate were now clearly visible. It read Mass 57 at the top, but the bottom number was partially obscured by the woman's leg. She could only see the first five numbers: 324 52.

She reached for a pad and pencil to jot them down. "I wonder how many license plates from 1957 start with those five numbers, if the records at the Department of Motor Vehicles even go back that far."

"Wouldn't hurt to check. A nice car like that might even still be around. Too bad there's no way to get the VIN."

Mary wasn't as curious about the car itself as she was about the owner of the car. Maybe it belonged to the woman in the photo since she was leaning her hand on it.

Mary stared at the photo, but her eyes glazed over a bit in thought. Maybe if she could find the woman—if she was still alive—Mary might be able to discover why someone was so determined to steal this photograph. Had it been wrongly placed in her basement? Perhaps someone simply wanted it back. But why wouldn't they have just asked her for it? If it didn't belong to her, she would have gladly given it back.

She returned to the ever-persistent thought that something *in* the photograph was troubling to someone. But what could be so bothersome? It seemed like a perfectly innocuous photograph to Mary. Of course, she couldn't ignore the fact that the woman in the picture was not Uncle George's wife. But like she had discussed with Betty, Mary found it hard to believe that her uncle hadn't been faithful to Aunt Phyllis. There was simply no reason to doubt his fidelity. And anyway, even if this woman had been in an indecent relationship with Uncle George in 1957, who around today would care enough to go to the trouble of stealing the photo?

Jean might care, Mary thought to herself. She had been so close to her father and they were such a proud family. But Jean could have simply asked Mary to take it down. There would be no reason for her to risk breaking into the shop.

Her head was spinning with possibilities and she hated that tiny sliver of suspicion that Jean might be involved. She simply couldn't picture her cousin dressing in black, breaking a window, and entering the shop to steal the photograph. No, the intruder was still out there, and now, more than ever, Mary wanted to find him—or her.

Mary closed her eyes and took a deep, calming breath. *Please, Lord, give me clarity and guide me in the right direction. Help me make sense of all this.*

When she opened her eyes, she decided that looking up the car's owner would be the most logical next step. She knew it was a long shot after so many years, but she couldn't walk away from this puzzle until it was solved.

Henry, who had been quietly studying the printouts, finally stepped away from the counter. "I'd better get going," he said, stretching his back. He gave her hair a quick tousle like he used to do when they were teenagers. "Good luck solving this mystery—too bad one of the detectives in our favorite mystery books can't help you."

She chuckled. "Wouldn't it be fun to pick one? Difficult, though. There's Miss Marple or Hercule Poirot—"

"Philip Marlowe or Nero Wolfe… Each with their own strengths."

"And weaknesses," Mary added. "But they were always able to find the answer. That's the difference between fiction and real-life mysteries, isn't it? Some of life's mysteries are never solved."

"Very true," Henry said as he moved toward the door. "I'll see you again soon."

"Absolutely. And thanks again for all the wonderful books." Mary followed him. "And your help with the photo. I really appreciate it."

"Anytime." He stared at her for a long moment, then turned around and walked out the door.

Mary watched him through the window until he disappeared from sight. Then she walked over to the box of books he'd brought and carried them to the back room. She was torn between sorting through the mysteries in the box or the mystery connected to that photograph. She was surprised to find herself wanting to do both. But no, there was something even more pressing. She needed to talk to Jean.

NINE

◆◆◆

Mary decided to walk to Uncle George's house, hoping the fresh air would help clear her head. The day was glorious with the clear blue sky overhead and the bay waters shimmering under the warm sun.

Her uncle's house was located on the edge of Ivy Bay, near the shore. The path took her past a salt marsh and thick shrubs of white and pink beach roses on the dunes. The scent of the roses mingling with the salty sea air brought her instantly back to her childhood. Those were halcyon days, and so many of them had been spent with Jean. They'd built sand castles on the beach together and dreamed of the castles they'd live in someday, once they each found their Prince Charming.

Mary had found hers and she liked to think that Jean had done the same. David was a hard worker and had always treated his wife well. Mary had spoken with both David and D.J. at Uncle George's funeral, but there had been so many people there that they'd only been able to chat for a short time. She wished David had been able to come to Ivy Bay to help Jean with the house, but then again, maybe Jean needed this time to herself.

As Mary neared the house, she wondered how to broach the subject of the surveillance recording. She even practiced some questions out loud. "Hey, Jean, I was looking for the intruder on the surveillance disk and I saw you on there." No, that wouldn't do. "Jean, is there some reason you told us you arrived here on Wednesday when the disk clearly shows you were in Ivy Bay on Monday?" No, that sounded too accusatory, which was the last thing that Mary wanted.

If Jean had arrived in Ivy Bay on Monday, there might be a good reason that she hadn't wanted to share with Mary and Betty. A reason that Mary didn't want to force her to acknowledge. But there was something she could ask Jean that would seem perfectly natural. She could ask her about the mystery woman in the photograph. After all, Mary hadn't yet talked with Jean about the break-in, so the conversation could potentially come up naturally.

Mary walked up the tree-lined drive that led to a large white house with green shutters. The colonnade still looked majestic to Mary, the double pillars evenly spaced along the wide front porch. The house stood three stories tall, with a dome-shaped cupola at the very top that served as a lookout over the sea.

She passed the blue rental car in the driveway, then made her way up the steps to the front porch and rang the doorbell.

A few moments passed, then Mary heard the sound of footsteps on the other side. The door opened, and Jean greeted her with a smile. "Hi, Mary. What a nice surprise."

"How are you doing, Jean? You've been on my mind." *In more ways than one*, Mary thought. She studied her cousin's face. Jean looked pale and tired, but her voice was light.

"I'm better than the last time you saw me." Jean stepped onto the porch. "In fact, I'm on my way to meet some old high school friends for lunch."

"That sounds fun. I won't keep you, then, although I did want to ask you one question while I was here."

"Oh?"

"Yes, I didn't mention it when I saw you yesterday, but someone broke into my bookshop last Monday night."

Concern flooded Jean's brown eyes. "Oh no! Was anything taken?"

"That's the strangest part. The only thing taken was one of the old photographs of the shop that I e-mailed you. It was the one with your dad and a woman I didn't recognize."

Jean's brow furrowed. "That *is* strange. Do you know who did it?" Her cousin's reaction deepened Mary's conviction that she couldn't be involved, but Jean still hadn't said anything about walking past the bookshop on the evening of the break-in.

"Not yet, I'm sorry to say." She reached into her bag for her photocopy. "It might just be a silly act of vandalism, but it's got me curious." She handed the photo to Jean. "Do you recognize the woman standing next to your dad?"

Jean didn't hesitate. "No, I don't. I wondered about that when you e-mailed those pictures to me. I assumed she was one of his customers." She handed the photocopy back to Mary. "I sure don't remember ever seeing her before." Then she glanced at her watch. "I'm sorry, Mary, but I'd really better get going. I'm already running late."

"Of course," Mary told her, making room for both of them to walk down the porch steps. "Have fun at your lunch."

"Thanks, I will," Jean replied. When they reached the driveway, she asked, "Can I drop you anywhere on my way?"

"No, you go ahead," Mary told her. "I've enjoyed walking today. It's so beautiful out."

Jean reached out to give her shoulder an affectionate squeeze. "Okay, I'll see you soon, then." Then she climbed into her car and drove off.

Mary's cell phone rang before she'd even had time to process their conversation. She pulled it out of her pocket. "Hello?"

"Hey, it's Betty. Sorry I missed you this morning. I'm on my way back from the flea market and wondered if you'd like to meet for ice cream at Bailey's."

Mary smiled. "Ice cream? Before lunch?"

"I know, but I've always been a big believer in having dessert first."

Mary remembered how many times her sister's sweet tooth had gotten her into trouble as a child. One time, their mother had actually found Betty on the stairs eating a bowl of sugar with a spoon.

"That sounds great, Bets. I've been dying to visit Bailey's and just haven't found the time yet." She could also use a listening ear. "When should I meet you?"

"I can be there in about fifteen minutes. Does that work for you?"

That was about how long it would take her to walk back to Main Street. "It's perfect. See you soon."

Mary arrived at the ice cream store at the same time that Betty pulled up in her car.

"Should we rethink our plans?" Mary asked as Betty exited her car. The long line of customers out the door was surprising to Mary. "They look pretty busy."

Betty waved the comment away. "There's always a line during the summer. Trust me, it will be worth it."

Mary and her sister walked to the end of the line and stood on the sidewalk in the shade of a majestic elm tree. The day was comfortably warm, and a yellow warbler sang on a branch above them. Betty looked regal as always with a gorgeous pair of pressed chinos and a light-blue blouse.

"You're looking awfully pretty today," Betty said to Mary. Mary smiled self-consciously while lightly fluffing her curly gray locks and pulling on the hem of her lightweight cardigan. She had at one time been insecure about the graying of her hair, but eventually she had come to appreciate it. Her hair still had a nice thick texture and although she kept it relatively short, she liked the bounce it still had. Her hair had always been one of her greater assets, and allowing it to gray naturally was something she'd decided to embrace. "I was just thinking the same about you, my dear," Mary said. "I love your blouse."

"Oh, this old thing?" Betty said. "I was just thinking that I feel rather un-put-together."

Mary harrumphed. "You couldn't look that way if you tried," she said. "So tell me the story of the ice cream shop. This line is incredible."

"Well, the Baileys make all the ice cream they sell and, I have to admit, it's almost as good as yours," Betty said.

One of Mary's favorite hobbies was making her own ice cream. She'd started years ago, after receiving an electric ice-cream maker as a Christmas gift from her husband.

She'd always teased him that the gift was for both of them, because he liked to eat ice cream as much as she liked to make it. "I haven't made any ice cream in a very long time—not since John became sick," Mary said with a hint of sadness she couldn't mask.

"I know, Mar. Maybe it's time to start again. Why not make a batch for the church ice-cream social?"

"But doesn't the church supply the ice cream?"

"Sure, but people have been known to bring their own recipes...."

Mary shifted on her feet. "I've just started attending services there. I'd feel strange taking my own ice cream when I'm not a member."

"Nonsense," Betty said cheerfully. "I've been telling everyone at Grace Church that you're planning to join, and I know they'd be thrilled to see you and your ice cream on Sunday." Then her eyes widened. "I almost forgot to ask—what happened at the bank? Did you get the recording?"

Mary glanced around her, not wanting to reveal too much in the crowd. "I'll tell you everything after we get our ice cream," she said softly.

Betty arched a curious brow but didn't say anything. A few moments later, they found themselves at the counter.

The shop reminded Mary of a vintage ice-cream parlor, with its bubblegum-pink-and-white-striped wallpaper and the matching pink padded stools, each with a shiny chrome pedestal base, lining the counter at the front of the store. Small, round wrought-iron tables, all painted white, were scattered throughout the shop. Everything was crisp and clean, a place of cool refuge on a warm day.

"Hello there, Betty," said a pleasantly plump woman on the other side. She wore a white bib apron with the words *Bailey's Ice Cream Shop* embroidered in bright pink floss across the front, and her name tag identified her as Tess.

Mary chuckled. "It's a bad sign when the owner of the ice cream shop knows you by name...."

Betty gave Mary a mock glare, and the woman laughed sweetly. "Not at all," Tess said. "I like to get to know all my customers." She glanced at Mary. "I see you brought a friend with you today, Betty."

"This is my sister, Mary Fisher," Betty said. "She moved here from Boston recently and is set to open Mary's Mystery Bookshop just across the way from you."

Tess's mouth gaped slightly as she looked at Mary. "Is that right? I've been meaning to get myself over there and say hello, but we've been so busy I haven't had a chance. I'm Tess Bailey, by the way. It's nice to meet you."

"Nice to meet you too." Mary smiled. "I've felt the same way about you." She had just started to worry that the people behind them were getting antsy when two more employees emerged from the back of the store and started taking orders.

"These are my daughters," Tess said. "Paige and Jamie. They're both in high school. My two older sons have already flown the coop." The girls waved politely, and Mary and Betty said hello.

Betty turned to her sister. "This is definitely a family business. Tess's husband Blake works here too."

Tess smiled. "He works hard, that's for sure, but I'm the self-proclaimed mad ice-cream scientist. He's not allowed in my kitchen." She let out a hearty, infectious laugh.

"You know, Mary makes ice cream too," Betty said. "She's amazing at it, actually." Betty nudged Mary as if to remind her of their earlier conversation. "Her flavor combinations are always surprising. And surprisingly delicious. She reminds me of you, actually, Tess!"

"Is that right?" Camaraderie sparked in Tess's green eyes. "What are some of your favorite flavor combinations, Mary?"

Mary had to think a moment. "Well, I love espresso almond and strawberry macaroon. I also like to make tea-flavored ice creams. I've had success with Earl Grey ice cream and a chai latte ice cream."

"Sounds lovely. It's always fun to meet a fellow ice-cream artist." Tess glanced at the long line behind Mary and Betty. "Now I should probably get back to work.... What can I get for you, ladies?"

Mary had already scanned the delicious-looking menu and decided what she wanted. "I'd like a single-scoop cone with black walnut ice cream," Mary said.

"Good choice." Tess dipped the silver ice-cream scoop into the tub in front of her and started filling the cone.

"I'll have the same, but make mine a double," Betty told her.

They paid for their cones and made their way to an empty table away from the other customers. Mary took a bite of her ice cream. She loved the creamy texture and the subtle flavors of vanilla and cinnamon that she detected beneath the main ingredients. "This is delicious."

"Didn't I tell you?" Betty said as she pulled out a chair and sat down.

Mary hooked her handbag over the back of her chair and joined her sister at the table. The black walnuts in her ice cream had a perfect crunch, and she took another bite while Betty looked at her expectantly.

"Well?" Betty said at last. "So tell me about the recording."

Mary had gotten momentarily caught up in the ice cream, but the thought of the surveillance disk raised her heart rate a little. She wasn't sure where to start. "Well, there were two significant parts to it."

Betty leaned forward. "Two parts? What do you mean?"

Mary took a deep breath. "The first one is a shocker. I saw Jean on the recording. Looking at my shop. At 10:03 PM."

"Huh? Jean? Our Jean?" Betty shook her head. "But that's impossible, Mar. She didn't get into town until Wednesday."

"I know that's what she told us," Mary said softly. "But she was on the recording. She walked past the bookshop the night of the break-in."

Betty's eyes widened. "You don't mean…"

"I hope not," Mary interjected, anticipating what she was about to say. "But it does have me wondering why she didn't tell us that she arrived in Ivy Bay on Monday. And why she hasn't mentioned that she went by the shop."

"Maybe we misunderstood her. Maybe she arrived on Monday."

Mary slowly shook her head. "I don't think so…. I remember specifically asking her about when she got here, and her exact words were, 'this afternoon.' She even wanted a rain check when you invited her for supper because she wanted to get settled in."

"That's right," Betty said, frowning. "I wonder what's going on."

"I don't know. I was just leaving Uncle George's house when you called. I was hoping she might mention it when I told her someone broke into my shop that night."

"And did she?"

"No. And she seemed genuinely surprised about the break-in, but..."

Betty nibbled her lower lip. "But what, Mar?"

"But I can't seem to shake this smidgen of suspicion I have that she might be involved somehow. That's why I need to find out who broke into my shop, so I can eliminate that suspicion once and for all."

"And without letting her know that you saw her on that recording," Betty said, reading her mind.

"Exactly. I know it would hurt Jean terribly if she thought I suspected her. It hurts me to even think it. And I *believe* it's not true; I just need to prove it."

"What about the police chief? Maybe he could help."

"I thought about that," Mary admitted. "But he would see Jean on the surveillance disk, and I'm sure he'd ask her about it." He might even wonder if she'd had black clothes in the tote bag she'd been carrying and changed into them before returning to the bookshop a half hour later.

"And that's what we want to avoid," Betty said, nodding thoughtfully.

"If at all possible." Mary hoped she was making the right decision.

"You said there were two parts to the recording," Betty reminded her.

"Oh yes. This is where it really gets strange." Mary took a deep breath, ready to forge ahead.

She began to tell Betty about the figure in the black hooded sweatshirt and how that person had looked through the window. She also mentioned how enlarging the image of the photo allowed her to see more details in the picture. She reached behind her and grabbed the photocopies out of her bag. "Here they are."

Betty leaned in for a closer look. "What am I supposed to see?"

"Well, there's the partial license plate number on the car parked in front of the shop. And the woman is holding a book behind her back. Don't you think that's a little odd?"

"I'm not sure," she said tentatively. "What do you think it means?"

"I don't know, but I want to find out." Mary glanced at Uncle George's smiling face in the photograph. "Maybe I'm being silly, but I just got the sense that whoever was peering through my window was making sure the coast was clear before they broke in and stole the photograph. If someone was specifically after the photograph, which I'm becoming more and more convinced of, then they must have seen it hanging in my shop at some point."

"But you haven't even opened yet."

"I know," Mary said. "But there have been a few people who have stopped by—like Eleanor's book club group."

"Oh, Mary." Betty's hand fluttered to her chest. "I can't believe Eleanor or one of those other ladies in the book club broke into your shop."

"I'm not saying that at all." Mary took another bite of her ice-cream cone. "But I think it's a good idea to make a list of the people who were in the shop between the time I hung up the photo and when it was stolen."

"How long was that?"

"Well, I hung up the picture on Friday and I was in the shop on Saturday. I wasn't there on Sunday but was back on Monday, and it was stolen on Monday night. So that means there's a three-day window." She pulled a notepad and pen from her bag. "The book club was there on Friday afternoon to look around. So that means Eleanor was there; not that I think she did it."

Betty smiled. "Yet you're writing her name down, anyway. I wonder if my sister-in-law has ever been on a suspect list before."

"She's not really a suspect. I'm just trying to figure things out." Mary looked up at her sister. "Luckily, I remember the other women in the group. Eleanor has a way of introducing people memorably." Mary wrote down the names Virginia Livingston, the member of Ivy Bay's founding family; then Frances Curran, the retired Dartmouth professor; then Madeline Dinsdale, the artist.

Betty nodded as she looked at Mary's list. "That's everyone." She pointed to Madeline's name. "I've seen some of her work in the Gallery. She's very rich and very reclusive. Eleanor considered it quite a coup when she convinced Madeline to join her book club."

Mary finished her cone, licking a dab of ice cream off the tip of her thumb. "It's a pretty small group for a book club, isn't it?"

"It's meant to be small. As you know, Eleanor considers it very exclusive—by invitation only."

Mary smiled. "Lucky you."

"I think it will be good for me to spend some time with those ladies." Her face grew wistful. "I sort of dropped out of life after Edward died, and it's been a little difficult to get myself back out there again." She brightened. "Maybe you're a good influence on me."

Mary laughed. "That would be a first." When they were children, Betty was almost always the good one, while Mary was the risk taker. More than once, she'd lured her big sister into one of her crazy schemes.

Betty smiled as she looked down at the list. "So is there anyone else you should add?"

"There's Paul Becker," Mary said, writing down the name of the attorney who had briefly owned the store before Mary bought it. "He stopped in on Saturday with some spare keys to the shop. He looked around awhile too, so he may have seen the picture."

"Did he say anything about it?"

"No," Mary replied. "No one had said anything about it." She tapped the tip of her pen against the table, trying to think of anyone else. "Bob, the mailman, stopped by, but he didn't come inside."

Betty finished her ice-cream cone and wiped her fingers on her paper napkin. "What about that guy who painted your shop?"

"Kip?" Mary jotted down his name. "Yes, he was there. But not after I hung up the picture. I suppose he might have seen it on the front counter, though, before I hung it." She looked up from the list to find Betty staring at her. "What?"

"You really are becoming Nancy Drew, aren't you? You're even making a suspect list." Betty grinned. "In fact, you should probably add me to that list too. I was in the shop shortly after you bought the building."

"You're right." Mary playfully jotted her sister's name on the list but then crossed it off. "Nope, this Betty here is definitely not guilty. Breaking windows isn't her style. She's more of a lock picker."

"Very funny." Betty's blue eyes twinkled. "But seriously. You should see yourself right now. Talking about this mystery makes you light up."

Mary tried to describe the feeling. "I guess it's like when Gram and I used to try to figure out the mystery novels I'd read out loud to her. That was so much fun."

Betty nodded. "I remember. You always did like ferreting out the clues in those stories."

"Besides," Mary said brightly, "my curiosity about that photo has made me get out there and meet people in Ivy Bay. I've touched base with Toad again and met Mason Willoughby, who gave me a wonderful tour of the Gallery. Neither of which would have happened if I'd just let it go."

"So what's next?"

"Well..." Mary thought for a moment. "I'm convinced that the picture was stolen for a reason, so there must be a clue in it somewhere." Mary tapped one finger on one of the printouts in front of her. "The first step is to find out who owned this car." Mary looked at her watch. "But I'll have to approach that subject tomorrow, because there's just too much work at the shop today. I'm getting woefully behind on inventory." Mary thought of the stacks and stacks of books she still needed to organize before the grand opening. For now, this investigation would have to wait. She had a bookshop to prepare.

TEN

◆ ◆ ◆

The next morning, the glazier arrived at her shop.

"I've got some good news and some bad news," he said, after he had studied the window.

Mary didn't want to deal with any bad news, but she squared her shoulders and said, "Which one do I want to hear first?"

He rubbed one meaty hand over his jaw. His name tag read Tiny, which didn't describe the man standing in front of her. Just the opposite, in fact. He towered over her and looked like a man who did a lot of heavy lifting. "Let's start with the good news. There shouldn't be any problem with putting in the new glass today."

She breathed a sigh of relief. "And the bad news?"

"I noticed that you've got some water damage on the door frame." He removed a small corner of the plywood. "See here?" Tiny dug his thumbnail into the frame. "The wood is soft, a sign that there's a slow leak. The interior part of the frame is still good enough for me to install the glass, but if this doesn't get fixed soon, you're going to have a real problem on your hands. It should have been done six months ago— the last time I replaced this glass."

She blanched. "This window was broken before?"

He shook his head. "It was just a crack. The owner called me up and said he wanted it fixed before he put the place up for sale. I noticed the damaged frame back then and advised him to replace it. I guess he didn't tell you."

No, he hadn't told her. It made Mary wonder if there was anything else Paul Becker had kept from her. She'd just seen him last week when he'd stopped by the shop to give her the spare keys. He'd always seemed sincere and honest. Maybe this was just an oversight. Then again, he was on her "suspect" list.

Tiny moved toward the door. "Do you want me to go ahead and get started?"

She hesitated, wishing she could ask John for advice. He'd always been such a good sounding board for her, so often the voice of reason when she felt uncertain about something.

Now she turned to God, praying to Him for guidance. *Heavenly Father, please tell me what to do.*

Tiny glanced at his watch. "I've got a full schedule today, ma'am."

"Oh, of course, I'm sorry." Mary cleared her throat. "For now, go ahead and replace the glass. I'll deal with the frame later."

He nodded and headed outside. His truck was parked in front of her store; several large panes of glass stood in the back, secured by rods and clamps.

Mary knew she'd be too distracted by Tiny as he repaired the window to get any work done, so now seemed like the right time to make a trip to the Department of Motor Vehicles.

She scooped up Gus and carried him to the back room. She opened a can of cat food for him and placed it in his bowl before leaving the room and closing the door behind her. She didn't want him to get in Tiny's way or get injured while they were making repairs.

When she returned to the front of the shop, she saw that Tiny and his assistant had removed the plywood board and were now prepping the frame for the new glass.

Mary walked over to the counter to find the list she'd been preparing. She added another item: *Replace damaged door frame and hang Open/Shut sign*. Betty had found an adorable vintage sign that had Open on one side and Shut on the other at one of her flea market visits, and Mary thought it would be perfect for her shop. Yesterday afternoon, she had called Kip and arranged for him to come by around noon to take a look at her list and figure out the tools he would need. She hoped he would be able to actually start the repairs soon. She was especially glad now that she had chosen the opening date she had; the last thing she wanted was for her very first customers to be browsing among the bangs and clanks of construction. And while she vaguely worried that they wouldn't be done in time for the opening, she had seen Kip work, and he was efficient and thorough. She hoped he'd come through for her again.

She jotted her cell-phone number on the bottom of another Post-it.

"I'm going out for a while," she told Tiny. "If you need me, just give me a call on my cell phone. I left the number on the counter."

"Okay. We should be fine here," he told her, pulling a rag from his pocket and wiping his hands with it. "We'll be breaking for lunch soon, but we should finish by early afternoon."

"I'm sure I'll be back before then." Mary picked up her bag and headed for the door as Tiny and his assistant resumed working.

———

Mary walked to the Department of Motor Vehicles, which was located in a one-story brick building out by the highway. There were six people lined up at the counter, so she moved to the back of the line.

The line moved slowly, making Mary glad she'd brought a book with her. Just last night she had begun reading, for what felt like the zillionth time, *Wuthering Heights*, a book she certainly planned on selling at the bookstore. It was indeed a mystery, and from the beginning Mary had planned to push the boundaries of traditional definitions of mystery novels. She had kept an open mind while buying books and planned to continue that philosophy as time went on.

Twenty minutes later, just as Catherine's ghost appeared at the window, Mary finally reached the front of the line.

"May I help you?" asked the middle-aged brunette behind the counter.

"Hello, my name is Mary Fisher and I have a rather strange request."

"Okay," the clerk said with a tentative smile. "What is it?"

Mary placed the slip of paper with the partial license plate number on the counter between them. "I'm trying to determine the owner of this car. The strange part of the equation is that this plate was issued in 1957 or shortly after. Any thoughts?"

"Well, you're missing the last number on the license plate. All the plates from that era have six digits."

"Do your vehicle registrations go back that far?"

She grimaced. "They do, but we rarely have requests to view them. Hold on while I check with my supervisor." The clerk picked up the paper and walked to the end of the counter before disappearing behind a door.

Mary waited. And waited. More people joined the line behind her, and she could tell they were becoming antsy. Finally, the clerk reappeared and handed the slip of paper back to Mary.

"Any luck?" Mary asked, taking it from her.

The clerk nodded. "The records are filed in the storage room in the cellar. You're welcome to look at them, if you'd like."

Mary hated cellars, but if going down there meant getting closer to solving her mystery, she'd give it a try. "Sounds great, thanks."

The teller waved to a young man sweeping the floor behind her. "Hey, Bill, will you take this lady to the dungeon?"

The dungeon? Even worse than "cellar."

"Sure thing," he said, setting the broom aside. He reached into a closet and pulled out a flashlight. That wasn't a good sign.

"This way," Bill told her, heading toward the door at the end of the room. He was tall and lanky, with a sweep of blond hair that kept falling into his eyes.

"What's the flashlight for?" She tried to keep her voice casual as the man opened a heavy steel door and ushered her into the stairwell.

"Oh, it's just precautionary." He waved off her concern. "Sometimes the electricity goes out down here and it's black as midnight without any windows."

Just perfect. Mary waited for him to lead the way and then followed him down the steep stairwell. The air around her grew cool and musty. When they reached the landing, she saw row upon row of gray, steel file cabinets.

Bill reached to turn on the overhead lights, and a series of fluorescent panels lit up the ceiling. It was cramped and smelled a bit mildewy in the cellar of the DMV, but not as bad as she'd expected.

Mary thanked Bill, who stood in an almost military position while waiting for her, then turned to the row of file cabinets in front of her. She opened the top drawer of the first cabinet, pleasantly surprised to find that the files were organized by months and years. Unfortunately, the years didn't seem to be in any sort of order.

Decades of dust invaded her nostrils as she sorted through the files and she reached for a tissue just in time to catch a sneeze. She paused for a moment, feeling another sneeze approaching, then the sensation passed.

Mary turned her attention back to the first file cabinet, which contained vehicle registrations from 1933, 1947, and 1961. She began moving down the row of file cabinets, looking in each one for files from 1957.

The lights flickered above her, and she glanced over at Bill. "Got that flashlight ready?"

He held it up in the air. "Sure do."

She moved on to the next file cabinet and opened the top drawer. "1941, 1964, 1952," she read out loud, until she reached the last section. "1957. Got it!"

Bill hung back while Mary pulled out twelve thick files and set them on the rickety table next to the stairs. She flipped through the paper documents in the January file. The registration contained the name and address of the car owner, as well as the year, make, and model of the car. The license plate number of each vehicle was written in ink at the top right-hand corner of each page. She needed to find all the Cadillac Eldorado Broughams that had been registered in 1957 and see if the license plate number matched up with the first five numbers of the license plate in the photograph.

This could take a while.

She tried to pick up her speed as she moved onto February. The lights flickered again, and Mary felt the urgency shoot through her. She moved even quicker now, nervous that Bill's prediction would come true and they would lose the light.

The lights kept flickering as she searched through March, April, and May.

"Here's one," she said, excitement flowing through her as she pulled it from the file. The car had been registered to a man named Leroy Steckler in May 1957 and had a license plate number of 324 526. She stared at the name, finding it vaguely familiar. But try as she might, Mary couldn't remember where she'd heard it before. She set the registration aside and continued searching for other matches.

By the time she reached the August registrations, she could tell that Bill was starting to grow restless. He paced in small circles, and every once in a while, he'd exhale a long sigh.

"You don't have to stay down here with me," Mary suggested. "Just leave the flashlight, and I'll be fine."

"We're not allowed to leave people down here alone," Bill replied. "It's one of the many rules of the DMV. I don't get it. Why would anyone want to steal a bunch of dusty, old records?"

He didn't expect an answer, and she didn't have one for him. Before the break-in at her shop, she never would have believed someone would want to steal that old photograph. That was the reason she was here now, digging through all these dusty files and suppressing the urge to sneeze.

The lights flickered again and went out. For a moment, Mary was drenched in darkness. Then a beam of light shone from the spot where Bill had been leaning against the wall. "You okay?"

"Yep, I'm fine," she said, still finger-deep in the August file. "Can you bring that flashlight over here?"

His audible sigh reached her through the darkness. Then she heard the sound of his footsteps as the beam of light bounced around the room. When he reached her, he aimed the light at the file in her hands. "Can you see okay?"

"Just fine, thanks," she replied, resuming her search. She was just about to close the file for the month of August when she reached the last document and saw that it was a Cadillac Eldorado Brougham and the number in the top right-hand corner was 324 521.

"Here's another one!" Mary pulled the document from the file. She knew Bill didn't really care about what she was looking for, but she was happy to share her discovery with him nonetheless. She thought of Henry; he'd be proud of her for finding these files. She looked forward to telling him about them.

"Congratulations," Bill said with a mix of sarcasm and genuine satisfaction. "Now can we go upstairs?"

"Soon," she promised. Mary looked over the document. According to the registration, the car with the license plate number 324 521 was registered to Fred Vargo in August 1957.

Mary resumed her search, but she didn't find any more matches in the remaining months of the year, a fact that thrilled her. It meant one of these two men was the owner of the car in the photograph.

"Do you mind if I take these registrations upstairs and make a copy?" she asked him.

"I'll do it for you myself if we can leave now." He plucked the papers from her hands and headed toward the stairs. Mary followed him, realizing that she'd been so focused on identifying the owner of the car that she didn't have a plan for what she'd do once she'd succeeded.

As Mary made her way back to the bookshop, she considered how to locate the two men named on the car registrations. If she was lucky, they'd each still be at the same address listed on the registration. She didn't know if they were still alive or if the car had anything to do with why the picture was stolen, but it was a start.

She arrived at the bookshop just as Tiny and his assistant were emerging from the Black & White Diner next door.

"Good timing," she said with a smile, walking through the front door.

Tiny patted his large stomach. "Good food. I always eat there when I have a job in Ivy Bay."

The two men headed for the back of the truck. All the original window glass had been completely removed, along with the old putty.

Mary stood out on the sidewalk, holding her breath as they removed the pane from the truck and gingerly carried it over to the frame. The sun reflected off the glass, blinding her for a moment. She moved slightly, her shoulder brushing into someone behind her.

"Hi, Mrs. Fisher," Kip said, walking up next to her. "You must be excited to finally have the window replaced."

"I think I'm more nervous than excited," Mary admitted as they watched the two men fit the glass into the frame. It was a delicate process, and Mary could feel her shoulders tensing as she watched.

When Tiny finally stepped back, Mary clapped her hands together. "You did it!"

Tiny grinned proudly. "Good as new."

"Thank you so much, Tiny." Mary shook his hand.

"How's it going, Tiny?" Kip greeted him.

"Hey, Kip. Goin' well. Let me just show you the damaged areas of the door frame."

"Sounds good."

While Tiny pointed out the repairs that needed to be made, Mary admired the new window. Her shop looked like itself again. The new window made all the difference, letting in the extra sunlight the board had blocked. Of course, the shop was otherwise filled with light, but since the front counter was so close to the door, the slight darkening of the room felt significant to Mary. Now that the window was fixed, she could already feel herself moving with a lighter step, remembering a Bible verse she had memorized that seemed to fit the moment: *Light is sweet, and it pleases the eyes to see the sun* (Ecclesiastes 11:7).

A few minutes later, after Kip had taken a look at the rest of Mary's list and scoped out the areas that needed repair, he approached her. "Looks like I've got some work to do."

Mary shrugged ruefully. "I guess this sort of thing happens to a two-hundred-year-old building. When can you start?"

"As soon as tomorrow. I know you've got a big opening planned." He looked down at the list she'd handed him. "I'll do my best to have everything on here completed by next week."

Mary sighed in relief. Kip was a godsend. "That would be great. Thanks, Kip." She walked over to the counter and unlocked the top drawer, retrieving a spare key to the front door that Paul had given her. "I'll give you a key now so I don't forget. Is there anything else you need?"

"That should do it." He folded the Post-it and put it in his pocket. "I'll get on it as soon as I can."

"Thanks, Kip. You're a lifesaver."

He waved off the comment, clearly uncomfortable with the compliment. "Definitely not a lifesaver. Just a regular old handyman."

"Well, you've been very helpful and kind, and I'm grateful for you," Mary said.

He gave a modest nod and headed out the door. Mary turned from the door and let Gus out of the back room. Then she spent some time cataloging books on her computer and admiring the new window glass. She cleaned off the finger-prints Tiny and his assistant had left behind and polished the wood tables and chairs until they glowed.

When Mary finished up at the bookshop, she headed home. The sun was shining, the sky was blue, and the beach beckoned. Someday soon she wanted to go out on the water, perhaps even on Henry's fishing boat. But she had a different kind of fishing to do first.

ELEVEN

Mary knew it was a long shot, but she needed to check out the addresses listed on the car registrations, so she decided to make two stops before she went home for the day. It was early afternoon, but she wasn't sure how long she'd be on this errand. And even if she headed back to the bookshop again later, she wouldn't mind a stop at home to check in on Betty.

According to the file, Fred Vargo had lived on Plover Lane, a street on the outskirts of town. She headed there first, her car window down and the warm breeze caressing her hair.

Gus sat nestled in his carrying case on the passenger seat. Gulls flew overhead as they made their way to the edge of town. Even if Vargo no longer lived at 22 Plover Lane, there might be a neighbor who remembered him or his family.

As she drove, Mary noticed fewer and fewer houses. "I don't know about this, Gus," she said out loud. "Maybe he lived in a farmhouse."

She turned onto Plover Lane and slowed to a stop. There were no houses on either side of the street. One side of the block was a park, with picnic tables and a small playground, and the other side was filled with red cedar trees and native grasses. There might have been a house there once, but she saw no sign of it now.

"I don't think we're going to find Mr. Vargo here," she said with a disappointed sigh. Gus replied with a soft meow.

"One more stop," she said, turning the car around and heading back into town. The other car owner Leroy Steckler had lived at 19 Cherry Mew, according to his car registration. That was closer to home, and she knew there were houses along that street. She only hoped it wasn't another dead end.

When she reached Cherry Mew, she slowed the car, looking for the address. "There it is, Gus, number nineteen."

She parked along the street and climbed out of the car, leaving the window cracked for Gus. A woman about Mary's age rounded the side of the house wearing garden gloves and carrying a foam kneeling pad.

"Hello there," Mary called out, walking up the drive.

The woman tucked the kneeling pad under one arm and peeled off her gloves. "Hello. Can I help you?"

"Yes, hello. I'm Mary Fisher and I'm looking for a man named Leroy Steckler."

"That's my stepfather," the woman said, tilting her head to one side. "Do you know him?"

Mary hesitated, not sure how to begin. "I used to spend summers here when I was a child and I think your father might have known my uncle George."

The woman smiled. "Well, why don't we go ask him?"

Mary stared at her. "You mean...he's here?"

She laughed. "Yes, he's on the deck in the backyard, telling me how to weed the garden. He and I could both use a distraction. My name is Miranda, by the way. Miranda Bodell."

"It's nice to meet you, Miranda." Mary followed her into the backyard, feeling as if she could perform cartwheels. She couldn't believe her luck in finding Mr. Steckler at the same address that he'd listed on his 1957 vehicle registration. But why not? Many people spent their adult lives in one home. Her grandparents had, and she knew Betty's sister-in-law, Eleanor, still lived on the estate where she'd grown up.

"Hey, Dad," Miranda called out as they entered the backyard. "You have a visitor."

Mary could see a thin, elderly man seated in a chair on the deck. Wispy white strands of hair covered his freckled scalp, and he pushed the glasses up on his nose as she climbed onto the deck.

"Hello," he said, his piercing green eyes staring at her from under a pair of bushy white eyebrows. "Do I know you?"

"I don't think we've ever met before." Mary pulled up a chair beside him while Miranda headed toward a flower garden near the fence that bordered the yard. "I'm Mary Fisher. I used to spend my summers in Ivy Bay with my grandparents, Charles and Ida Nelson."

"Well, what do you know," he exclaimed. "My wife and I used to attend the same church with the Nelsons. We knew them well." He looked her up and down. "I remember two little girls they used to bring to church in the summertime. Don't tell me you're one of them."

Mary smiled at the disbelief in his voice. "I'm all grown up now, as you can see, but I was actually the youngest girl. My older sister is Betty Emerson. She moved to Ivy Bay after she married her husband."

"I remember the Emerson family," he said. "I worked as an electrician and did some jobs at their estate. Which one of their kids did she marry?"

"Edward," Mary told him.

He nodded his approval. "He was one of the good ones."

Mary scooted her chair closer. "Actually, there's someone else I hope you might know." She pulled the enlarged printout from her bag and handed it to him. "This is my uncle George Nelson in front of the shop he owned in 1957. I just bought that same shop and found this picture in the cellar."

"I knew George." Leroy studied the picture for a moment. Then his mouth dropped open. "And would you look at that! A '57 Cadillac Eldorado. I had one just like it."

"Is there any chance this is yours?"

"Oh, I'm sure." He pointed to the car. "I got hit by a crazy driver, so my car had a bit of a dent in the front fender on the driver's side. I don't see a dent in this car."

"Maybe this picture was taken before your accident."

He shook his head. "Nope, my accident happened right after I drove off the dealer's lot. It didn't turn out all that bad, though." He grinned. "I ended up marrying that crazy driver. Never did get that dent fixed.... It ended up being our little reminder of how my wife and I met."

Mary smiled, already growing fond of Leroy. He was one sharp cookie, and she loved the fact that he'd known her grandparents and uncle, people who had been such an important part of her life. And even if the car wasn't his, perhaps he would be able to help, anyway. "I don't suppose you recognize the woman in the picture?" Mary said.

He twisted his mouth as he studied the mystery woman. "Can't say that I do, but she's definitely a looker."

"Dad!" Miranda said with a playful roll of her eyes. "Sorry, Mary, he's never been one to hold back his true feelings."

"Oh, it's okay," Mary said with a laugh. "My grandfather was the same way."

Leroy ignored them both and continued to look at the picture. Then he snapped his fingers. "Wait a minute; she was Fred's girl."

"Fred Vargo?" Mary asked, her pulse quickening.

Leroy nodded. "He had a way with the ladies. And cars, for that matter. He and I drove the same vehicle, so maybe that's how you got us messed up." Mary smiled at his deduction. He looked at the photo for a moment longer and then looked up at her pointedly. "What's this all about, anyway?"

"Let's just say I'm looking into my family history," Mary said. "Once I learned you owned a '57 Eldorado, I was hoping you might be able to tell me something about this picture."

Leroy's piercing gaze didn't leave her face. "Sometimes family history is better left alone."

What a strange comment, Mary thought. She was almost tempted to believe he knew more than he was admitting, but he had been so forthcoming and genuine, she couldn't doubt his sincerity. "Perhaps, Mr. Steckler," she said with a soft voice, "but it's important to me."

Leroy sighed. "Well, I just remember that Fred and your uncle got into a fistfight. It didn't last too long from what I was told, but Fred walked around with quite a shiner for a while."

Mary couldn't picture her sweet uncle in a fistfight. She'd never even heard him raise his voice. "Do you remember what they fought about?"

He shrugged his narrow shoulders. "I heard it was over a girl. Maybe this girl, since she and your uncle look pretty friendly here."

Her heart sank at the possibility that he was right.

"I wish I could remember her name," Leroy continued, tapping his knee with one hand, "but I'm drawing a blank."

She waited, hoping it would come to him, but after several minutes, he shook his head and handed her the photocopy. "Sorry, I'm not going to remember. It's just been too many years."

She took the photo from him. "Thanks so much for your help. I really appreciate it."

"And I appreciate the visit. Stop by again sometime, and I'll tell you some stories about your grandpa Charles. He was a fine man."

"I will," Mary promised, looking forward to it. Then she thought of one more question. "What about Fred Vargo? Do you know anything about him or his family or friends?"

He shook his head. "I sure don't. After a while, I didn't see him around Ivy Bay anymore. I'm not sure what happened to him."

After chatting a little while longer, Mary said her good-byes to Leroy and Miranda and walked back to her car. She still didn't know the name of the mystery woman, but at least now she knew the woman was connected to Fred Vargo. And if Uncle George and Fred Vargo had come to blows over her, maybe putting the old photograph on display had evoked an emotional reaction in someone else. A reaction that had resulted in theft.

When she arrived home, it was late in the afternoon. Mary opened the front door and called out, "Bets, wait until you hear…" Her voice trailed off when she saw her sister and Eleanor seated on the living room sofa. Across from them were the other ladies of the book club: Virginia Livingston, Frances Curran, and Madeline Dinsdale.

"Oh, I'm sorry," Mary said, closing the door behind her. "I didn't realize you had a book-club meeting today. I didn't see any cars outside."

Gus jumped out of her bag and onto the floor, apparently unfazed by their guests.

"We all walked here," Virginia said, looking at Mary through a pair of periwinkle-blue eyeglasses that matched her summer dress. "It's such a beautiful day."

"And this isn't an official meeting," Eleanor clarified, sitting primly on the sofa with her ankles crossed. She wore an ivory skirt suit, and her dark hair was smoothed back into a neat chignon. "Frances called an impromptu gathering of the group because she wanted to talk to us about a philanthropic project she has in mind."

Frances turned in her chair to face Mary. "Actually, I was hoping you might be able to help."

Mary glanced at her sister, then back at Frances, who was dressed in a casual pair of khaki clam diggers and a white top. Her short gray hair had a youthful edge to it. "What did you have in mind?"

"Well, as a bookshop owner, I'm sure you love books as much as I do," Frances began. "I was reading about a tornado in the South recently, and one small-town library lost every book in its inventory. I'm sure the same type of thing happens during other natural disasters. So I thought we might sponsor a disaster-aid book drive to send new and used books to libraries that need them."

Mary's opinion of Eleanor's exclusive book club just went up several notches. "I think that's a wonderful idea. How can I help?"

Frances glanced at the other members. "Well, I thought your bookshop might be a good place for the first book drive. It's right on Main Street and it will attract people who love books."

"This wouldn't be an ongoing project," Madeline interjected, fingering the long string of yellow and purple beads around her neck. The artist wore a gauzy black tunic blouse and a pair of black slacks. "We think it will be more productive to have our book drives on set dates."

"That's right," Virginia said, as Gus curled around the leg of her chair. She reached down and picked him up, setting him in her ample lap. "I've been on enough charitable committees to know that people don't have very long attention spans. It's better to go big for a short period of time than to do things in dribs and drabs."

"That's why I was thinking the grand opening of your shop would be a perfect time for our first one," Frances said, smiling up at Mary. "We'll be advertising the book drive in the local paper, so naturally your grand opening will be mentioned as well."

Betty clapped her hands together. "Oh, I think that's a wonderful idea!"

Mary agreed, but she'd want to help even if it didn't benefit her business. "That does sound wonderful. Please count me in."

"We haven't made any final decisions yet," Eleanor said, her voice cool. "I'm certain Betty will let you know what we decide to do after our meeting concludes."

Betty winced and sent Mary an apologetic smile. "I'm sure we'll be done soon."

The last thing Mary wanted was for Betty to feel bad. "Please take your time. It was nice seeing you again, ladies, but I just thought of an errand I need to run." She said it to be polite, but she really did have a place she wanted to visit. She left the house with a spring in her step.

TWELVE

———◆◆◆———

Seagulls flew low over the dock as Mary made her way past the bait shop to the floating walkway. The well-kept boat bay was located on the canal that separated Cape Cod from the mainland and was the domain of both pleasure boaters and commercial fishermen.

She was about to ask someone where to find Henry's boat, *Misty Horizon*, when she saw the man himself by a dock piling.

She walked toward him, watching as he worked a knot out of a fishing line. The water sparkled behind him, making him seem much younger than his sixty-three years.

"Ahoy," she said with a smile, walking up to him.

He stood up straight when he saw her. "Well, this is a nice surprise. What are you doing here?"

"I hoped I'd find you here. I brought you some ice cream from Bailey's to thank you for the books you gave me, and for the help with the photograph." She handed him the thermal cooler with a pint of pistachio-nut ice cream.

He stared for a moment at the thermos and then looked back at Mary. "You didn't have to do that." His voice was tender, as if this kind of gesture hadn't been paid him in a while.

"Well, it's not for purely altruistic reasons," she said lightly. "I've also been wanting to see your boat, and this seemed like the perfect time to do it."

He tilted his face up to the clear blue sky. "You couldn't ask for a better time. Even when the fish aren't biting, I don't really mind on a day like this."

Mary moved closer to the edge of the dock. "Is this your boat?" she asked, pointing to the sleek watercraft behind him. It was white with navy-blue accent stripes running from the stem to the stern. The chrome trim and fixtures gleamed under the bright sun.

"That's her." Henry reached out and rubbed her white hull. "Do you want to take a spin?"

She grinned up at him. "I thought you'd never ask." Then she performed a mock salute. "Permission to come aboard, Captain?"

He laughed. "Permission granted."

She climbed up the ladder, Henry standing close by to offer his hand in case she needed help. Once they were aboard, he handed her a life jacket.

"Let's go!" He maneuvered the boat away from the marina, gradually picking up speed as he reached the more open waters of Cape Cod Bay.

Mary sat on a chair, enjoying the tingle of the sea spray on her face and the fresh air filling her lungs. She watched Henry, his feet set apart and his broad hands controlling the boat with ease.

To Mary's delight, he took her past many of the bay's most beautiful spots. She saw the lighthouse in a neighboring town and classic historic inns that lined the coast. Seabirds flew overhead, one occasionally diving for a fish or coasting low over the rippling water.

She turned around to see Ivy Bay in the distance and thought she could spot the tall white spire of Grace Church. Little Neck Beach was already filling with people, but they looked like colorful dots from this distance.

After about thirty minutes, Henry slowed the boat and let it drift on the calm waters. "I think it's time for a snack." He sat in the chair beside her and took the ice cream out of the cooler. Then he popped off the lid. "If this tastes as good as it smells, I'm in for a treat."

She watched him take a bite. Then he looked up at her with a wide smile. "I think I owe you another boat ride someday for ice cream this good."

"Next time I'll bring you one of *my* special recipes," she promised. Then she sat back and enjoyed the view. And the company.

When Mary returned home, she slowly opened the front door of the house and took a cautious peek inside. She saw Gus looking back at her as he sat in the empty living room. "Is the coast clear?" she whispered.

Gus bounded her way and sniffed at the Pizzeria Rustica pizza box she had picked up on her way home.

Mary walked inside, breathing a sigh of relief that the book club had left. Now she could finally talk to her sister.

She carried the pizza into the kitchen and set it on the table. Then she headed over to the French doors leading to the backyard. She could see Betty bent over a row of cucumber plants in the garden, a wide-brimmed straw hat shading her face from the sun. Mary loved the vision of her sister doing another thing she loved, gardening. Betty's hobbies like interior decor and gardening had kept her active and healthy. Mary felt a tinge of pride for her sister. And more than pride; Mary was simply impressed. Rheumatoid arthritis was often a prohibitive condition, but Betty had done everything she could to defy it.

Mary opened the door and walked onto the patio. "Hey, Bets. I'm home. How's the garden going?"

"Good!" Betty called out, setting a cucumber into the basket beside her. "I'll be there in a minute."

Mary walked back inside and headed toward the cupboard. "No pizza for you, little man," she said to Gus. She opened a can of cat food for him and placed it in his bowl. Then she retrieved some plates and forks and set them on the table.

Betty walked into the kitchen a few minutes later. "It's warm out there today." She reached up to wipe her damp brow with the back of her hand. "But we'll have fresh cucumbers and onions for dinner."

"And pizza," Mary said, setting the box on the table. When Mary moved in with her sister, they hadn't discussed how to split up household chores like cooking and cleaning. But one of the reasons she'd wanted to live with Betty was so she could take over several of those tasks so Betty could get a break. "I figured you wouldn't have much time to cook after your meeting and I certainly don't feel like cooking."

"*Mmm*." Betty let out a relieved sigh. "Sounds perfect." She walked over to the sink and began rinsing off the vegetables.

Betty glanced over at Mary, her face contrite. "I'm so sorry if Eleanor made you feel uncomfortable earlier. She's really a good person at heart."

Mary smiled. Betty always looked for the best in people— that was one of the things she loved most about her. "Don't worry about it. I'm perfectly fine. I actually went out to visit Henry at his boat. We took a ride. It was lovely."

Betty looked at her and wiggled her eyebrows. "Lovely, was it?"

Mary blushed and kept her composure. "Yes, it *was* lovely. I suspect he'll once again become a very good friend." Her emphasis was on the word *friend*.

"Whatever you say, sis," Betty said with an exaggerated wink. Then she pulled out a knife, and Mary walked over to the sink and gestured for Betty to hand it to her.

"Let me slice those cucumbers. You sit down and cool off, okay? Your face is a little red."

"That's from bending over so much." But Betty didn't object. She handed over the knife, walked over to the refrigerator and retrieved a bowl of sliced red onions. Mary could detect a slight limp in Betty's step.

"I've been pickling these in vinegar for a few hours," Betty said. She set the bowl on the table, practically plopped into one of the kitchen chairs, and plucked an onion from the bowl. "*Hmm*, these are good. Just the right amount of tartness."

Soon, Mary and Betty were settled at the table and digging into their pizza.

"*Mmm*, this is so good," Betty said.

"I know. It's the real deal," Mary said, loving the authentic Italian pies the place baked. She had chuckled when she'd met the store's owner, Anthony Cantuccio, who described his pizzas as "better than any of those knockoffs you get in New York." He'd recommended the special pizza of the day—mozzarella, artichoke and sun-dried tomato—and Mary couldn't resist.

"So how did the window installation go?" Betty said, pulling a string of mozzarella.

"Great! The window's fixed, and Kip even agreed to make some other repairs for me before next week." Mary pulled some cheese off her slice and tilted her head back to take it in.

"I'm glad." Betty set her pizza down and hid a yawn behind her hand. "And what about the DMV? Any luck there?"

Mary told her about the two car registrations she'd found and her meeting with Leroy. "He's such a nice man. Do you know him?"

"I don't think so, but he sounds like someone I'd like to meet."

"He is." Mary knew it was time to tell her sister *everything* that Leroy had told her. "He even warned me not to dig too deep into family history."

Betty's brow furrowed. "What does that mean?"

Mary told her about the fistfight between Uncle George and Fred Vargo—a fistfight apparently provoked by the woman in the picture.

Betty sat back in her chair, a stunned look on her face. "I don't believe it. Not Uncle George!"

Mary knew just how she felt. "I only met Leroy today, but he doesn't seem like one to exaggerate. Still, it all happened a long time ago, and he said it was what he heard, not something he witnessed for himself."

"So it could be based on a rumor," Betty said hopefully.

"Maybe. He did see Fred's black eye himself, though, so that much seems to be true." Mary wished she knew what to believe. How could she solve a mystery when the only apparent clues were in a photograph dating back more than fifty years? At least those were the only clues she'd found so far.

"I called Jean this afternoon," Betty said abruptly. "I could tell she'd been crying. I think we were right not to say anything to her about all of this yet. I'm not sure she could handle it."

"That's strange. She seemed better when I saw her yesterday. But I guess that's part of the grief process." Mary tried to avoid the roller coaster of emotions by keeping herself busy, but it wasn't easy.

"She's probably been going through her dad's things today, and the emotions got the best of her," Betty said. "We both know how overwhelming that can be."

Mary nodded. Even now, John's personal belongings were packed away in the closet in her room. Mary couldn't yet bring herself to go through them—afraid she might fall apart if she did.

"I can only imagine how much stuff Uncle George must have in that house," Betty said, a wan smile tugging at her mouth. "Remember how he was always trying some new get-rich scheme? He once tried to talk Dad into investing in underwater cars. He was certain that was the wave of the future."

Mary nodded, happy to be thinking of their father. "I do. Dad never wanted in on any of Uncle George's investments, though. He always said he'd taken enough risks in the war."

"That's right." Betty breathed a wistful sigh. "Even though they were brothers, the difference between them was like night and day."

Their father had died from a heart attack. Uncle George had given a beautiful eulogy and helped their family deal with all the business matters that had to be handled.

Just thinking about it made her feel guilty for doubting her uncle. And for doubting Jean. But it was too late to let the mystery go now. If she did, those doubts would never entirely fade away. She'd rather know the truth, no matter what path the truth took.

They ate in silence for the next several minutes, each caught up in their memories of the past.

Then Betty took her last bite of pizza and laid a hand over her midsection. "I ate too much."

"Me too, but that pizza hit the spot." Both Mary and Betty settled back into their chairs. "So what do you have planned for the rest of the evening?"

"Actually, I'm feeling pretty beat," Betty said. "I think I'll lie down for a little while."

"Good idea. You go ahead. I'll clean up here."

She watched Betty slowly make her way to her bedroom at the back of the house. It used to be Edward's office, but after he passed away, Betty had turned it into a bedroom so she wouldn't have to climb the stairs anymore.

That left the second floor of the house as Mary's domain. There were four bedrooms and a bathroom up there. One bedroom belonged to Mary, and the others had been children's bedrooms but now served as guest rooms.

After she finished washing the dishes, Mary headed upstairs, Gus close at her heels. The second floor was warmer than below, so when she walked into her bedroom, she turned on the overhead ceiling fan.

Gus liked to watch the fan, although it seemed to make him a bit dizzy. It cracked Mary up whenever he did it. He sat on the floor, his head tilted upward as the fan blades went around and around.

Mary stood for a moment, before deciding to look at the other framed photograph that she'd found in the cellar. She'd brought it home over a week ago to fix the cracked frame, and she'd stored it in the closet, intending to deal with it when she wasn't quite so busy. She knew there was nothing particularly special about the photo, but then again, she hadn't thought the stolen photograph was particularly important either.

She walked over to her bedroom closet and opened one of the sliding doors. She reached up to the top shelf, feeling blindly for the picture, when her hand gripped a baseball. She paused for a moment, a lump forming in her throat. She pulled her hand down to look at the ball.

The baseball had turned a little gray over the years, although she could still see the signatures of the ballplayers on it. Carl Yastrzemski and Sparky Lyle, just to name a couple. It must have fallen out of one of the boxes of John's things she had stored.

John had caught this baseball at a Red Sox game in 1970, shortly after they'd become engaged. He'd been so proud of it. Mary had arranged for the players to sign it and gave it to him as a wedding present. The funniest part had been when John thought he'd lost his beloved baseball when it went missing for a week before the wedding. It was a story he'd told their children, Jack and Elizabeth, over and over again. She smiled to herself, remembering. He used to tease her that he'd been so worried about his missing baseball that he didn't have time to get cold feet before the wedding.

Mary gently moved her fingers over the old baseball, remembering how many times John had held it in his hands. She wished she could hear him tell the story once more or hold one of his big, strong hands again.

"Lord, bring me through this pain," she prayed. "I miss him so."

After a long moment, Mary lovingly placed the ball in a box with John's other things. It hurt too much to think about what she'd lost. She'd deal with her grief and bittersweet memories later.

She once again reached on her tiptoes and began to feel around on the top shelf. She quickly found the photograph and pulled it down gently, not wanting to do any further damage to the frame. She wiped a layer of dust off the glass surface.

The frame was identical to the one on the stolen photograph, as she remembered, and just as she had recalled, the image itself showed only the back of the building and the small, weedy backyard. There were no people or cars or bicycles in this picture. As she studied the image, she realized that the courtyard today looked almost the same as it had in 1957. She realized, not for the first time, that it wouldn't take too much work to fix up the backyard a little. She could clear out the weeds and plant some flowers, maybe even add a nice bench. She resolved to talk with Betty about it—one of these days.

Mary's eye moved to the crack in the oak frame, near the top right corner. The crack was slightly curved, and the wood moved between her fingers as she tested the depth of the break.

She knew there was some wood glue in the craft room downstairs, so she decided now was as good a time as any to try to repair it. She tucked the picture under her arm and then checked her face in the hallway mirror, wiping away a stray tear.

"No tears tonight, Gus," she said to the cat. "Let's go do some gluing."

Gus blinked at the sound of his name, got up and walked through the open bedroom door, his path a little wobbly from watching the fan spin for so long. Mary felt a little wobbly too, but she had faith that God would keep her on the right path.

Once she reached the craft room, Mary examined the crack again. It looked like she might be able to glue it without having to take the frame off. She preferred to do it that way, not wanting to tear off the original backing.

Then she noticed a faded ink stamp on the bottom corner of the brown paper backing. It was in the shape of a circle and inside the circle was "Bratt Frame Shop 1957."

Mary delighted in the discovery. She'd assumed this photograph and the one that had been stolen were in their original frames, but this was confirmation. Apparently, these pictures had been hidden away in the shop for over fifty years, but why? Had Uncle George simply wanted to keep a picture of his secret girlfriend? She shook that thought from her head. If that were the case, why was there a matching set of photographs showing the front and back of the building? No, there had to be another reason.

Gus padded out of the craft room, leaving her alone. The evening was quiet and peaceful. She hoped Betty was resting well so they could enjoy a fun weekend together.

She applied a thin line of wood glue to the crack and pressed the edges firmly together. After holding the edges for several minutes, Mary realized that there would need to be some kind of constant pressure on the frame until the glue dried. She opened a wardrobe in the room to look for something that would do just that. The wardrobe stored all kinds of crafty and utility items like clothespins, twine, and packaging tape. Her eyes fell on a large, heavy-duty rubber band. "That might do it," she said to herself.

She placed the sturdy rubber band around the cracked end of the frame and watched as the broken edges began to slowly pull apart. The rubber band wasn't strong enough; she needed something stronger. She picked up the ball of twine and cut off a long piece of it. Then she began to wind it tightly around the frame, over and over again, before finally tying a knot.

This time, when she let go of the frame, the broken edges stayed together. She set the frame on the end of the craft table, wanting to give it plenty of time to dry.

As she walked out of the craft room, she noticed a glow of light coming from the living room. Then her sister's cry pierced the silence. "Mary!"

THIRTEEN

❖

Mary rushed toward the living room, noticing a white trail of toilet paper snaking from the hall bathroom into the living room. She paused by the open bathroom door just long enough to see that the room was empty. Then she continued into the living room.

The scene inside the living room made her mouth gape. There was toilet paper everywhere, stretching over the floor and crisscrossing the furniture in a crazy pattern.

Betty stood frozen in the middle of the floor, looking at her once-pristine living room. She slowly turned to Mary, a bemused expression on her face. "I think the hall bathroom might be out of toilet paper."

Gus sat on the floor next to the sofa, an innocent expression on his furry face. But the shreds of white toilet paper hanging from his whiskers gave him away.

"Gus," Mary exclaimed, "I can't believe you did this!" Then she turned to her sister. "Oh, Bets, I'm so sorry."

Betty let out a long sigh and her shoulders dropped. "Don't worry about it," she said, a small smile teasing her lips. "I couldn't get comfortable in bed, so I thought I'd come out here and try to take my mind off my aches and pains." Her smile widened. "It worked, but not quite like I had planned."

Mary walked over and picked up her cat. "Gus, what's gotten into you tonight?" She stroked his head. "He's never done anything like this before."

"It reminds me of the time some of Evan's friends did the same thing to our front yard as a prank. It took days to get all the toilet paper out of the trees. At least this will be a lot easier to clean up."

Mary set Gus back on the floor and pushed up her sleeves. "Don't worry; I'll clean up this mess. Why don't you fix yourself a cup of hot tea and go relax in the kitchen until I'm done?"

"I'm fine," Betty assured her, reaching down to pick up a strip of toilet paper at her feet. "It will probably help me feel better to do a little stretching."

Mary bent down and began scooping up the scraps of toilet paper on the floor. "I don't know how to explain this. Maybe Gus is still adjusting to the new surroundings. I'm sure he'll settle down soon."

Betty picked up some toilet paper off the sofa. "At least he only focused on one room instead of the entire house. Somehow, he got hold of the toilet paper roll in the hall bathroom and went to town." A chuckle escaped her. "Just my luck that I'd replaced the empty roll with a jumbo size just this morning."

Mary tried to stop herself, but laughter bubbled up in her throat as she pictured Gus on a mad dash through the living room with the toilet paper streaming behind him. "I'm sorry. I know it isn't funny."

A smile flitted over Betty's mouth. "It's pretty funny. In fact, stop what you're doing. We've got to take a picture of this, or no one will ever believe it."

Mary waited while Betty used the camera on her cell phone to snap some pictures of the living room. She was relieved Betty was taking this so well, but she was still worried that Gus might wear out his welcome.

When Betty was through taking pictures, they resumed picking up.

Mary carried two handfuls of toilet paper over to the small wastebasket under the Chippendale writing desk. "I finally found that other picture in my bedroom closet upstairs. I was gluing the frame when I heard you call for me."

"I hope I didn't scare you," Betty said. "I was just so shocked when I walked into the living room and I wanted you to see it."

It had scared her, but Mary was just relieved it was nothing too serious. "No, I'm fine. I'd just found something interesting on the back of the picture frame, though. It was a stamp from the Bratt Frame Shop, dated 1957."

"Really?" Betty straightened up and looked over at Mary. "So Uncle George had the pictures framed when he owned the shop?"

"It seems so." Mary began unwinding the toilet paper that was wrapped around the legs of the coffee table. "Do you know if the Bratt Frame Shop is still around?"

"No, it closed about a decade ago. The owners were in their eighties when they finally sold the place and they've both passed away since then."

Mary dropped two more fistfuls of toilet paper into the wastebasket and then looked around the room for more toilet paper. They'd picked up most of it, but she spied a few tattered pieces in the corner by the potted ficus tree.

She still wondered why Gus would do such a thing. He'd been off his food for the first couple of weeks after they'd moved here but had regained his appetite.

After they had finished cleaning up the mess, Mary realized that Gus was no longer in the room. She went in search of him, heading up to her bedroom first.

She walked through her open bedroom door but didn't see Gus sleeping on top of the bedcovers or anywhere else in the room. Then she bent down and looked under the bed. A pair of blue feline eyes stared back at her.

"There you are," she said, reaching for him. He came to her arms without protest, letting her scoop him up. She sat down on the side of the bed, stroking the top of his head. "What got into you tonight, Gus? You were very naughty."

He blinked up at her but didn't look contrite.

"You must never do anything like that again," she warned him. "We don't want Betty to kick us out of here."

She knew her sister would never do such a thing, but she didn't want Betty to be uncomfortable in her own home either. Mary had insisted they share the maintenance and utilities, although the mortgage had been paid off long ago. When Mary had first broached the subject of moving to Ivy Bay, they'd both agreed that it would make more sense to live together than to set up two separate households.

After tonight, she hoped Betty wasn't having any regrets about taking in Gus.

———

Mary was too wound up to sleep, so she decided to take a moonlit walk on the beach. As she moved closer to the shore, the cares of the day began to slip away. A warm breeze caressed her face, and the deep bass of a boat horn sounded in the distance.

When she reached the beach, Mary kicked off her sandals and dug her toes into the warm sand. She loved seeing the lights from the moored boats dance on the water. Moonbeams made the waves shimmer as they rippled over the bay.

She wasn't completely alone here, glimpsing a young couple walking hand in hand along the shoreline, their heads close together. Just past them was a bonfire with a group of people circled around it, but it was too far away for her to hear them.

Mary walked closer to the water, enjoying the peaceful night and savoring the magnificence of God's handiwork. She'd seen it hundreds of times, but it never failed to fill her with awe.

"The earth is the Lord's," she recited out loud, "and everything in it, the world, and all who live in it; for he founded it on the seas and established it on the waters" (Psalm 24:1–2).

As she looked over the water, she thought how different this Friday evening was from the ones she used to spend in Boston. Lizzie and her family used to come over for supper; then they'd all play a board game together or sit out on the deck and talk, if the weather was warm enough.

Mary clasped her arms around her chest, missing those family times together. John was gone now, and Elizabeth was busy raising her two adorable children. She hadn't seen them since she'd moved here, and that had been almost a month ago. Those memories were bittersweet, but Mary knew that she was in the right place, and the beauty and comfort of Ivy Bay was well worth the distance.

She took a deep breath of sea air, feeling as if her life had come full circle. As a teenager, she used to come to the beach at night and wonder what the future held for her. She'd been excited about all the changes in her life but a little apprehensive too, just like now.

Mary walked along the beach, the full moon lighting her way. The gentle lap of the waves on the shore provided a peaceful rhythm to the night. At this precise moment, she couldn't think of anywhere else she'd rather be.

An hour later, Mary headed back to the house. The windows were dark except for a low glow in the kitchen window. Betty had left a light on for her. She kicked her sandy shoes off on the deck, walked inside and locked the door behind her.

She walked into the craft room to check the broken frame. She examined the repair job, gingerly touching the crack that was barely visible now that the two broken edges had come together. Satisfied, Mary carried the picture into the kitchen.

"Hold on," she said out loud, coming to a halt. She set the picture on the end of the kitchen counter and spun on her heel, realizing she'd almost forgotten to activate the security system. She walked to where the alarm box was located and turned the system on.

As she walked back into the kitchen toward the stairs, Mary noticed that there was still food in Gus's bowl. She didn't think it was possible for Gus to have a guilty conscience, but she still felt badly about the toilet paper incident. Tomorrow, she'd find a way to make it up to her sister.

On Saturday morning, Mary went grocery shopping at her favorite local market, Meeting House Grocers. When she returned home, she set the shopping bags on the kitchen counter and noticed that the framed picture still lay on the counter where she'd left it the night before. She gently scooted it out of the way to make room for the grocery sacks.

Betty sat at the kitchen table in a light-blue terry-cloth robe, sipping a cup of coffee and reading the newspaper spread out in front of her. She looked up as Mary set the grocery bags on the counter. "Hey, I thought you were still asleep. Where have you been?"

"I made an early trip to the market." Mary grinned. "We're going to make ice cream." She felt a sense of levity at the prospect of the relaxing Saturday ahead of her, and she took comfort in knowing that Kip would be working at the bookshop today. The work needed to be done, and she was glad that Kip would be the one to do it. She looked forward to a day away from the shop.

Betty's face lit up. "Well, this is a nice surprise."

"I was hoping you'd like the idea." Mary began to unload the first sack, setting four pints of cream on the counter, along with a dozen eggs and a bag of sugar. Then she looked up at her sister. "As a matter of fact, I'm making your favorite ice cream. Consider it a peace offering from Gus and me."

"Cranberry?" Betty clasped her hands together. "Please tell me it's cranberry."

Mary smiled. "Of course. And I'm using Gram's recipe."

Betty breathed a wistful sigh. "I haven't had good cranberry ice cream in ages. I hope you're making enough to take to the church ice-cream social tomorrow."

"I am." Mary walked over to the cupboard to retrieve a saucepan. Then she walked over to the spice rack. "Oh, good, we have ground cardamom. I almost bought some, but I thought I'd seen it here before."

Betty watched as Mary gathered the supplies to make ice cream. "Can I help?"

"Definitely. If you can prepare the cranberries, that would be great. Just take them out of the freezer, give them a good rinse, and then put them in a saucepan with a cup of sugar and a tablespoon of the cardamom. I like to crush the cranberries a little bit to help them absorb the spices."

Betty rose from the table. "My mouth is watering already."

Mary poured cream and sugar into another saucepan and headed for the stove. "Oh, and you can toss a cinnamon stick in the pan too. Then just give it all a good stir and let it set until I finish making the custard."

Betty started following her directions, mixing the cranberries and other ingredients together while Mary stirred the cream and sugar together as it heated on the stovetop.

A few minutes later, Betty said, "Hey, Mary."

Mary glanced over at her sister and burst out laughing. Betty's face was covered with red spots, each one the size of a dime. "I can't believe you did that!"

Betty giggled. "Hey, I was just following your example. Remember when you tried to convince Grandpa you had the measles so he wouldn't make you clean out the garage? He'd called the doctor before Gram realized you'd speckled your face with cranberry juice."

"That's right." Mary began to laugh again. "Grandpa kept describing the spots to her and insisting they were measles…and"—the laughter was starting to build—"when she pressed her cheek against my forehead to check for a fever, she could smell the cranberry juice."

Betty was by then doubled over with laughter, the kind of deep belly laugh that Mary hadn't heard from her sister in a very long time.

"It's not that funny," Mary noted, unable to stop laughing herself. "I not only had to clean Grandpa and Grandma's garage, but they made me clean out Uncle George's garage too."

"And Uncle George nicknamed you Spot," Betty said, catching her breath.

"Don't remind me." Mary and Betty simultaneously let out a jolly sigh after the laughter slowed, and Mary turned her attention back to the saucepan, removing it from the stove and covering it with a lid. Then she moved to the other side of the counter and plugged in the standing mixer. She was just getting ready to separate the egg yolks from the whites when the back door opened and Betty's son walked inside.

Evan Emerson was in his midthirties and looked just like his father had at that age. He had the same rich brown hair, the same deep green eyes, and the same proud bearing.

"Mom?" he said, hurrying toward her. "What's wrong? Are you sick?"

Betty met Mary's gaze and they both started laughing again, this time even harder than the first.

Evan folded his arms across his broad chest and looked between the two of them. "Okay, what's so funny?"

"Oh, hon, I'm fine," Betty said, catching her breath again and reaching up on her toes to kiss his cheek. "These spots are just cranberry juice."

Now Evan looked even more confused. "You put cranberry juice on your face? Is that supposed to be some kind of new beauty treatment?"

"No, just an old joke between Aunt Mary and me."

Evan walked over to the counter and gave her a hug. "Hey, Aunt Mary. It looks like you're corrupting my mom. She's never been one to dabble in cranberry juice before."

Mary smiled. "I always did get her in trouble when we were younger."

Betty retrieved a dishcloth from the drawer and wet it under the faucet. Then she began scrubbing at her face. "So what brings you here?"

"I came to pick up the cat." He turned to Mary. "Betsy and Allison are so excited. They can't wait to dress up Gus in their doll clothes."

Mary's heart dropped down to her toes.

"Evan," Betty chided. "Don't tease her." Then she looked at Mary. "He's joking. He's not taking Gus. I sent him the pictures from my cell phone last night."

Evan grinned as he leaned back against the counter. "Yes, I'm joking. Although, a cat smart enough to TP the *inside* of a house could be a lot of fun to have around."

Evan reached out and plucked a cranberry from the saucepan. "Hey, that tastes good. What are you making?"

Betty lightly slapped his hand out of the pan. "Aunt Mary's making cranberry ice cream," Betty replied. "You can have some at the church ice-cream social tomorrow. Keep your paws out for now."

"Sadly, we won't be able to make it," he said. "Mindy's parents are celebrating their fortieth wedding anniversary tomorrow afternoon." Together, Mindy and Evan had two daughters, ten-year-old Betsy and eight-year-old Allison.

"How about I bring you a batch of ice cream, if you'd like," Mary said. "I'd love to see the girls."

"That'd be great, Aunt Mary. Stop by anytime," he said, pushing himself away from the counter. "Well, I'd better get going. Mindy gave me a long list of stuff to get for this anniversary party. I just wanted to stop in and say hello." He leaned down to kiss Betty's cheek. "Yum. I can still taste cranberries."

Betty gave him a playful pat on the arm. "See you later, honey."

"Bye," he said, heading toward the door, "and don't forget to save some of that ice cream for me."

Mary finished the custard and then began to prepare the top-of-the-line stainless steel ice-cream maker John had bought her. When it was ready to go, she blended the custard and cranberry mixture carefully together and poured it into the electric ice-cream maker. She'd just turned it on when the doorbell rang.

"I wonder who that could be," Betty said. The laundry dryer buzzed. "I'll get the laundry, you get the door."

Mary smiled. "Got it." She wiped her hands on a dish-towel, hurried into the living room and opened the door.

Henry stood on the other side, grinning and holding a small cooler. "How about an offer you can't refuse?"

FOURTEEN

◆◆◆

M ary's heart skipped a beat. "What's the offer?"

He held up the cooler. "Free fish for the price of a walk. Are you in?"

He was right; that was a great offer. "I'm in," she said with a smile. His timing was perfect; she had just finished preparing the ice cream, and now all it needed to do was set in the machine. She opened the door wider to show Henry inside, admiring his short-sleeved shirt with palm trees on it. It went well with his dark green shorts and a pair of brown leather sandals.

"I had a great catch this morning, so I thought I'd share the bounty." Henry followed Mary into the kitchen and set the cooler on the table. "They're already deboned and filleted, so you can put them right in your refrigerator or freezer."

Betty walked out of the laundry room. "I thought I heard a familiar voice. How are you, Henry?" She walked over to give him a hug.

"I'm great," he said. "Mary and I are going for walk. Would you like to join us?"

Betty glanced at her, and Mary felt her cheeks grow warm. "I think I'll pass today, but thank you for the invitation."

"As you wish," Henry said with a stately nod.

"Henry brought us some fresh fish too," Mary told her sister, opening the small cooler and peering inside. There were fish fillets stacked all the way to the top. "Wow, that is a lot of fish."

"It sure is," Betty agreed, peering over her shoulder. "Thank you, Henry. That's so nice of you."

He grinned. "My pleasure."

Betty pulled the cooler toward her. "Why don't you two go ahead and start your walk while I take care of the fish? I'll even cook some up for lunch. Can you join us, Henry?"

"I wish I could," he said. "But I've got another charter trip scheduled this afternoon. Rain check?"

"You got it," Mary told him. Then she turned to Betty. "Don't worry about the ice-cream machine. I'll be back before it's finished."

"Enjoy the walk," Betty said, giving them a wave as they headed out.

"Where shall we walk?" Henry asked Mary when they were outside. "The beach or around the neighborhood?"

That was a tough call as both routes appealed to her. But at this time of day in June, the neighborhood would probably be a little less crowded than the beach. "Let's take a walk around the neighborhood. I love to look at all the blooming plants in the front yards this time of year."

They made their way around the front of the house to the sidewalk and began a leisurely stroll. All the homes had big, lush front yards, filled with trees and flowering bushes. Some were cottages and others stately old houses, but they each contributed to the unique heritage and charm of Cape Cod. The day was beautiful, but there was a crispness in the air that suggested to Mary that it would probably rain later.

"So the last time we talked," Henry began, "you were going to try to find out if the Department of Motor Vehicles had any records matching the car in that photograph. Did you have any luck?"

"As a matter of fact, I did." She waved to Sherry Walinski, who was watering a small tree in her yard, and then looked up at Henry. "I found out that the car in the picture belonged to a man named Fred Vargo. Does he sound familiar?"

Henry hesitated for a long moment and then shook his head. "I'm afraid not. Is he still alive?"

"I'm not sure. The house address on his vehicle registration doesn't exist anymore, but I did find out that he's connected to the woman in the photograph. I met a man named Leroy Steckler." She began telling him about her meeting with Leroy, including the purported fight with Uncle George. Then she paused, knowing that Henry didn't have the full story. She'd been reluctant to tell him before, but she didn't want to keep anything from him.

"There's something else that's been bothering me." Mary looked straight ahead as they walked. "I saw my cousin Jean, George's daughter, on that surveillance recording. She walked by the bookshop about thirty minutes before I saw the hooded figure. I'm sorry I didn't mention it before, but..."

Henry stopped walking and turned to her, concern swimming in his eyes. "Mary, what's wrong?"

She took a deep breath. "It might not mean anything, but Jean showed up at the house last Wednesday and told us she'd just arrived in Ivy Bay that day. When I saw her on the recording, I knew that she'd lied."

Henry puffed out his cheeks, releasing a long breath of air. "That doesn't sound like the Jean I knew. She was always on the quiet side, and she didn't have a deceptive bone in her body."

"Exactly." Mary looked into his green eyes. "That's what has me so troubled. Why didn't she want us to know she was in town on Monday, unless..."

He arched a brow. "You think she might be involved?"

"That's just it, Henry. I don't think she's involved, but there's something strange going on here and it's connected to that photograph. I want to rule Jean out, but the more I learn, the more my doubts grow."

He reached out one broad hand and cupped her shoulder. "Mary, you've always been one of the best women I know. This will all work itself out and, no matter what happens, you'll handle it with your usual grace."

Mary blushed at his kind words, already feeling better. She hadn't wanted to admit it before, even to herself, but her conversation with Leroy had shaken her resolve a little. She had such wonderful memories of Uncle George and Aunt Phyllis and Jean. She didn't want anything to change that.

"You're right," she said at last. "I'm going to keep moving forward."

"That's the spirit," he said, giving her shoulder a squeeze before he turned and started walking again. "Just let me know if you need any help. I'm just a phone call away."

A short while later, he glanced at his watch and frowned. "Looks like I'd better get back to the marina, but thank you so much for the walk. I'm sure glad you agreed to my offer."

"Free fish in exchange for a nice stroll around the neighborhood? What's not to like?"

He chuckled. "True enough."

"Will I see you at the ice-cream social tomorrow?"

"You can count on it."

As they walked back to the house, Mary realized that she'd always been able to count on Henry. Which was just one more reason for her to love her new life in Ivy Bay.

———

That evening, Mary and Betty sat in the living room enjoying the fire burning in the hearth. Mary leaned back in the armchair, her stockinged feet close enough to the blaze to be toasty warm. A summer squall raged outside, the crashing thunder had sent Gus under Mary's bed shortly after supper, and he wouldn't come out no matter how much she'd tried to coax him.

As she lounged in the chair, Mary felt rested and refreshed, content with the cranberry ice cream finished and in the freezer. Now she found herself ready to figure out the next clue in her real-life puzzle.

Betty sat on the sofa, her heating pad next to her hip. She was working on a puzzle in her jumbo crossword book. "What's a word for 'flightless bird'?" Betty asked.

"How many letters?"

"Three."

Mary thought for a moment. "Does *emu* fit?"

"It does." Betty filled in the word, and Mary noticed that her fingers moved with painstaking slowness.

Mary reached for the laptop computer that hummed on the table beside her.

Her fingers hovered over the keyboard as she considered what to type in the search engine first. She settled for simply starting with Fred Vargo Ivy Bay Massachusetts. There were no hits—at least none that fit the profile of the car owner she was looking for.

She brought up an online directory of the Cape Cod area and searched for Fred Vargo. Again, there were no hits. Then she simply entered Vargo Massachusetts in the search box. A moment later, four names came up. One was an Alex Vargo in Mashpee. There was a Zach Vargo and a K. B. Vargo in Barnstable, each separate listings, and a P. Vargo listed in Ivy Bay.

"Find anything?" Betty asked from the sofa.

"Some possible relatives of Fred around Cape Cod, and one Vargo in Ivy Bay." She jotted down their phone numbers on her notepad. "Now I just need to figure out what I'll say when I call them."

"I think you should just tell them the truth."

Mary arched an amused brow in her sister's direction. "That I have a picture of a car from 1957 and I'm trying to track down the owner?"

Betty smiled as she filled in more boxes on her crossword puzzle. "I suppose that would sound a little bizarre."

"I'll probably tell them what I told Leroy—that I'm looking into some family history and that Fred might be able to help."

Betty nodded her approval. "I think that sounds like a good approach." Then she looked down at her puzzle. "Now can you tell me a six-letter word for literary alter ego?" Betty asked.

"*Hmm*, that's a tough one." Mary turned to her. "Pen name?"

Betty turned to her paper and shook her head. "Doesn't fit."

Betty's sentiment was perfect. That described why Mary felt so compelled to follow even the slimmest of clues—because the facts of the story just didn't fit. Not just compelled, she realized, but intrigued. And a little frustrated. She felt barely closer to figuring out why someone would break in and steal that photograph from the day the break-in had happened. She had an inkling that she was on the right track, but the puzzle pieces still seemed so disconnected.

Mary's gaze moved to the window as a crackle of lightning illuminated the dark clouds, its electric tendrils sailing over the water. Rain pattered against the windowpanes, and the wind howled in the chimney.

She opened a new Word document on her computer, wanting to organize her thoughts and ponder some of the questions that had been nagging at her. Placing her fingers on the keyboard, she typed the first question:

1. *Why would someone break into a shop just to steal a seemingly worthless photograph?*

That intruder had bypassed a display case full of rare books—some of them worth hundreds of dollars—not to mention a brand-new computer, Mary thought to herself. It once again furthered her suspicion that there might be a personal angle to this case—something in the photo itself that upset someone enough to steal it. She began typing more questions:

2. *Who is the woman in the photo and why was she photographed with Uncle George?*
3. *Who is Fred Vargo?*

4. *Who is the figure in the black hooded sweatshirt?*
5. *Why was Jean near the shop the night of the break-in?*
6. *Why did Jean lie about her arrival date?*

"Oh, I think I figured it out," Betty announced. "It's Jekyll."

Mary looked over at her, confused. "What?"

"The answer to the crossword puzzle clue about a literary alter ego," Betty reminded her. "It's Jekyll, from Dr. Jekyll and Mr. Hyde."

"Bravo!" Mary turned back to the computer, ready to figure out her own puzzle. But as she returned to her Internet search, her eyes began to feel heavy. She set the computer aside and rose to her feet. "I think I'll make a few phone calls and then get to bed early. See you in the morning for church."

"Sounds good, Mar. Good night."

Mary picked up the notepad and headed up to her room. Her cell phone lay on the nightstand, where she'd put it earlier in the day to charge. As she reached for it, Mary noticed a message on the screen that she'd missed a call.

She pressed the View button on her phone to see who had called her, and Kip's name came up. She noticed that the call had come in several hours ago and hoped that didn't mean there was a problem with the repairs at her shop.

Mary pressed a button to dial his number and waited while it rang several times. To her disappointment, she got his voice mail, instructing her to leave a message. When the tone sounded, Mary said, "Hello, Kip, this is Mary Fisher. I'm sorry I missed your call. Give me a call back whenever you get a chance."

She disconnected the call and sat down on the edge of the bed. She set the list of telephone numbers beside her, working up the nerve to make the first phone call.

Mary dialed the number for P. Vargo first, since that was the only number in Ivy Bay.

"Hello?" A woman answered.

"Hi, my name is Mary Fisher. I'm looking for someone named Fred Vargo. Do you know anyone by that name?"

"Same last name, but no, I'm sorry. Don't know any Freds."

"Well, it's actually possible this person is no longer living. I believe Fred resided in Ivy Bay in the 1950s."

"I wish I could help you," the woman said, "but I'm drawing a blank."

"Okay, thank you for your time." Mary gave the woman her phone number in case anything came to her later and then moved on to the next number. It belonged to Zach Vargo in Barnstable. That was close enough that there could be a connection.

He answered on the first ring. "Yo."

"Hello." Mary repeated the same information she'd given to the Vargo woman in Ivy Bay.

"Fred." The man rolled the name around on his tongue. "Fred. *Freeeed.* Nope."

His vernacular told her that he probably was a child of a more recent generation rather than the fifties. Still, he could be related to a Fred Vargo, so she was going to give him all the time he needed to remember.

"He would be in his seventies now," Mary pressed. "Perhaps a distant relative?"

"I got nothin'," the man said at last. "I don't think I know any Freds. Sorry."

Mary could hear the distinct noises of a video game in the background and sensed he wasn't giving her question his full attention. He hung up before she could thank him for his time.

When she tried to call K. B. Vargo, the number had been disconnected. That left her with one Vargo—Alex Vargo in Mashpee.

Mary dialed the number, hoping she'd saved the best for last. Maybe he could point her in the right direction.

"Hello," a woman's voice sounded over the line.

"May I speak with Alex Vargo, please?"

"This is Alex." That threw her. She'd been expecting a man, not a woman. Mary explained that she was looking into family history, then asked Alex if she knew a Fred Vargo.

"I had an uncle named Fremont Vargo. Could that be who you're looking for?"

Mary's heart rate rose a bit. "Possibly. Is your uncle still living?"

Alex snorted. "Oh my, no. He fought in the Civil War. We're talking family history, right? I guess that makes him my great-great-great-uncle. Or maybe it's great-great-great-great? I'm not sure. I'll have to check my genealogy chart."

"That's all right. I'm looking for someone a little younger than your uncle Fremont. Hate to bother, but are you certain there's not a Fred on that chart somewhere?"

"I sure can't think of one."

Mary was stymied. There were only four Vargos in the area and none of them had ever heard of Fred. She gave Alex her phone number and then rang off.

The storm outside had finally eased itself into a nice, steady rain. She walked over to the window and parted the curtain, watching the tiny rivulets of water drizzle down the glass.

She stood there for a long time, missing John and thinking about her children and grandchildren. She hoped Emma and Luke could come for a visit soon—she knew Lizzie would appreciate the break. It wouldn't be for her grand opening, though. Lizzie had teared up when she found out the date Mary had announced—she had already booked a flight to visit Chad's parents. Mary considered changing the date but she had already told several key people in the community, including several local shop owners who were helping promote the event, and she didn't think it would be a good idea to confuse things right off the bat. And her son Jack's pediatrics practice was always so busy and his daughter Daisy was at summer camp, so they weren't able to make it either.

Mary was disappointed, but she knew this was one of the bittersweet by-products of having adult children—they inevitably lived their own lives. She wished she could find time to go visit them too, and she would soon, but she wanted to get her bookshop up and running first. Thinking about her grandchildren, she realized that she needed to get more children's books into her shop. And make it more kid-friendly. As a librarian, her passion had been helping children learn to love books. There were so many distractions these days, with video games and television, that it was difficult to convince kids that there was something even better waiting for them between the pages of a book.

Each time one of her grandchildren celebrated a birthday, Mary sent them a book inscribed with a special message. She believed one of the greatest gifts you could give a child was a lifelong love of reading.

Turning away from the window, Mary reached for a note-pad and began drawing some ideas for a children's area in her bookshop. She let the pen loosely sketch the vision that began to form in her mind. She grew more and more excited. She had some money budgeted for miscellaneous projects, and this one certainly fit the bill.

She continued to sketch. She wanted the children's area to be cozy and inviting but not the centerpiece of the entire shop. She hoped it would be a place where kids could snuggle in and lose themselves in the world of books.

After she'd finished some preliminary sketches, Mary began getting ready for bed. Now that the worst of the storm had passed, Gus had come out from his hiding place and padded out of the room.

She turned on the lamp on her nightstand and climbed into bed, still buzzing from her idea of a children's area. She breathed a contented sigh. This was always her favorite part of the day. She could read uninterrupted until she fell asleep.

Wuthering Heights was still stashed in her handbag, and she decided against getting out of bed again. She'd just open a new book for now. It was often like this; she'd have several books going at once.

Mary reached over and plucked a book from the top of her reading pile. It was one of the books Henry had given her. She adjusted her pillow and opened the book to a short verse that introduced the first chapter.

I like to see a thing I know has not been seen before.
That's why I cut my apple through to look into the core.
It's nice to think though many an eye has seen its ruddy skin
Mine are the very first to spy the five brown pips within.

—*Author Unknown*

It was an interesting start to a mystery novel and already had her thinking about the meaning behind the verse for this story. She relaxed into her pillow and began to read. Her eyes became heavy, and she allowed herself to drift off, the book flapping open beside her.

An ear-splitting screech jolted Mary out of a sound sleep. It took her a moment to get her bearings. She sat up in bed, her heart pounding in her chest as the sound reverberated all around her.

"The alarm!" she realized, throwing the bedcovers aside and swinging her legs to the floor. "It's the alarm." She'd never actually heard it before, but the noise was deafening.

Mary ran toward the open doorway as the high-pitched siren assaulted her ears. She couldn't think about anything except getting to her sister.

FIFTEEN

·◆◆·

M ary breathed a frantic prayer as she hurried down the stairs. "Lord, protect us and keep us safe. Please let my sister be all right."

It occurred to her that she could run straight into whoever had set off the alarm. If there was an intruder in the house, neither one of them was safe. She forced herself to pause for a moment at the bottom of the stairs and look around the dark, empty kitchen. Now she wished she'd grabbed her cell phone and called the police.

Betty's bedroom door opened, and her sister stood in the door, a small silver canister in her hand. She held up her other hand, motioning for Mary to stay put. Then she stepped out of her doorway and rounded the corner to the laundry room.

A moment later, the alarm was suddenly cut off. Mary's ears still rang from the noise, but at least now she could hear herself think. She saw Betty emerge from the laundry room and hurry toward her.

"Are you all right?" Betty said in a half whisper.

Mary reached out for her hand. "Yes, are you?"

"I'm fine." Their hands clung to each other as they slowly moved into the kitchen.

"What happened?" Mary whispered. "Did someone try to break in?"

"I don't know."

Mary looked around them. The noise had sent Gus running under the couch, but there was nothing out of place.

"I don't hear anything," Betty said, as they moved slowly out of the kitchen and toward the living room. "If you see something, tell me." She held up the canister. "This pepper spray is supposed to stop someone at a minimum of thirty feet away."

"Have you ever used it before?" Mary whispered.

"No, but after Edward died, Evan bought this for me and made me practice with it in the backyard so I'd know how it worked."

The living room was empty, with no sign of a break-in. They checked all the doors and windows, as well as the hall bathroom, the dining room, and Betty's craft room, but they all looked undisturbed. It took them only a few minutes to search the entire first floor, and by the time they were finished, Mary's heart had resumed a normal rhythm.

"Thank You, Lord," she breathed, "for keeping us from harm."

"Amen," Betty murmured beside her.

As they walked back through the dining room and into the kitchen, Mary saw a man's face pressed against the glass of the door. She screamed.

Betty grabbed her and held up the canister of pepper spray. "What is it? What do you see?"

Mary pointed to the door and realized she recognized the face behind the glass. She placed one hand on her chest, feeling her heart racing beneath it. "It's all right," she told Betty. "It's D.J."

"D.J.?" Betty said, confused, as she looked at Jean's son standing on the other side of the glass. At twenty-one, he was about six feet tall, and his shaggy brown hair was damp from the rain.

Mary hurried over to let him in. "D.J., what's going on?"

He walked inside, wearing a pair of black shorts and a black shirt with a guitar on it. "Hey, I'm sorry. I rang the front doorbell, and when nobody answered, I came around to the back door to see if anyone was still up."

Betty glanced at the digital clock on the stove. Mary followed her gaze and saw that it was after midnight.

He wiped his feet on the throw rug in front of the door. "I didn't mean to spook the cat. He must have set off the alarm when he saw me because I hadn't even touched the door when the siren started going off."

Betty and Mary looked at each other, perplexed. Then Mary glanced over at Gus, who still sat on the kitchen floor. She couldn't imagine any possible way that he could set off the alarm, but what she found even more curious was why Jean's son had shown up here so late.

"I just drove in from Chicago," D.J. explained, "to surprise my mom. I knew she was feeling pretty sad, about..." he hesitated, his eyes expressing loss, "...about Grandpa, so I wanted to try to cheer her up. But she didn't answer the door at Grandpa's house and she's not answering my calls or texts either. So I thought she might be over here."

"I'm afraid not," Mary said, handing him a kitchen towel so he could wipe the rain off his face.

"Come on in and sit down," Betty told D.J. "Do you want something to eat or drink?"

He perked up. "I'll take a soda, if you have one."

Just then, the phone rang and D.J. stepped toward it. "Hey, maybe that's her."

"It's probably the security company," Betty said, walking over to answer it. She picked up the receiver and pressed the Speaker button. "Hello?"

"Mrs. Emerson, this is Glenda with Assurance Security," said a woman's voice. "We have a report of your alarm going off. Is everything all right?"

"Yes," Betty said, glancing over at Mary. "It was a false alarm."

"So there are no signs that someone tried to enter your home?"

Mary looked over at D.J. and saw him twisting the dishtowel in his hands.

"No," Betty said. "We're fine."

"Very well," the woman said. "I recommend that you reactivate the security system immediately and contact us or the police if you have any concerns."

"Thank you," Betty said. "I will."

Mary ushered D.J. to the kitchen table. Then she retrieved a can of soda from the refrigerator. "Did you drive all the way from Chicago today?" she asked. Betty disappeared into the laundry room for a moment to reactivate the system, then joined them at the table.

"Yeah." D.J. popped open the soda can and took a long gulp. "I don't have money for a hotel or anything, and my car's too small to sleep in, so I had to marathon it."

"How long did that take?" Mary asked.

He shrugged and took another drink of his soda. "About eighteen hours, I guess. I left before dawn."

Despite the anxiety still tight in her stomach from the alarm, Mary was pretty touched. For a son to drive such a long way to comfort his mother seemed to Mary a wonderful expression of devotion.

"You must be exhausted." Betty reached out to rub his shoulder. "I'm sure your mom was probably sleeping or she would have heard her cell phone ring."

"I pounded on her door too," D.J. said, scowling a little. "Mom's always been such a light sleeper. I guess I shouldn't be surprised, though, since she..."

His cell phone began to beep and relief washed over his face as he looked at the screen. "Mom *finally* answered my text." He pushed his wire-rimmed glasses up on his nose, pushed the chair back and stood up. "Sorry again for causing such a racket. I'm going to head over to Grandpa's house now."

"Wait," Mary said, rising to her feet. She wanted to know what he'd been about to say before Jean had texted him. "You were telling us that your mom was a light sleeper, but something had changed...."

"Yeah," D.J. said, not meeting her gaze. "I don't even remember now." He grabbed his soda off the table. "I'd better get going."

D.J. headed back out the French doors, leaving Betty and Mary alone once more.

Gus emerged from under the kitchen table and padded over to his food dish. He dug into the leftovers from earlier in the day, still acting unconcerned about all the commotion.

"How odd that D.J. blamed the alarm on Gus." Betty stared at him. "You don't suppose…"

Mary looked from her sister to her cat. "Oh, Bets, there's no way. But that wasn't the only odd thing about D.J. tonight. It is so sweet that he drove all the way out here, and I give him lots of credit for that. But is it just me, or did he seem nervous? And he evaded my question about his mother."

"I noticed that too." Betty looked pensive. "But at least Jean won't be alone in that big house anymore. That's something to be grateful for."

Mary nodded. She'd always liked D.J. He was smart and outgoing, but tonight he'd been…different. She just couldn't put her finger on it. She also couldn't forget the sight of his face pressed against the glass door. That was exactly what the hooded figure had done on the surveillance recording. She shook that thought from her head, not wanting to add D.J. to her suspect list too.

Mary walked over to the refrigerator. "Now, how about a hot cup of cocoa so we can relax and go back to sleep?"

"That sounds nice." Betty retrieved two ceramic mugs from the cupboard and carried them over to the kitchen table.

As Mary pulled the carton of milk out of the refrigerator, she noticed the framed photograph she'd repaired still sitting on the counter. Her gaze moved to the doors, and she realized it could easily be seen from there.

She stood frozen in the middle of the kitchen, the carton of milk still in her hand. "Betty?"

Her sister looked over at her. "What's wrong?"

"Do you think it's possible that D.J. saw that picture and tried to get in, not realizing he'd set off the alarm?"

"Oh, Mar, no! Not D.J." Betty met her gaze, the same doubts now in her eyes that were plaguing Mary.

"It's odd that he came around to the back of the house when we didn't answer the doorbell." The doubts began to build. "I didn't hear a doorbell ring, did you?"

"No, but I was asleep." Betty rubbed a hand over her eyes, clearly exhausted. "Besides, if he'd tried to break in, wouldn't he have run away when the alarm went off?"

"Maybe. Or maybe he realized we might see his car from the window and thought it was best to pretend it was an accident. He did try to blame Gus."

Betty nibbled at her lower lip. "You're right; that is one possible scenario. Another is that he really did just get here tonight and accidentally set off the alarm. It is pretty sensitive."

Like her sister, Mary wanted it to be true, but she wasn't sure what to think anymore. She turned back to the stove to stir the cocoa, aware that they both needed sleep tonight. Tomorrow, she'd figure out a way to turn up her investigation a notch. She remembered Henry's encouraging words and took strength from them.

The next morning, Mary sat in a middle pew at Grace Church, trying to put the alarm scare out of her mind and focus on the serenity that being in church inspired. The church was located north of Main Street on Water Street. The tall white spire on the century-old building was visible from almost every point in Ivy Bay.

At the first service she attended after moving to Ivy Bay, Mary had felt a little uncomfortable. She'd loved her old church back in Boston, where she and John had been members since they were first married. They'd raised their children in that church, and she'd taught Sunday school there for over ten years. John had been a longtime member of the finance committee and had frequently served as an usher.

Now, as she sat next to her sister, Mary was starting to feel as comfortable in this church as she had in the one back home. This church was beautiful, with a row of stained-glass windows along each side, each portraying a scene from the Bible. The white vaulted ceiling rose high in the air and a pair of ceiling fans were suspended from it.

A polished mahogany pulpit stood at the front of the church, behind a spindle-style mahogany railing.

Betty leaned toward her. "Do you see Jean?"

Mary looked around. "No. She said she'd be here, didn't she?"

Betty nodded. "Maybe her plans changed after D.J.'s late arrival last night, but surely they'll make it to the ice-cream social."

Before Mary could reply, the minister, Pastor Frank Miles, appeared at the pulpit. "Good morning!"

"Good morning," the congregation responded in unison.

"Rejoice in the day the Lord has made and be glad in it," he said. Mary liked the soothing tenor of his voice. The minister appeared to be in his early fifties and was tall and slim. He smiled as he announced the first hymn. " 'Joyful, Joyful,' on page 87."

The organ played the opening bars, and Mary's heart lifted at the familiar tune. She quickly flipped through her hymnal, finding the correct page just in time to join in the opening verse with the rest of the congregation.

> *Joyful, joyful, we adore Thee,*
> *God of glory, Lord of love;*
> *Hearts unfold like flowers before Thee,*
> *opening to the sun above.*
> *Melt the clouds of sin and sadness;*
> *drive the dark of doubt away;*
> *Giver of immortal gladness,*
> *fill us with the light of day!*

This had been one of John's favorite hymns and singing it this morning made her feel closer to him, and closer to Grace Church. She looked around her as she sang, realizing that a church family wasn't confined by a building or a town or even a state or a country. These people shared their beliefs. They might be strangers now, but their faith formed a connection that would only grow as she got to know them.

Mary took a deep breath and sang the second verse.

> *All Thy works with joy surround Thee,*
> *earth and heaven reflect Thy rays,*
> *stars and angels sing around Thee,*
> *center of unbroken praise.*
> *Field and forest, vale and mountain,*
> *flowery meadow, flashing sea,*
> *singing bird and flowing fountain*
> *call us to rejoice in Thee.*

When they finished the hymn, the minister invited the congregation to be seated. Then he began to read the announcements. Mary found her mind wandering, thinking again about the alarm going off last night. She'd moved the repaired photograph back to her room, dismayed to see the cracked frame had come apart again. Apparently the crack was just too deep to be mended with glue.

She couldn't help herself; she thought about D.J.'s visit. Was it possible he really was trying to steal that photograph? But why? Unlike the one that was stolen, there was truly nothing in the second photo that looked the least bit unusual. Perhaps she needed to enlarge it like Henry had done for her with the first photograph.

The pastor opened his Bible. "I'd like to begin with a Scripture reading from Matthew. Now that tourist season is upon us, I thought this one especially fitting."

Mary reached for the pew Bible, wanting to follow along as he read the Scripture.

"Then the King will say to those on his right," Reverend Miles began. "Come, you who are blessed by my Father; take your inheritance, the kingdom prepared for you since the creation of the world. For I was hungry and you gave me something to eat, I was thirsty and you gave me something to drink, I was a stranger and you invited me in" (Matthew 25:34–35).

He looked up at the congregation. "We will have many strangers among us in the next several weeks. Most of them will be friendly and a few might annoy us, but we need to remember that we are all children of God. One of my favorite quotes, which is attributed to both T. H. Thompson and John Watson, goes like this: 'Be kinder than necessary, for everyone you meet is fighting some kind of battle.'"

It was a good message and one that Mary wanted to carry with her as she searched for the person who had broken into her shop. She still believed that the break-in hadn't been done out of mischief or malice but for a more personal reason. A reason she was more determined than ever to find out.

SIXTEEN

"Your cranberry ice cream is going fast," Betty noted as she joined Mary who stood under the shade of an elm tree on the church lawn.

"I'm glad people like it." Mary spooned up another bite of her ice cream, glad they liked her too. Several of them had come up to introduce themselves and welcome her to Ivy Bay. They'd also commented on her bookshop and how excited they were to have a new shop in town.

Pastor Miles approached them. "Hello, ladies." He turned to Mary. "I hear you're responsible for that delicious cranberry ice cream."

"Guilty," she replied with a demure smile, nodding toward her sister. "Betty helped me make it yesterday. We had a lot of fun."

Pastor Miles smiled at Betty. "I'm sure it's nice to have your sister living with you." He took a bite of ice cream. "How do you like living in Ivy Bay?"

"I love it here," she said honestly. "And I really enjoyed your message today."

"Thank you," he said. "I hope that means you'll consider Grace your church home."

"You can count on it," Mary promised, honored at Pastor Miles's personal invitation. "In fact, after I get my bookshop up and running, I'd love to talk to you about becoming a member."

His eyes twinkled. "Just give me a call, and I'll be glad to meet with you."

"I'll do that." Mary's gaze fell on an older couple seated on the other side of the elm tree and she recognized Frances Curran.

She excused herself as Betty and Reverend Miles continued to chat and walked over to the other side of the tree. The couple were seated in a matching pair of forest-green folding lawn chairs with "Dartmouth" stamped on the back of each in bold white letters.

As she rounded the lawn chairs, the man rose to his feet.

"I hope I'm not interrupting," Mary began.

"Oh no, not at all." Frances Curran stood up, placing one slim hand on her husband's arm. "Albert, this is Mrs. Mary Fisher, the woman who is opening the new bookshop on Main Street." Then she turned to Mary. "And this is my husband, Dr. Albert Curran."

"Nice to meet you," Mary said, reaching out to shake his hand.

"The pleasure is all mine," he replied. He was a stately gentleman, with white neatly trimmed hair and a pair of silver-framed glasses. He was dressed in a gray suit with a crisp white shirt and a forest-green tie.

"Mary is from Boston and is the sister of Betty Emerson," Frances told her husband. "She just moved to Ivy Bay a few weeks ago."

"Then we have something in common," Albert told her, his tone warm and friendly. "Frances and I are recent settlers here too. We moved here just shy of a year ago."

"I couldn't help but notice your lawn chairs," Mary said. "Did you enjoy working at Dartmouth?"

"We loved it!" Frances exclaimed. "I was a literature professor there, and Albert taught in the medical school."

"We met at Dartmouth," he said, "although we were both students at the time. I guess that explains why we like the place so much."

Mary smiled. "So where are you two from originally?"

"I'm from Providence," Albert said, turning to his wife. "You didn't really have a hometown growing up, did you, dear?"

"I'm the daughter of an army colonel," Frances explained, "so I lived all over the world when I was a child, but no place permanently until I married Albert."

"That means fifty-three years in one place," Albert said, chuckling a little. "When I told her I wanted to move, she was ready."

"So how did you choose Ivy Bay?" Mary asked them. "Do you have family here?"

"Our grandchildren live in New Bedford," Albert explained, referring to the city across Buzzard's Bay from Cape Cod, "and we wanted to move closer to them."

"And we think Ivy Bay is lovely," Frances added. "So here we are!"

"We were just about to have a second serving of ice cream," Albert said. "Would you care to join us?"

"Thank you," she said, sensing that he'd asked out of politeness rather than any interest in getting to know her better, "but I think I'll wait awhile."

"It was nice to see you again," Frances said as her husband headed toward the ice-cream table. "And I'm so glad we get to launch our disaster-aid book drive at your grand opening. I'll be in touch with you soon to work out the details."

"I'm at the bookshop most days," Mary told her, "so feel free to stop by anytime."

"I will," Frances said, following her husband to the ice-cream table. "Enjoy your afternoon."

Mary looked around the church lawn and saw Virginia Livingston speaking with Eleanor and Madeline a few yards away.

They, along with Frances, were among the names on her potential suspect list, which, she realized, she really needed to spend more time thinking about. The list was flimsy at best, but it still had potential to be helpful. She thought about Jean's place on the list and sighed. She looked back to the book-club women. It seemed unlikely that Frances was suspect, since the woman didn't seem to have any connection to Ivy Bay before moving here last year. But Virginia's roots in Ivy Bay went all the way back to the founding fathers, and Eleanor's weren't far behind. She didn't know much yet about Madeline, or Paul Becker, who was also on the list. She looked around but didn't see him among the crowd.

"Hey, Spot."

Mary turned around to see Henry grinning at her. She placed her hands on her hips, trying to look annoyed but failing miserably. "Excuse me?" she said with a mock grimace.

He held up the bowl of cranberry ice cream in his hands. "You didn't think I'd forget your nickname, did you? When I heard you made this delicious ice cream, I remembered the summer you gave yourself a case of the cranberry measles."

She smiled, realizing once again how far the two of them went back. "At least you never called me by that awful nickname," she said. "Until now."

"I'll never do it again." He held up his right hand in a three-finger salute. "Scout's honor."

Since Henry had been an Eagle Scout, Mary knew she could believe him. She took a step closer to him. "I was just visiting with the Currans. Do you know them?"

He squinted in their direction. "Not really. I've chatted with the doctor a couple of times at the marina. He has a boat that he takes out almost every day. A very nice boat, I might add." Then he turned back to Mary. "Why do you ask?"

"Just curious," she replied, not wanting to get into the details at the ice-cream social. "How about Madeline Dinsdale? Is she a native of Ivy Bay?"

"Don't think so. She moved here from New York, oh, about five years ago, I'd say. Of course, you could ask her yourself...." He lowered his voice. "Do these questions have anything to do with the break-in at your shop?"

Mary leaned in slightly. "They're just some of the few people who saw the photograph hanging in my shop before it was stolen," Mary replied. Then she told him about D.J. setting off the security alarm last night and his odd behavior.

"He blamed Gus?" Henry asked in disbelief.

She chuckled, realizing how silly it sounded. "Yep. Gus is a smart cat, don't get me wrong, but I'm afraid D.J. was just making excuses."

Sherry, Mary and Betty's neighbor, approached them. "Great ice cream, Mary." She looked up at Henry. "Have you had the cranberry ice cream yet?"

"I have," he said, "and I think I'll go have some more before it's gone."

"You better hurry," Sherry told him. "They just opened the last quart."

Mary watched Henry walk away. Then she turned her attention back to Sherry.

Sherry dug her spoon into the ice cream and took a bite. "There's some spice in here that is just divine, but I can't place it."

"It's cardamom," Mary said, happy to give out the secret. "I don't use it a lot in my ice creams, but it works well with certain flavors."

"So what do I have to do to get the recipe? Learning to make ice cream could be my new project for summer vacation. I'm more than ready to get away from that high school for a while."

Mary smiled. "I'll be happy to give it to you."

As she spoke, a thought suddenly occurred to Mary. She had a picture of a mystery woman she couldn't identify, but if the woman had been a student at Ivy Bay High, maybe she could match it to a yearbook photo. She touched Sherry lightly on the arm. "Speaking of school, Sherry...I have a question for you. Does the high school keep all the old yearbooks?"

"I assume so. There's a whole pile of them in the school library, but I'm not sure how far back they go."

"Do you mind if I stop by the high school tomorrow? I'd love to take a look at them!"

"I don't mind at all." Curiosity gleamed in her eyes. "Is there something specific you're looking for?"

"Just some people from the past," Mary said. She liked Sherry and knew she wasn't a gossip, but she didn't want to give away too much. "I thought it might be fun to look through some of those old yearbooks, if it's not too much trouble."

"Of course not. You can stop by any time tomorrow," Sherry said. "It gets pretty lonely at school during the summer. I'm used to a bunch of kids popping into my office every five minutes during the school year, so it will be nice to have a visitor."

They chatted for a few more minutes until Mary went to look for her sister. She found Betty chatting with an elderly woman with gray hair that was wound into a tight bun. She carried a cane but seemed steady on her feet.

"Oh, there you are," Betty said when she saw Mary approaching them. "I want to introduce you to Hazel Pritchard. Hazel was Evan's kindergarten teacher. I told her she had to come by this afternoon so she could try some of your cranberry ice cream."

Hazel smiled as she held up her empty bowl. "I don't get out much these days, but this ice cream sure made it worth it for me to put my Sunday clothes on."

Mary smiled. "Thank you. I'm so glad you liked it."

Hazel pointed her cane past Mary. "There's another one of my students." Then she raised her voice. "Kip Hastings, come on over here and say hello to your old teacher."

Mary turned to see Kip walking toward them. "Well, hello there, Kip," Mary said. "Nice to see you somewhere other than my bookshop." Mary gave him a knowing wink—he'd already worked so hard for her.

Kip greeted everyone and leaned down to give Mrs. Pritchard a kiss on the cheek. "How are you, Mrs. Pritchard?"

Mrs. Pritchard grinned with pride. "I hear you're getting married. So when's the wedding date? And more important, am I invited?"

Kip laughed. "Of course you're invited. If it wasn't for you, I still wouldn't know how to tie my shoes."

Mary remembered the call from Kip that she'd missed yesterday. She wanted to ask him about it, but he and Hazel were now engrossed in a conversation about the upcoming wedding.

Betty pulled Mary aside. "Jean and D.J. aren't here. I don't know about you, but I'm really starting to worry. I know Jean's grieving for her dad, but we've hardly seen her at all these past few days."

Mary nodded. "I'm a little worried too. I think we'd both feel better if we paid her a visit. And while we're there, let's try to find out what's really going on."

SEVENTEEN

$\blacktriangleright\blacklozenge\blacklozenge\blacklozenge\blacktriangleright$

Mary and Betty walked up the wide front porch of Uncle George's majestic house. They'd gone there straight after the ice-cream social, determined to see their cousin.

"It's been ages since I've been inside this house," Mary said as she reached out to ring the doorbell. "We didn't even come here after the funeral."

"Jean wanted it that way," Betty reminded her. "But they had a very nice dinner in the church basement after the service."

Mary looked up at the house. "Remember when we used to slide down the banister?"

"*You* used to slide down the banister," Betty said with a smile. "Uncle George never cared if you did it, but Aunt Phyllis was always afraid you'd fall off and break a leg."

"And I loved playing hide-and-seek here." Sweet childhood memories washed over Mary as if they'd just happened yesterday. "There were so many places to hide in this old place, I'm surprised we never got lost."

"It sure would be easy to get lost in a big old house like this. Maybe that's why no one is answering the door." Betty rang the doorbell again. "Both her rental car and D.J.'s car are in the driveway." Betty's look of concern mirrored Mary's feelings.

"Maybe the doorbell isn't working, or she's upstairs and can't hear it," Mary suggested.

Betty pulled her cell phone out of her purse. "Let me try calling her. Maybe she's just out for a walk."

Betty dialed Jean's cell phone number and looked at Mary. After a few moments, she said, "Jean's not answering. I don't have D.J.'s number, do you?"

"No. I guess we'll just have to try her later." They started down the steps when Mary heard the front door open behind them.

"Hey, girls," Jean called out to them, her tone light. "What brings you by? Sorry I didn't make it to church to-day, but I was up most of the night talking with D.J." Pride glowed in her eyes. "Can you believe he drove all that way just to surprise me?"

"He's a good son," Mary said, and meant it. "How have you been?" Mary asked, genuinely concerned. Although she sounded cheerful, there was something about Jean's manner that seemed...forced. Was she just trying to put on a brave front in the face of her grief, or was there some-thing more?

"Oh, I'm just fine," Jean assured them. "D.J.'s still asleep, so I was cleaning out one of the upstairs bedrooms and had the radio turned up. I didn't hear you at the door until I came downstairs to get another box." She sighed. "I never realized how much stuff Dad had stored away."

"We're free the rest of the afternoon," Mary said, glancing at Betty. "We'd be glad to stay and help."

Betty nodded. "We sure would. Mary and I were just talking about all the fun times we used to have in this house. It would be like old times."

A ghost of a smile haunted Jean's mouth. "It was fun back then, wasn't it? Mom used to have a fit whenever she'd catch Mary sliding down the banister."

"I don't think I'll try that today," Mary said, moving toward the front door, "but you never know."

Jean turned slightly to block her path and gave them an apologetic smile. "Thanks, girls, really. I appreciate the offer to help, but I'd prefer to do this on my own. I hope you understand."

"Are you sure?" Betty asked gently. "I know it's been difficult for you losing your dad. We loved him too."

"I know you did." Jean reached out to squeeze Betty's hand. "Both of you. And that means more to me than you'll ever know." Her voice cracked and tears flooded her eyes.

Mary embraced her. The plan she had to question Jean evaporated in the face of her tears. They were real tears too, the kind of deep, gut-wrenching sobs that shook her entire body. Mary's questions could wait until later. Right now what Jean needed was her prayers. *Lord, please put Your loving arms around my cousin and give her comfort and peace that passes all understanding. She needs You so.*

Betty moved in, circling her arm around Jean's shoulders, her own eyes bright with tears. After a while, Jean's sobbing eased and she took deep gulps of air. "I'm so sorry. I don't know what comes over me sometimes."

"You don't have to apologize," Mary said gently.

"Thanks," Jean said, pulling a tissue from her pocket and wiping her eyes. "You two mean so much to me. You know that, right?"

"Of course we do," Betty assured her, rubbing one hand gently over Jean's back. "And we feel the same way about you. That's why we want to help. So give us a call anytime, day or night."

A soggy chuckle sounded in Jean's throat. "I will. And I promise not to set off your security alarm. I was mortified when I heard that my son got you both out of bed in the middle of the night."

"At least now I know what the alarm sounds like," Mary said, wanting to make the best of the situation. Jean felt bad enough already. "And we had a nice cup of cocoa afterward, so no harm done."

Betty glanced at her, as if surprised she was letting it go this easily. Mary was tempted to delve into Jean's and D.J.'s strange behaviors, but this was the first time that Jean had really opened up to them since she'd arrived. If Mary started asking questions right now, no matter how innocently she'd phrased them, Jean might close them off again.

"Thanks again for stopping by," Jean told them. "It means a lot to me."

"Please don't be such a stranger," Betty said. "We want to see more of you and D.J. while you're here."

"We'll get together soon," she promised. "I just need a little more time and I'm sure D.J. will be a big help. He can always make me smile."

"We'll see you soon," Betty said, giving her a wave as she started down the steps.

They said their good-byes, and Mary followed her sister down the steps. When she reached Betty's car, her cell phone rang and she saw Kip's number on the display panel. She'd looked for him at the ice-cream social after he'd finished his long conversation with Hazel, but he had disappeared.

"Hello?" Mary said, answering the call as Betty climbed into the driver's seat.

"Hi, Mary, this is Kip," he said, his voice upbeat. "I just listened to my voice mail."

"Oh, good. I missed your call on Saturday and wanted to make sure it wasn't anything important."

He chuckled. "Not to worry. It's just that the key you gave me wouldn't work in the lock."

Mary sank into the passenger seat. "So you couldn't get inside the shop on Saturday?" A wave of anxiety flooded over her. She had already worried about getting the repairs done in time before the opening, and that was with a full day of work on Saturday. Why hadn't the key worked?

"No. I tried to reach you, but you didn't seem available. I'm really sorry about that, Mrs. Fisher. But don't worry, there's still plenty of time to do those repairs before your grand opening. I can be at your shop first thing tomorrow morning."

She was glad he had somehow read her mind and tried to dissolve her anxiety. She told herself that if Kip wasn't worrying about time, she wouldn't either. She thought about bringing up the children's area she had envisioned, but perhaps that would have to wait until after the grand opening. It did seem rather ambitious at this point. Before she said anything to Kip, she decided she'd wait to see how his current work progressed. "Okay, I'll see you then," she said, ending the call.

"What's going on?" Betty asked, clearly sensing Mary's concern.

"That spare key Paul Becker gave me didn't work."

"That's odd." Betty's brow furrowed. "Didn't Paul stop by your shop specifically to give that key to you?"

"Yes, he did." Mary pulled on her seat belt, wondering if he'd simply made a mistake. *Or had he been looking for a reason to visit her shop?*

Mary grew suspicious. But then again, if Paul had a key, why would he have needed to break in? Either way, Mary decided it was time to pay Paul Becker a visit.

———

On Monday morning, Kip was waiting at the front door when Mary arrived at the shop. She'd left Gus at the house, not wanting him exposed to the sawdust and fumes while Kip was making repairs. She just hoped her cat behaved himself. He'd been on his best behavior since the toilet paper incident, but Betty still didn't trust him.

"Good morning," Kip greeted her. "It looks like it's going to be another beautiful day." He inhaled deeply. "It smells like it too. I'm going to have to stop by Sweet Susan's on my way home tonight. I can't resist her cupcakes."

"I know what you mean," Mary said. She'd already tried Susan's baked goods a couple times, and they were astoundingly good. It would be a blessing and a curse, working right next to a bakery.

She sorted through her key ring until she found the one that opened the front door. "How's everything going for you,

Kip? By the sound of your conversation with Hazel yesterday, the wedding plans are coming along nicely."

"They are. Heather is the most organized person I know." He grinned. "I just do what she tells me. I've found it's easier that way."

Mary laughed. "Then it sounds to me like you've got the makings of a good husband."

They entered the shop, and Kip started unloading his toolbox. Mary walked over to the counter and turned on her computer. "Say, do you have that key I gave you? I'd love to find out why it didn't work."

"Sure thing." Kip pulled the key from his pocket and handed it to her. "Why don't you give it a try first? I sure couldn't get it to work, but maybe you know a secret jiggle or something."

Mary smiled and inserted it in the front door. The key went in smoothly, but it wouldn't turn to the left or the right. She pulled it out and tried again, but to no avail.

"I went through the alley and tried the back door too," he said, "but that didn't work either."

"The locks are keyed the same on the front and back doors." Mary dropped the key into her purse. "I have some errands to run today"—her first plan was to visit Ivy Bay High School—"and I can stop by the hardware store and make you a copy of my own so that you don't have to wait for me anymore to get started. That is, if you don't mind working here without me."

"I actually prefer it that way. The time alone is nice for me. Plus, some of my clients like to give advice as I work, which can slow me down."

"You don't have to worry about that with me. I don't know anything about construction."

"Then it sounds like you've got the makings of a perfect client," he teased, strapping on his leather tool belt.

She left him to his work while she carried her bag into the back room and placed her sack lunch in the refrigerator. She'd called Paul's law office on her way to the shop and made an appointment for one o'clock that afternoon. That left her plenty of time this morning to visit the high school and look through those old yearbooks for the mystery woman in the photograph.

A half hour later, Mary had stopped by Jimmy Shepard's hardware store to get a couple of extra keys made and was now walking through the doors of Ivy Bay High. The principal's office was framed with clear acrylic walls and lay straight ahead of her.

Sherry stood up from her desk as Mary approached. "You're here nice and early this morning," she said.

Mary gave Sherry a friendly hug. "I wanted to get a good start on my day."

Sherry reached into her desk drawer and pulled out a set of keys. "All the yearbooks are in the school library. Just follow me."

When they reached the library, Sherry unlocked the door and let Mary inside. "The annuals are over here." Sherry led her to a book rack in the back of the library. She started thumbing through them. "Wow, these really go back a long way. At least they're sorted in chronological order."

"This should keep me busy for a while."

Sherry headed toward the door. "Let me know if you need anything."

"Thanks." Mary studied the volumes in front of her.

The mystery woman in the photo appeared to be in her late teens or early twenties. Since the photo had been taken in 1957, that gave her a range of years to go by.

She stood up on her toes to reach the annuals dating from 1950 to 1957. As she was pulling the yearbooks from the shelf, she caught sight of the one from the year her mother had graduated from Ivy Bay High. She grabbed that one too, realizing she'd never seen a copy of the leather-bound year-book in her parents' home.

Mary carried them all to the nearest table, setting the 1943 edition aside and sorting the rest with the earliest edition on the top. Then she pulled out a chair, the metal legs scraping against the linoleum floor. The sound echoed in the empty library.

She sat down, feeling right at home. She loved every-thing about a library—the sounds, the sights, and even the smells. It evoked something in her that Mary couldn't de-scribe, a feeling that was even stronger in her new bookshop. She was fulfilling the dream she and John had shared for so long and truly felt as if she was following the path God had set before her.

Now solving the mystery of the stolen photo seemed to be part of that path.

She set the enlarged version of the photo on the table in front of her and opened the first yearbook, planning to com-pare the faces of the female students with the woman in the photograph.

It was a slow process, and she paused more than once for a closer comparison of a yearbook photo with the one on the table in front of her. She also glanced at the names of all the students as she scanned the photos, looking for the surname of Vargo. She might find Fred himself in one of the yearbooks or perhaps a sibling or cousin.

When she was halfway through, she decided to take a break.

After rising out of the chair, Mary stretched in place and then began walking around the library. She felt so comfortable here among the stacks, glancing at familiar titles and thinking of how she could use paper shelf talkers and other hooks at her shop to encourage people to pick up a book.

When Mary returned to the table, she reached for the 1943 edition that featured her mother, too curious to wait any longer.

She turned to the senior pictures, and her heart leaped at the sight of her mother's serene smile. She'd been such a pretty young woman. "Esther Randlett," she whispered, her fingers smoothing over the page.

She breathed a happy sigh as she looked at the other pictures in the yearbook. She saw Uncle George's photo, along with the ever-kind visage of Aunt Phyllis.

As she paged through the yearbook, she searched through the names of the students for Fred Vargo. Since an Ivy Bay home address had been listed on his car registration, she knew there was a good chance that he'd gone to high school here. If she could just find Fred or the mystery woman in one of these yearbooks, it might lead her to someone who could explain the significance behind the stolen photo.

Then another photo caught her eye—not the picture itself, but the name beneath it: Hazel Vargo.

Another Vargo. The *only* one she'd seen so far. She did some quick math in her head and realized that the Hazel in the yearbook would be close to the same age as Hazel Pritchard, the retired kindergarten teacher she'd met at the ice-cream social. Could Vargo be her maiden name, and if so, was she related to Fred?

Excitement buzzed through her as she studied the photograph of the young Vargo girl. It was hard to tell after so many decades, but she thought she saw a resemblance to the woman she'd met yesterday.

Mary approached the remaining yearbooks with a fresh energy, carefully comparing the photo of the mystery woman with the former students of Ivy Bay High. She found Eleanor Emerson and Virginia Livingston in the 1956 edition, neither of whom looked like the mystery woman.

A short time later, Mary closed the last yearbook and sat back in her chair. The girl in the photograph hadn't been a student at Ivy Bay. So where had she come from?

At least she'd found a possible connection to Fred Vargo. If Hazel was related to him, she might even be able to lead Mary to the truth behind the photograph.

EIGHTEEN

When Mary arrived back at the bookshop, Kip was working away. He stood by the door, a tool belt slung around his hips as he measured a section of the door frame. A portable radio sat next to his toolbox, playing a jazzy tune.

"How's it going?" she asked, the hope she felt over the discovery in the yearbook penetrating her voice.

"Pretty good," he said, turning toward her and smiling. "I've repaired the bookshelf and now I'm working on the frame."

"Perfect. Keep up the good work," she said. Then she handed him the spare key. "This one should work," she said.

Kip took the key and inserted it into the lock. It slid in perfectly. "Yep, it works," he said. "Thanks."

She glanced at the clock. After she found the name Hazel Vargo in the yearbook, she'd wanted to rush over to Hazel Pritchard's house and ask if Vargo was her maiden name. But she needed to slow down. One name in a yearbook was a pretty slim lead.

It was just past eleven o'clock in the morning, which meant she had plenty of time to think things through before her one o'clock appointment with Paul. As a former owner of this building, he might have seen those photographs or even known something about them. She'd start there and get as much background information as possible.

She moved to the counter, surprised to see two sealed cardboard boxes on top. "Hey, Kip, any idea where these boxes came from?"

Kip turned to look. "Yeah, a UPS guy dropped them off a couple of hours ago. I went ahead and signed for them. Hope that's okay. I thought they might be more books for your grand opening."

"That's perfect. Thanks." Mary pulled a box cutter out of the drawer and sliced through the first box. Kip was right, it was full of books. But she was confused; she hadn't ordered them. She checked the mailing label and saw they came from Boston, but the address didn't look familiar to her.

When she opened the second box, she saw an envelope sitting on top of the books. She opened it and began to read the letter inside.

> *Dear Mary,*
>
> *We all miss you, but we're so excited about your new venture as the owner of a mystery bookstore. We wanted to do something to show our support, so we've gathered together some of our favorite mysteries as a gift for you. Hope you have a wonderful summer. Come back and visit us soon!*
>
> *Connie Casswell*

Tears of gratitude filled Mary's eyes. She blinked them away as she started looking at the books her friend Connie and the rest of her fellow staff members at the north

Boston library had sent her. She'd worked with them for so many years. That had been one of the hardest things about moving to Ivy Bay—she'd left so many good friends behind.

Mary began pulling the books out of the box and placing them on the counter. She reached for the stamp and ink pad on the counter, the one she'd had made when she'd first opened her business. It had the name and address of her bookshop, which she stamped on the inside back cover of every book. It would be an inexpensive form of advertising for her shop and would help her keep track of her inventory.

She stamped all the books that Connie and her old friends at the library had sent her, thrilled to see that many of them were children's books. Each stamped book was set next to her computer to be cataloged.

A tendril of excitement wound through her. It was all coming together now. Mary's Mystery Bookshop would be open in just over a week. The dream she and John had shared of running a mystery bookshop was finally coming true.

She finished her work, walked out the front door with a wave to Kip, and headed to her car for her appointment with Paul. On her way out, she almost ran into Jean.

"Mary, just the woman I was coming to visit!" Jean's smile was bright and warm, a perfect complement to the sunny day. "You in a hurry?" Jean said, shifting her large shoulder bag to her other arm.

Mary embraced Jean in a quick hug. "I wish I could stay and visit, but I have an appointment in a few minutes. What are you up to today?"

"I had to get some groceries at the market and thought I'd stop by to see for myself this alleged bookshop you've been working on."

Mary smiled, though suspicion threatened to surface. She pushed it aside. "I'd love to give you a tour. But I'm on my way out. How about later this afternoon?"

Jean peered through the open doorway where Kip was measuring a piece of wood. "Would you mind if I just take a sneak peek now? I promise I won't bother your handyman. I really needed a break from the house and want to keep my momentum going."

"I guess that's fine," Mary said, a little surprised by the request. "And I'm sure it goes without saying, but I wouldn't go down in the cellar. The stairs are wobbly and haven't been repaired yet."

"Really? Those stairs were even wobbly when I was a little girl!" Jean laughed wistfully as she looked at the building. "You know, this place hasn't changed that much since my folks owned it. At least on the outside, that is." Jean reached out to pat Mary's arm. "I don't want to keep you any longer. You go on to your meeting. I'll see you soon. Just can't wait to see all you've done with the place!"

Mary watched Jean step into the bookshop. Her cousin's emotions seemed to be all over the place. She wondered if she should try to postpone her meeting with Paul and stay with her. But maybe Jean really did just need a change of scenery. And perhaps, she even wanted some time alone at the bookshop to reminisce. Of course, Kip would be there, so Jean wouldn't be completely alone.

Mary fished the directions to Paul's law office out of her handbag and realized it was right next to Pizzeria Rustica, the charming place where she'd picked up pizza just the other day for her and Betty. She put the directions back in her purse and set on her way. She had some questions to ask that only he could answer. *Lord*, she prayed as she walked, *as always, I could really use Your help. Please continue to guide me and help me keep my spirit focused on You.* Her gaze forward, and her heart centered, she started out.

———

Paul's law office was a small building located in a historic Victorian cottage, south on Water Street, tucked between a yarn store and the pizzeria. Mary walked inside and approached the receptionist. The older woman stared up at her through a pair of thick glasses.

"Hello." Mary offered her hand. "I'm Mary Fisher."

The receptionist shook Mary's hand firmly with a pursed mouth. "I'm afraid you're late for your appointment, Mrs. Fisher. Let me check with Paul to see if he can still fit you in."

The receptionist got up from her chair and disappeared down a hallway. Mary looked at the large, gilded mirror behind the desk. She could see her reflection in it and took a moment to pinch some color into her cheeks and tame a few stray curls.

A few moments later, the receptionist returned. "Paul will see you now. Please follow me."

Paul stood up as Mary entered and extended his hand. "Hello, Mary. How are you?"

"I'm fine, thank you." She shook his hand, noting that his brown suit hung a little looser on his stocky frame than it had when she'd bought the building from him. Paul was in his midforties, with thinning brown hair and pale blue eyes.

"Please have a seat," Paul said, motioning to a chair. "What brings you here today?"

Mary dug into her bag and retrieved the key. "I wanted to return this to you." She held the key toward him. "Unfortunately, it doesn't fit any of the locks at the shop."

"I know," he said, casually pulling the center drawer of his desk open and picking up another key. "I mixed them up."

So it had *been a careless mistake*, Mary thought to herself.

"Sorry for the inconvenience," Paul said as they exchanged keys. "You sure didn't have to make an appointment to return it."

"Oh, I suppose not." Mary tucked the key into her bag and smiled up at him. "But I was actually hoping to ask you a few questions, if you have time."

Paul leaned forward, a gleam of curiosity in his eyes. "You get the first hour of consultation free, so ask away. Are you having some legal difficulties?"

"Oh no," she assured him. "Nothing like that. I wanted to ask you about the old photographs." Mary sat back in her chair and waited to see his reaction.

"Old photographs?" he echoed. He looked genuinely confused.

"You might have seen one of them hanging in my shop last week when you dropped off the key."

He slowly shook his head. "Not that I can remember."

"They were photographs of the building, taken in 1957," she said, hoping to jog his memory. "One photo was of the front of the building, and the other was of the back."

His face cleared. "Oh, *those* photographs. Yes, I do remember them."

"You do?" she said in surprise.

"Yes, I found them in the cellar sealed up with a few books. That was right after I bought the building."

Books? That was a new wrinkle. Uncle George had obviously stored away those two photographs for some reason. Were the books special too?

"Do you happen to remember any of the book titles?"

He shook his head. "Sorry, I didn't pay that much attention to them. I thought the photos looked kind of cool, though." Paul rocked back in his swivel chair. "I had planned to hang them on the wall too, but then I decided to sell the place when my wife found this location. I decided that I just didn't need all that space." Paul waved away the tangent. "Anyway, so I never got around to it." He tilted his head to one side. "May I ask why you are asking me about them?"

Mary guessed that he either didn't know one of them had been stolen or was pretending not to know. She continued carefully. "Well, I find them interesting and nostalgic, and wondered if you knew more about them. Do you know anything about the people in the pictures?"

"I can't help you there. I'm like you—I just thought they were interesting and retro. I'm glad you found them."

"Me too," she said, feeling sad that she'd found and then lost one of them. She looked at Paul, who began to tap his pencil rather rapidly on the desk. She would take the hint, but she had one more question.

Mary wondered about the book the mystery woman had tucked behind her back in the photo. Had that been in the box too, at some point? She assumed Paul must have decided to keep the books because they weren't in the box.

"Did you have any plans for the books that were with the photographs? I'm planning to sell used books at my shop and can always use more inventory."

"Sorry," he said. "I actually donated them to the library. There weren't that many of them—maybe four or five."

"Oh, that's okay. Thanks, anyway." She stood up and lifted the strap of her bag over her shoulder. "And thanks for taking the time to chat with me, Paul. I wish you all the best."

"Likewise." He pushed back his chair and stood up, then moved to open the door for her. "Please let me know if there's anything else I can do for you."

Mary bid him good-bye and headed out the door. She might not have learned much from Paul, but she was ready to eliminate him as a suspect. He'd been totally open to her questions, and his body language was as comfortable as can be. Not like a man who was trying to hide something.

When Mary returned to the shop later that afternoon, she found Kip still hard at work.

"Hi, Mrs. Fisher," Kip greeted her.

"Hi, Kip," Mary replied. "Looks like you're making progress."

"Yep. Happy to say it's going faster than I expected," he said.

"Great." Mary carried her bag back to the counter, careful to avoid the scrap wood and sawdust on the drop cloths. She glanced over at her Gram's rocker, hoping he'd protected it well.

But the rocker wasn't there.

She looked around the shop and spotted it near the children's book section, as far as possible from the construction area.

"That's it," she said out loud.

"That's what?" Kip asked.

"That's where Gram's rocker belongs." She walked over to the area she called the children's section, although it was really just a corner of her shop to put up posters and add colorful pillows. But seeing her gram's rocker there made her realize it needed to be even more inviting.

She thought again about the plans she'd sketched for a children's area. Kip had said things were moving faster than expected. Maybe she could gauge his reaction when she mentioned it.

"Hey, Kip, are you still trying to make extra money?"

He put down the foursquare in his hand and walked over to her. "As much as possible," he said. A brief wave of sadness crossed his face, but then he composed himself and offered his usual friendly expression. "Why do you ask?"

Mary hesitated. What was she thinking? She had so much on her plate right now, and clearly, so did Kip. Between getting ready for her shop to open and trying to solve the photo mystery, did Mary really want to take on another project? It did seem like Kip sincerely needed the money, though.

Lord, what should I do?

She thought about John and how he'd handle decisions like this. He'd look at the pros and cons. The biggest pro was making her bookshop even more perfect for the grand opening. The biggest con was the possible time constraints that it might put on her.

But how much time could it cost her, really? The plan she liked most was a simple one, and Kip was an excellent worker.

"Mrs. Fisher?" Kip said, interrupting her thoughts.

That's when she realized how long she'd left him standing there while she was thinking it through. But it had been enough time for her to make her decision.

"What would you think about building a children's nook for me, Kip? I've been thinking it'd be the perfect touch to the shop."

He arched a brow. "What exactly did you have in mind?"

She walked over to the counter and pulled out some of the sketches she'd put there earlier. After laying them out on the counter, Mary selected the one with a simple, clean design that wouldn't cost her much in materials, labor, or time.

Mary handed the sketch to Kip. "I'm envisioning two waist-high bookcases, each one about four feet deep and twenty feet long. I want them angled from each wall so it forms a diamond shape with a small gap in between the bookshelves for an entrance."

"Do you want to put a gate on it or anything?"

She smiled up at him. "Oh, Kip, that's brilliant. Let's put a garden gate there. We just have to make sure it's lightweight and easy to open, whether you're going in or out."

Kip studied her rough sketch. "That could look pretty cool, actually."

"So you can finish it in time for the grand opening?"

He scratched his head in silence for a moment, a smile slowly growing on his face. "You know, it would be an honor for me to build it," he said. "And it shouldn't be too difficult to finish on time. What color do you want the shelves?"

She looked around her shop, realizing that she had satin-wood bookshelves everywhere. "I'd want this children's nook to stand out but not be glaring, so let's paint them white. Then later, I can add flowers and butterflies—things that will make it look like a garden."

He folded up her sketch and stuck it in his shirt pocket. "I'm about finished here today, so I think I'll head over to the hardware store and get the supplies now. That way I'll have them when I start work tomorrow. I've got to work on the stairs too, but...one step at a time!"

"Thank you so much," Mary said, truly grateful for his enthusiasm. "I'll see you tomorrow."

Kip pivoted to leave, but then he turned back to Mary and said in a low voice. "By the way, is that lady all right?"

She looked at him, completely confused. "What lady?"

"The one who came in here after you left for your appointment. She's still here, you know."

Mary blinked in surprise. "Jean is still here?" She'd looked around the shop several times already and hadn't seen her. And why would Jean stay here so long? She'd told Mary she only wanted a quick peek. "Where is she?"

"I think she's still in the cellar."

"Still?" A chill crawled down Mary's spine. "How long has she been down there?"

He shrugged his shoulders. "Maybe twenty minutes or so. I just figured she had your permission. She acted like she knew the place pretty well."

"She does," Mary replied vacantly, trying to make sense of Jean's behavior. There was nothing down in the cellar. *Nothing she knew about anyway.*

NINETEEN

◆▸◆

Mary held tight to the railing as she descended the cellar stairs. "Jean?"

The cellar light was on, but she couldn't see her cousin in the dim recesses of the large room. She concentrated on the stairsteps, negotiating the unstable ones with care before she reached the landing.

"Jean, are you down here?" Then she saw a movement in a far corner, and her cousin emerged out of the shadows.

"Hello, Mary."

Mary hurried toward her, grasping her gently by the arms. Her skin was cold and clammy. "Oh, Jean, you had me worried there for a minute. What have you been doing down here for so long?"

"Just looking around," she said, her voice flat.

"But Kip said you've been down here for at least twenty minutes." Mary noticed that she'd been crying again. She wanted to get her upstairs and get her warm. "There's not that much to see except spiders—and you hate spiders."

Jean's face crumpled. "There are worse things in life than spiders, Mary."

Mary stared at her cousin, willing her to open up. "Jean, please tell me what is going on with you."

Jean pulled a small camera from her pocket. "I'm fine, Mary. I was just taking some pictures for the family scrapbook. I got a little emotional, that's all."

Now Mary was even more perplexed. "You want pictures of the cellar for your family scrapbook?"

"Just pictures of this building, since it was part of Mom and Dad's life. I didn't want to use the one you e-mailed me because I have no idea who that woman is with Dad." Her voice cracked. "I'm sure there was nothing going on between the two of them, but it's just strange. Why is it still around after all these years?"

"I don't know," Mary answered truthfully. That question had been nagging at her too. The building had been through several owners in the past five decades—she'd discovered that when she'd signed the deed. Somehow, those photographs had survived that many owners moving in and out of the building.

"But there are other things that confuse me too," Mary continued gently. "Like the fact that you lied to us about when you arrived in Ivy Bay. You arrived last Monday, Jean." She didn't have to try to keep her tone and demeanor soft; she *felt* soft toward her cousin. She wanted her to be innocent.

Jean didn't try to deny it. She closed her eyes, looking very tired. When she opened them again, Mary saw raw pain in their deep brown depths.

"David left me, Mary," Jean whispered.

Those words took Mary's breath away. "Oh, Jean. When—"

"Two weeks ago; he just walked out the door." Tears spilled onto her cheeks. "He just said he didn't want to be married to me anymore."

Mary reached out to hold her, letting her cry in her arms. "I'm so sorry." Even as she said the words, relief flowed through her that there was an explanation for Jean's odd behavior. Jean wasn't a thief; she was an abandoned wife. And that also seemed to explain D.J.'s odd behavior when he had come to the house. It seems he really had just been trying to reach his mother, not only to comfort her after the loss of his grandfather, but also in the wake of his father's departure, which neither he nor Jean had been ready to talk about. Mary thought about the storm that had raged that night. Perhaps *that's* what had tripped the alarm.

"I didn't want to tell anyone because I'm still hoping there's a chance he'll come back." She wiped away her tears with a tissue. "But I couldn't stay in my house in Chicago a moment longer. I was such a mess. And I couldn't face you and Betty when I got here on Monday, so I lied about it because I just couldn't handle any questions."

Mary completely understood. If Jean had mentioned to Mary and Betty that she had arrived two days before contacting them, of course they would have questioned the delay.

"And that wasn't the only time I lied to you either," Jean continued, raising her head to meet Mary's gaze. "Remember when you stopped at the house on Thursday? I wasn't headed out to meet my old classmates; I just wanted to be alone. I guess I'll have all the alone time I want when I go back to Chicago."

Mary gently patted her back. "You're not alone. You have me and Betty and D.J." She knew it wasn't much of a consolation, but it was the best Mary could provide.

Jean pulled a clean tissue from her pocket. "I know. I have so many blessings in my life, even if I don't have my…husband." Tears pooled in her eyes again, but she blinked them back. "I'm *so* tired of crying. All I've done since I've gotten here is cry and go on long walks."

That would explain why Mary had seen her standing by the bookshop on the night of the break-in. She hadn't been scoping anything out; she had just been reflecting on the past.

"I really do appreciate what you and Betty have been trying to do by inviting me places and coming over to visit," Jean continued. "But I've just needed time by myself to sort out everything in my life."

Mary still wasn't sure how taking pictures of the cellar for twenty minutes would help her do that, but Jean seemed much too fragile at the moment to bring it up.

"You're going to be all right," Mary assured her, so sad for her cousin but also relieved to know that Jean was not the thief. "You're a Nelson, and we always land on our feet. I'll be praying for you and I know Betty will too." She hesitated. "Is it all right if I tell Betty what you're going through?"

"Of course," Jean said, taking a deep breath. "And tell her I'm sorry about lying to her. The last thing I want to do is alienate more of my family."

"You don't have to worry about that," Mary assured her. "Betty and I will always be here for you."

"Thank you," Jean said in a small voice.

"Are you ready to come upstairs now?"

"I suppose. I'm not afraid of spiders anymore, but I'm not that fond of them either."

That made Mary smile as she led her cousin back up the stairs. Kip was already gone by the time they emerged from the cellar.

Mary picked up her bag and put it over her shoulder. "Can I give you a ride home?"

"No thanks. I've got my car."

Mary moved closer to her. "If I can't give you a ride, can I offer some advice?"

Jean hesitated but then said, "What is it?"

"I think it would help if you could talk to someone like Pastor Miles at Grace Church. He's a very kind man, and from what I understand, he does quite a bit of pastoral counseling."

Jean gave her a watery smile. "Thanks for the advice, but I think I can handle this on my own. Like you said before, we Nelsons are a strong bunch."

"Just promise me you'll keep it in mind," Mary urged her.

"I promise."

———

Mary walked through the front door of her and Betty's home with a sense of heaviness at the news she'd just heard from Jean.

Gus bounded into the living room and stood at her feet. She scooped him up and cradled him against her chest.

"Hello there, big guy," she said. "Have you been good today?"

Gus began to purr as he placed both paws on her left shoulder. She carried him down the hall and into the kitchen, looking for her sister.

Betty emerged from the laundry room carrying a basket of folded clothes. "Hey there, Mar. I didn't know you were home."

"I just got here." Mary set Gus on the floor. "Do you need some help with that?"

"Thanks, I've got it," Betty said with a smile, setting the basket by the stairs. "I did some laundry today, and I've already sorted out my clothes, so you can take these upstairs."

"Oh, Bets," Mary said, grateful and frustrated at the same time. One of the reasons she'd moved in here was to help her sister, not add to her workload. "You didn't have to do my laundry."

Betty shrugged. "It's no bother at all. Besides, it makes more sense to have a full load." She walked over to the table and sat down. "Now, tell me about your day."

"First, tell me about yours," Mary said, joining her at the table. "Did Gus behave for you?"

"He was just fine. I actually barely saw him." She pointed to his food dish on the floor. "I noticed he didn't eat anything, though. I think he missed you."

Mary looked over at Gus, who was up on his two hind legs, peering into the laundry basket. "He's going to have to stay here until the construction is done at the shop. I hope that's okay."

"It's totally fine," Betty said. "How's the shop coming along?"

"Great." She told Betty about her idea for a children's nook, but her heart still felt heavy over Jean. "I'm going to put Gram's rocker in there. After how many stories she used to read to us in that rocking chair, it seemed like the natural place."

Betty clapped her hands together. "I think that's a great idea."

"Now I just need to think of more ideas to make the nook a fun place for kids." Then Mary grew more serious. "Something else happened today too. I saw Jean."

"Oh? Where?"

"She came to the shop just as I was leaving to meet Paul. I thought it was strange when she asked me if she could take a quick peek at the place while I was gone." Mary sighed. "And I have to admit that it made me suspect her of breaking into my shop even more."

"So what happened?"

Mary explained how she'd come back to find Jean in the cellar and the confession that spilled out of her. "She was pretty distraught. I have to admit the news came as a shock to me, and I'm so saddened by it, even though I'm certainly relieved to know that the break-in had nothing to do with Jean. She seemed fine when we saw her on Wednesday—even happy. Now I know she was just putting up a good front."

"Jean's always been so proud of her family," Betty said fondly. "She's a lot like Aunt Phyllis that way. I'm sure it was difficult for her to tell you that things weren't as rosy as she'd made them seem."

"Very difficult." Mary's throat tightened as she remembered the pain she'd seen in Jean's eyes. "I didn't know what to say to make her feel better."

"Maybe I could put her in touch with Pastor Miles. He's so good in situations like this."

"I actually suggested that to her, but she was a bit hesitant. I did tell her we'd pray for her."

"Of course we will. No time like the present," Betty said as she took Mary's hand in her own. They both bowed their heads and prayed for their cousin.

After the prayer was over, a serenity settled over Mary. She filled her sister in on the rest of the day, including her visits to the high school and with Paul Becker.

Betty sat for a long moment, a smile teasing her mouth. "You're rather good at this, aren't you?"

"Good at what?"

"Ferreting out clues and such. I never would have thought to look through some old high school yearbooks."

Mary grew thoughtful. "You know, I really didn't expect it to go this far when I first started looking into the theft of the photo. I just wanted to figure out why someone would steal it."

"And now you've discovered Hazel may be related to Fred Vargo. Amazing."

"I'm not sure how amazing it is," Mary said humbly. "I still don't have a prime suspect in the break-in, and my theory is based on what Leroy told me. If Uncle George was in a relationship with the mystery woman, maybe she or someone in her family is afraid the truth will come out."

Betty's brow furrowed. "After so many years have passed? We could walk right past the mystery woman on the street and not recognize her from that photo."

"I know *we* could," Mary said, nodding. "But someone who knew her during the time would recognize her." Plus, she couldn't shake the feeling that there was more to the theft of that photograph than a simple attempt to hide a decades-old affair. A surge of energy ran through her. She was getting closer to the answer. She could feel it.

TWENTY

On Tuesday morning, Mary stood in the living room, snuggling Gus in her arms. "You be a good boy today, okay? No television or video games or tripping alarm systems," she said, laughing to herself. "And no playing with toilet paper either." She hated leaving him home, but she'd start taking him to the shop again once the construction work was done. She set him down and headed out the door.

She planned to stop at the library before heading to the bookshop. She'd lain in bed last night reflecting on the day, and Paul's comment about the books he'd found with those pictures had come to mind. The books might not have anything to do with the mystery, but she couldn't forget the book that woman was holding behind her back. Those pictures and the books had been sealed up together, according to Paul. That might mean something.

A short time later, Mary arrived at the Ivy Bay Public Library. It was housed in a red brick building with white doors and windows. Mary found it surprisingly spacious as she walked inside. There were large skylights in the high vaulted ceilings, filling the room with sunshine and giving it a light, airy feeling. That lightness was echoed in the blond oak bookcases and furniture. Tables and chairs were arranged in cozy nooks and reading areas, giving patrons some privacy from the main area.

Mary walked up to the front counter to greet a trim woman in her midforties. She had short dark hair, and her pink cat's-eye glasses matched her blouse.

"Hello," she said cordially. This was her first visit to the library since she'd moved here. She wanted to check out the fiction section when she had more time, but today she was on a mission. "I'm Mary Fisher and I—"

"You're the bookshop lady," the librarian interjected. "Mary's Mystery Bookshop. I can't wait until it opens. I'm a big mystery fan, and we don't stock enough of them here. My name is Victoria Pickerton, by the way. I'm the head librarian."

"Well, then, you'll definitely have to come to my grand opening and take a look around. I'd love to have you there."

"I'd be happy to come." Victoria stood up a little straighter. "I wasn't sure you'd still be hosting it so soon after your store was broken into."

She knew the news had spread, of course, but it still came as a small shock to her whenever someone mentioned it. "Oh, it's definitely still on," Mary said with a determined look. "No way am I going to let some intruder keep me from opening my shop. I can hardly wait."

"Well, great then! I'll be there." Victoria folded her hands on the counter. "Now, how can I help you today?"

"Well, this may seem like an odd request. . . ."

"Those are my favorite kind," Victoria interjected. "Go on."

"I'm looking for some books that Paul Becker donated a few months ago.... Do you happen to have individual donor lists?"

"*Hmm.*" She thought for a moment and then hopped off her chair. "Well, we do keep records of donations. Wait right here, and I'll go see what I can find."

As Mary waited, she perused the nearby bookshelves, impressed with the high number of new fiction and nonfiction books on display. For as much as she liked libraries, she was surprised she hadn't made it here before. She picked up a book on garden designs that Betty might enjoy. She might check the book out for her sister since she'd left Gus home again.

"Found it!" With a proud grin, Victoria returned from the back room just as Mary reached the front desk. "Here is a list of the titles Mr. Becker donated."

"Perfect," Mary said. "Thanks so much." She was excited for even the remote possibility that there could be a clue about the picture, or of the mystery woman, in one of those books. She knew it was a long shot, but long shots were still all she had to go on. If the same book the mystery woman was holding happened to be on the list of books Paul donated, she may be able to learn something about the woman herself. On the other hand, it may be a dead end. And Mary still wasn't sure what she expected to learn about the woman based on the book she was reading. But at this point, she was too invested in determining why that photograph was stolen to give up now.

Mary surveyed the list. There were six books, each of them fiction, along with a bar-code number.

"Thank you," Mary said, setting off to find them. They were an eclectic lot of novels that had been written in the first half of the twentieth century. *The Great Gatsby*, *A Town Like Alice*, *The Hobbit*, *Gone with the Wind*, *A Passage to India*, and one of Mary's favorite mystery novels, *Rebecca* by Daphne du Maurier.

Mary began to gather the books. The library had multiple copies of a few of them, so Mary had to match the bar code on a particular book with the bar code on the list. Then she sat down at the table with them and closely examined each one.

They were different sizes and lengths and the covers were different colors, but they did have one thing in common. On the inside of the front cover, near the bottom corner, were the initials ST, along with a small sketch of a butterfly.

Mary searched her memory, trying to match someone who knew her uncle with the initials ST, but she simply couldn't think of anyone.

Fifteen minutes later, Mary carried all six of the books on the list to the checkout counter.

"Did you find what you were looking for?" Victoria asked.

"I hope so." She pulled her wallet out of her bag.

Victoria reached into a drawer and pulled out a membership form. "I'll just need to see some form of identification that shows you're a resident of Ivy Bay."

Mary had it ready for her. "Here you go. I used to be a librarian in Boston, so I know the drill."

Victoria's eyes widened in surprise. "I didn't know that. It's nice to meet a fellow bookworm. And I'm confident your bookshop will be a success, since you've got that kind of experience behind you."

"I hope you're right." Mary gave a nervous grin, finished filling out the form and slid it across the counter to Victoria.

Victoria worked up the file on the computer and then handed Mary a plastic card. She stacked up the books and pushed them toward Mary. "You're all set."

Mary bid her good-bye and headed out the door. It was another gorgeous day with temperatures in the upper seventies and a warm breeze coming off the bay. She wished she could spend the rest of the day on the white sand beach and read *Rebecca* again, but this time, she was more interested in the initials written on the book than the book itself.

———

Mary had left the library three hours ago and had been working ever since. Her e-mail in-box had become rather full since she started working on this mystery, and she couldn't ignore it any longer. Follow-up notes from book donors, purchase agreements, people interested in doing various events at her shop, and so on. She couldn't believe the attention her shop was already getting before it had even opened, but she took it as a very good sign.

She had also been able to track down Hazel Pritchard's maiden name on the computer. According to the list of teacher certifications on the state education Web site, her full name was Hazel Mae Vargo Pritchard. Mary still didn't know whose name was associated with ST, but she could feel herself getting closer.

She rubbed her eyes. They were starting to blur from staring at the computer screen for so long.

"You look like you could use a break."

She looked up from her computer to find Henry standing by the counter. With the noise of Kip hammering boards together for her new children's nook, she hadn't heard Henry come in.

"You read my mind," Mary said, pushing away from the computer. "I think I have a case of what my daughter Lizzie calls brain fog."

He smiled. "And I have the perfect cure—ice cream at Bailey's. My treat."

That was another offer she couldn't refuse, although she was tempted to. She'd been eating an awful lot of ice cream lately. Then again, it was summertime. Ice cream was as essential to summer as sunglasses or iced tea, she decided firmly. "Let me grab my bag from the back room and I'll be ready to go."

Henry walked over to chat with Kip while she made her way to the back room.

While there, she took a few moments to check the mirror above the sink. She ran her fingers through her curls and then called it good. She'd never be a fashion model, but the summer sun had given her a nice golden tan and brightened her gray hair.

She joined Henry back in the shop, draping her handbag over one shoulder. "I'm ready to go." Then she turned to Kip. "We're headed over to Bailey's for a while. Can we bring you anything?"

"No, thanks," he said. "Heather's picking me up at four today so we can sample wedding cakes, so I'd better not fill up on ice cream before then."

They left him to his work and headed to Bailey's. "Looks like we came just at the right time," Henry said. "No line."

"Hello, Mary," Tess greeted her, ice-cream scoop in hand. "I've been hearing rave reviews about that cranberry ice cream you made for the church social. I wish I could have been there to try it."

"People seemed to like it," Mary said modestly.

"Like it?" Henry echoed in disbelief. "They loved it. I had three bowls myself."

"I'd love to try some," Tess said. "I'm always interested in new flavors and taste combinations."

"Next time I make a batch, I'll drop a pint by your shop," Mary told her. "Although I think I'd be nervous for the ice-cream queen herself to try my amateur recipe."

"Nonsense. Now, promise you'll bring some by?"

She laughed. "Yes, I promise to bring you ice cream next time I make it."

"Now that's what I like to hear."

Mary and Henry placed their orders and then made their way to a corner table in the shop.

"Coconut ripple," Henry said, taking a tentative lick of his cone. "That's a new one to me."

"How is it?"

He gave a nod of approval. "Pretty good. How is your rosewater ice cream?"

"Interesting," she said, spooning up another bite and trying to identify all the flavors.

He chuckled. "Does that mean it's good or bad?"

"Good," she replied. "Definitely good." She enjoyed several more bites and then looked up to see Henry watching her.

"What?" she asked, dabbing her napkin over her chin. "Do I have ice cream on my face?"

"No, you look great. I was just wondering how you're coming along with the mystery. Any new developments?"

"Well, I found out that my cousin is having some personal problems, which explained many of the questions I had, especially after seeing her on the surveillance disk."

"But?" he said, letting the word linger in the air.

Mary smiled. Henry still knew her; that was clear. "But while I was initially very relieved, I'm realizing that it doesn't explain everything. Like why her son was outside our house at midnight and set off the security alarm? The one constant seems to be those 1957 photographs. The one that wasn't stolen was sitting on the kitchen counter at the time, in full view of the door where D.J. stood."

"So, you're back where you started?"

Mary nodded. "I guess. The thing is, I'm confident that Jean had nothing to do with the break-in. But until I can prove who broke into my shop, I can't really exclude any theories. And there's something else...."

Henry waited patiently as Mary tried to pull her thoughts together.

"I've been thinking a lot about Uncle George," Mary began. "And trying to remember what was happening in his life in 1957. I remember my aunt Phyllis telling us that sometime in the late fifties, Uncle George went to Virginia for a while to work. He was gone for almost a year and a half, and Aunt Phyllis was with him part of the time."

She dipped a plastic spoon into her ice cream and took a bite. "You have to understand that Uncle George, and especially Aunt Phyllis, just didn't do those kinds of things. They didn't just travel. And when they came back to Ivy Bay, they sold his auction house almost immediately."

Henry looked thoughtful. "That is pretty fast."

"I'm starting to think he might be the one I need to investigate. I loved him dearly, don't get me wrong," Mary said hastily. "There are just too many question marks about his past."

"But where do you start?" Henry asked. "Are you planning to ask Jean about it?"

Mary leaned forward. "Maybe, if the time is right. I'm on my way to talk to Hazel Pritchard this afternoon. It turns out her maiden name was Vargo. Like Fred."

His gray eyebrows rose an inch. "Well, there you go. Another lead."

She sighed. "I just hope it doesn't lead me to a dead end."

He gave her a sympathetic smile. "Well, let me know if I can help."

"I will," she said sincerely. "Although you're already bringing me fresh fish and treating me to delicious ice cream." She smiled, so grateful to God that she and Henry had resumed their friendship. "Fish and ice cream. What more could a girl want?"

TWENTY-ONE

❖◆◆◆❖

That Tuesday afternoon, Mary and Betty made their way to the Bay View Retirement Complex to meet with Hazel Pritchard. She'd started to ask Hazel some preliminary questions over the phone, but the woman had gotten confused and ended up inviting both Mary and Betty for a visit.

The complex was made up of a series of cute little duplexes in various shades of blue, green, beige, and gray. Each duplex had an attached garage on either side of it and they shared a brick patio in the back that looked out over Cape Cod Bay.

"It's so nice of you ladies to come and visit," Hazel said as they all sat at the table on her patio. She'd made iced coffee for all of them, and a plate of sugar cookies sat in the center of the table.

"It's lovely here," Mary said. "Thank you for inviting us."

Hazel folded her hands on the table and looked at Mary with a contrite smile. "I'm sorry we got our lines crossed on the phone earlier. I have slight hearing loss, but it doesn't bother me much unless I can't see the face of the person I'm talking to."

"It's no problem," Mary assured her, grateful that Hazel was so willing to talk with her.

"What I was able to hear," Hazel said, "is that you found a picture of me in my old high school yearbook. Ivy Bay, class of '43? Is that right?"

"Yes." Mary leaned forward, hope rising within her. If Hazel couldn't help her, she didn't know where to look next. "And your maiden name was Vargo, right?"

Hazel chuckled. "It sure was."

"Then you may remember our mother, who was in your same class," Mary said. "Esther Randlett?"

"Oh yes, of course I remember her. She had a terrific singing voice." Hazel studied Mary for a minute. "You look a lot like her, I can see."

Mary gave a wistful smile. "That's a wonderful compliment, Hazel. Thank you."

Hazel nodded. "Now what can I do for you ladies?"

"Well, I'm looking for someone named Fred Vargo. It's a long story, but basically, I have a picture that I'm curious about with a car in it that I think may have been his."

The woman's pleasant expression faded a bit. "I'm sorry to tell you that Fred passed away."

Betty touched Hazel's arm. "I'm so sorry to hear that. Were you two close?"

Hazel nodded. "He was my younger brother by about fifteen years. There were eight kids in my family, and I was the oldest. You don't see many families of that size these days. I was cooking and taking care of babies by the time I was nine...." Her voice trailed off, and she started to laugh. "Oh, listen to me go on. Tell me more about this picture? Do you have it with you?"

"I sure do." Hazel's hearing might trouble her a bit, but her eyes seemed sharp. The older woman had all the mannerisms of a good kindergarten teacher: She made direct eye contact and kept her voice gentle and even. Yet, there was a spark in the woman's green eyes that hinted she was much stronger than she looked.

Mary set the enlarged photo on the table in front of Hazel. "This is a photograph that was taken in front of our uncle's auction house back in 1957. And that"— Mary tapped on the car in the photo—"is a car that was licensed to Fred."

Hazel turned to Mary.

"So that's what brought you here?" Hazel asked. "A car in a photo?"

"It is," Mary admitted, knowing it might sound a bit flimsy. But in her mind, she hoped it would cause a kind of domino effect. She'd already identified the license plate on the car, then the owner of that car. Leroy had told her that the car was Fred's and that Fred and Uncle George had a fight over a girl—possibly the woman in the photograph, who had been Fred's girlfriend. What Mary needed to know now was how exactly the mystery woman was connected to Uncle George. And eventually, how all of them together might be connected to the break-in at her shop and the theft of the photograph. It was a tall order, Mary thought, certainly not for the first time.

"It's not just the car, though," Mary added. "I was told that Fred was dating the woman in the photograph. Do you recognize her?"

Hazel adjusted her bifocals and studied the picture. "I can't say that I do. I recognize George Nelson, though. He was always such a nice man."

Betty thanked Hazel for the compliment, and Mary smiled, but she tried to mask the disappointment she felt that Hazel didn't recognize the mystery woman. Who *was* she?

"I suppose it could be one of Fred's girls," Hazel continued. "He changed girlfriends more often than he changed cars. I think he was allergic to settling down."

"Did he ever marry?" Betty asked.

Hazel shook her head. "No, he was a bachelor until the day he died. He was engaged once, probably around the time this picture was taken."

"Do you remember her name?" Mary asked.

Hazel grimaced. "I was afraid you were going to ask me that. I think it might have been Starla...Stella, something like that. I regret to say I never even met her. I was married and had kids of my own by the time Fred graduated high school, so it was hard to keep track of him. And the engagement was broken off so quickly that I never got the chance to meet her."

"I understand," Mary said.

"I suppose, then, that you wouldn't know her last name?" Betty asked.

Hazel shook her head. "I'm sorry, I have no idea."

Still, it was a name. Perhaps Fred's fiancée—if Mary could locate someone on a tentative first name alone—would know something about the woman. She almost let out a weary sigh but then thought better of it. She couldn't believe the number of straws she'd grasped at, only to have none of them hold.

But she kept her countenance optimistic. "Do you know if Fred was friends with my uncle George?" Mary asked. She then thought of her uncle's get-rich schemes. "Or maybe even a business partner of some kind?"

Hazel placed her hand over her mouth, looking half shocked and half amused. "Oh my, no. Fred didn't care about going into any kind of business. He didn't really like to work much at all, to tell you the truth. He used to fix up old cars whenever he needed money." She sighed. "We always said Ma spoiled him too much because he was the youngest, but that's the way it goes. He even spent some time in jail, although our folks liked to pretend it didn't happen."

Jail? Until now, Mary hadn't really considered criminal activity as a motive for stealing the photograph, but why not? The statute of limitations would have run out on almost every type of crime, so she doubted that fear of prosecution could have led to the break-in, but she'd read enough mysteries to know there were a thousand reasons for people to try and cover up their crimes. Maybe the fistfight Leroy had mentioned hadn't been over a woman, but something else. "Do you remember when he went to jail?"

Hazel pondered that question for a moment. "It was in the sixties, I think. It turned out that some of the cars he'd restored had actually been stolen vehicles. He got out of more serious jail time by testifying against a crooked car dealer. Fred was *always* good at getting out of any serious trouble."

Hazel had given Mary a lot to chew on. "You've been so helpful," Mary told her.

Hazel laughed. "All I did was talk, which I like to do, so I'm the one who should be thanking you."

"We'll have to get together again soon," Betty promised her. "And next time, I'll bring the treats."

Hazel picked up the cookie platter and held it toward them. "Help yourselves to some cookies, girls. They're homemade."

As Mary bit into a crispy sugar cookie, she looked down at the photograph. The mystery woman's left hand was behind her back, making it impossible to see her ring finger. Even if she could, that wouldn't tell her the woman's name.

But she might be able to find out the name of Fred's fiancée if she kept digging, using every resource available to her. She just hoped it moved her one more step closer to solving this puzzle.

The next day, Mary made another trip to the Ivy Bay library.

"It sure is nice to see you again so soon," Victoria said. "Have you finished those books already?"

Mary smiled. "Not yet." She'd paged through them a few times but hadn't noticed anything significant aside from the initials. "But I wanted to ask you about newspaper archives. I'm hoping you have previous issues of the *Ivy Bay Bugle* on microfilm."

"Of course we do." Victoria rounded the counter. "We also have free Internet access, an interlibrary loan system, and several online newspaper subscriptions, as well as other resources. Do you want me to show you the way to the microfilm machine?"

"That would be great," Mary said, following the younger librarian.

"I'll just assume you know how to use it, so I'll save you my usual spiel. The microfilm rolls for the *Ivy Bay Bugle* archives are in the cupboard beside the machine. Just let me know if you have any questions, okay?"

"Thanks, I will," Mary promised, moving toward the cupboard and sorting through the microfilm rolls until she found the right one.

She pulled out a chair, sat down and turned on the microfilm machine in front of her. It only took a moment to place the roll of microfilm on the spoke and feed it into the reader.

As a librarian, she knew that many periodicals, newspapers, and even some older books were stored on microfilm because they took up far less space on that format than cluttering up precious bookshelf space or boxed up in a storage room somewhere.

Now that everything was going digital, many current periodicals, newspapers, and books could be found on a computer. In fact, the popularity of electronic books and fancy new e-readers made her a little nervous about the success of her bookshop. She believed there would always be readers who enjoyed the feel of a real book in their hands, but she couldn't deny the convenience and accessibility that digital technology could provide.

Mary scanned the index of the *Ivy Bay Bugle* and used the large knob on the side of the machine to scroll down. She was looking for engagement announcements, starting with 1957. If she had to, she'd look at other years too. She just hoped Fred Vargo and his fiancée had placed an announcement in the newspaper.

Mary's right hand slowed on the knob as she reached the first 1957 issue of the *Ivy Bay Bugle*. Then she perused the wedding and engagement announcements posted in the weekly newspaper. She scrolled fairly quickly past each weekly edition, her eyes on the lookout for the name Fred Vargo. Her hand was beginning to tire by the time she scrolled through the month of April.

Then she saw it.

"Bingo," Mary said, sitting back in her chair. There it was in black and white: Tuttle-Vargo Engaged.

Mary read the announcement, a tingle of anticipation running through her.

Mr. and Mrs. Leonard Vargo of Ivy Bay announce the engagement of their son Fredrick Lee Vargo to Miss Stella Frances Tuttle, the goddaughter of Miss Katherine Campbell of Ivy Bay. The wedding will take place in June.

Stella Frances Tuttle. ST. That fit the initials in the books that had been found with the photographs. And she knew only one Frances in Ivy Bay, and that was Frances Curran. Yet Frances said that she'd never been in Ivy Bay until she and her husband moved here a year ago.

Mary sat at the microfilm machine for several moments, wishing the engagement announcement had included a photograph. Then she could be sure that Fred's fiancée was the mystery woman. But the fact that the books from the shop had the initials ST, and that the woman in the picture was holding a book, seemed perhaps too coincidental to ignore.

Her gaze stayed on the page of the wedding and engagement announcements, and soon she noticed something interesting. All the other engagement announcements started with the names of the woman and her parents first. Only the Tuttle-Vargo announcement led with the names of Fred and his parents. Perhaps it was because Miss Tuttle's parents weren't listed, only her godmother.

It was also much shorter than the other announcements, not including such information as where they'd attended school or even the name of the church where they were to be married. Mary wasn't sure that meant anything, but she did find it curious. Just as she found the fact that a woman named Frances had seen the photograph in her shop only a couple of days before it was stolen and the fiancée of Fred Vargo had Frances for her middle name.

Mary thought back to her chat with the Currans at the ice-cream social when Albert had mentioned that they'd been married for fifty-three years.

On a hunch, Mary scrolled down to the 1959 archives of the *Bugle* and started searching through the weekly wedding announcements. Ten minutes later, she saw the mystery woman's face on the screen and almost fell off her chair.

Mary hastily turned around to reach for the copy of the stolen photograph in her bag, wanting to be sure. She held it next to the screen, comparing the two photographs. The woman's hairstyle was a bit different in the 1959 photo, but everything else was the same: the face, the eyes, the shape of her mouth.

Still reeling from the shock of finally discovering the mystery woman's identity, Mary took a moment to gather herself, then began reading the wedding announcement:

Miss Katherine Campbell of Ivy Bay announces the marriage of her goddaughter, Stella Frances Tuttle, to Albert Charles Curran, son of Dr. and Mrs. C. L. Curran of Boston. Vows were exchanged at a double-ring ceremony at 8:00 PM, June 28, in Rollins Chapel on

the Dartmouth campus in Hanover, New Hampshire.
O. H. Strayer, minister, officiated.

  Mr. Curran and his bride will continue their studies
at Dartmouth College this fall.

Now there was no doubt. The mystery woman in the
photograph was Stella Frances Tuttle Curran.

TWENTY-TWO

◆◆◆

As Mary drove home, her mind was still reeling. She needed to think about what she was going to do next. Three things were clear:

1. Frances Curran was the mystery woman in the photo.
2. She'd lied about the time she spent in Ivy Bay as a young woman. In fact, she'd made it seem like she'd never seen the town before moving here last year.
3. She'd had the opportunity to see the framed photo hanging in the shop before it was stolen. So why hadn't she said anything about it?

When Mary considered those three factors together, the most likely—and disappointing—explanation was that Frances and Uncle George had been having an affair when that picture was taken. Now that Frances was a happily married woman, she probably didn't want to take a chance of those tawdry details somehow coming out.

But something bothered her. Frances was a healthy, fit woman in her seventies. A woman of high standing in the community. Would she really break in, risking arrest, simply to steal a photograph of herself that no one had even recognized? Wouldn't that be just as scandalous if found out as a decades-old affair?

Mary considered alternatives. Perhaps someone *had* recognized Frances in that picture and had stolen it to use as blackmail. Mary sighed, knowing that was probably too far-fetched to be true. But she needed to consider all the possibilities so that some important fact didn't slip through her fingers. Because of that, she wasn't quite ready to talk to Frances about it yet.

Betty met her at the driveway. "You've got great timing. I'm about to go to one of my favorite places on Cape Cod. Why don't you come along?"

Mary didn't even care where Betty was headed—she just wanted to share this latest bombshell with her sister. She moved from her car to Betty's without saying a word.

Betty laughed as she settled in behind the driver's seat. "Now that's what I call cooperative. Aren't you even going to ask where we're going?"

"Nope, I want you to surprise me." Mary clicked her seat belt into place and turned toward her sister. "And I've got a surprise to tell you."

Mary spent the next ten minutes of the drive telling Betty what she'd discovered at the library.

"No," Betty sputtered, "it can't be!"

"That was my first reaction too. But Frances is the woman in the photo. That doesn't mean she broke into my shop necessarily, but at least we can now put a name with that face."

Betty glanced over at her, looking a little pale. "So do you think Frances and Uncle George...?"

Her sister didn't have to finish the sentence. Of course, Mary contemplated the same thing many times over but just couldn't see it. Then again, she couldn't picture the Frances

Curran she knew with the Fred Vargo that Hazel had described. "I'm not sure, and I don't know how we'd ever find out unless Frances told us herself."

"If she really did go to all that trouble to steal the photograph, I can't see her confessing to an affair she so desperately tried to hide," Betty replied. "Then again, if anyone could get the truth out of her, it's you."

Mary appreciated the compliment, even though she thought Betty gave her too much credit.

Betty parked her car and turned to Mary. "Well, my surprise isn't as shocking as yours, by any means, but here we are!"

Mary had been so engrossed in their conversation that she hadn't been paying attention to their surroundings. Now she stared out the front windshield. "I should have known..." Mary said with a smile. They had arrived at a flea market, one of Betty's favorite places.

"That's right," Betty said cheerfully. "It's one of the best flea markets on Cape Cod. You can find all kinds of treasures."

Mary wasn't quite as excited as her sister. Betty had a knack with interior design and furniture restoration. On the other hand, when Mary went shopping, she often tried to match purchases to whatever was in the display windows. She wasn't looking to buy anything, but she always enjoyed her sister's company and could use this time to think about what she wanted to do next.

The flea market was located about ten miles southeast of Ivy Bay and encompassed the area of a city block. Booths and long tables were set up under canopies, with everything imaginable on display. Mary saw fresh flowers, garden produce, an old bathtub, clothing in all sizes, and an array of dishware, crafts, and other items.

"Where do they get all this stuff?" Mary asked, following Betty from table to table.

Betty picked up a fabric remnant and fingered the cloth. "Mostly auctions and estate sales, although there are plenty of items on consignment here too. These booths stay full all summer long."

"A person could spend days here and still not see everything," Mary said as she and Betty began to peruse the merchandise. She'd had no idea how interesting this place would be. "Are you looking for anything in particular?"

"Oh, just browsing." Betty picked up a potato ricer and turned it over in her hand, but there was a knowing spark in her eye.

As they examined different items, they slowly began to drift apart. Mary spotted a stack of Hardy Boys and made a beeline for that table. She dug in to see if she could find some titles she didn't already have.

"Mary!"

Mary looked up to see Jayne Tucker, owner of Gems and Antiques, which sat across from Mary's store. Jayne was examining a dusty porcelain doll.

"Hello, Jayne." Mary set the stack of books she'd gathered on top of a nearby bookshelf and walked around toward her friend. "Is this where you get things for your shop?"

"Sometimes," Jayne said, smoothing the doll's cornsilk hair. "Though this visit is more for fun than anything. Rich is on a shopping trip to Europe right now, and I like to come here to find things he doesn't normally want to stock in the store." Jayne tucked the doll under her arm and grinned at Mary. "I see you've found some treasures."

Mary laughed. "I can't resist. This will be perfect for my new children's nook." They chatted for a few minutes and then Jayne headed off toward a display of antique toys. Mary and Betty spent the next hour scanning the tables and making purchases. By the time they were ready to go, Mary had two big sacks in her hands. "This place is like a treasure trove," she said excitedly. "I got some great books for my shop, and the prices were more than reasonable."

Betty held open her sack to reveal a small, rectangular-shaped package. "It's a lovely painting that will look great in my bathroom. I can't wait to show it to you."

"So are we ready to go?"

"Almost," Betty replied. "I just need to find out when they plan to deliver my bathtub."

"You bought a bathtub?" Mary asked in surprise. "But you just recently remodeled your bathrooms."

A mischievous smile crossed Betty's face. "Just come and see it," she said, drawing Mary by the hand toward the edge of the tent until Mary spied an old claw-foot tub.

"This is it!" Betty smoothed one hand over the rounded edge of the tub. "Isn't it great?"

The tub was at least a hundred years old, and the white porcelain now had a dull, gray cast to it. There were rust spots near the drain and paint peeling off the claw feet. Mary couldn't imagine why Betty was so excited about the old thing, but she gave her sister the benefit of the doubt. "What are you ever going to do with it?"

Betty looked at Mary, that mischievous spark returning. "You'll see."

On the drive home, Mary gazed out the passenger window at the birds in the salt marshes and the sailboats dotting the horizon against the deep blue backdrop of the sky.

"You're still thinking about Frances Curran, aren't you?"

Mary heard the worry in her sister's voice. "Yes, I am. And it sounds like you are too."

Betty nodded. "It's unsettling to discover that people you know have lied to you. First Jean, and now Frances. I know it's nothing personal, but it still feels strange. What is Frances trying so hard to hide?"

"Here's the question I keep asking myself," Mary said. "Frances had to have seen that photograph of herself when the book club came to look at my shop. Why didn't she say anything about it then?"

"I don't know," Betty said. "I'll admit, anyone would think that's suspicious."

Betty's words triggered an idea. Mary smiled at her sister. "You're right. And I think you've just helped me figure out the perfect way to approach her."

———

On Thursday afternoon, Mary stood on the doorstep of Frances Curran's house and rang the doorbell.

It was a spacious Queen Anne house, with neatly trimmed bushes in the front and yellow daylilies bordering the foundation. A pair of white wicker lawn chairs with soft pink cushions sat on the front porch. The brick driveway led to a detached garage that had the same white siding and black shutters as the house.

Mary could just glimpse a vehicle parked inside the garage, which meant someone was probably at home. She hoped that someone was Frances.

Betty had given her directions to the house and was eager to hear what Frances had to say. She was a little nervous, even after hearing Mary's plan, but she had every confidence in her sister.

Mary heard footsteps approaching the door and she took a deep breath, trying to remain calm. This meeting with Frances had a lot riding on it if she wanted to solve the mystery.

The door opened and Frances stood on the other side. Her eyes flashed with warmth when she saw Mary on the porch. "Well, hello, Mary," she said, "this is quite a surprise."

"Hello, Frances." At this moment, Mary almost wished the mystery woman had been Virginia or Madeline or even Eleanor. Frances had been so kind to her, and she didn't want that to change. *Lord*, she prayed silently, *give me the right words to say and the right way to say them.*

"Please come in," Frances said, waving her inside.

Mary stepped into a spacious living area with a pine floor, a high ceiling, and white wicker furniture adorned with a rich sapphire fabric. The white stone fireplace had family photos lined up across a wide pine mantel. She walked over to view all the pictures. "You have a beautiful home and a beautiful family." There were several pictures of two youngsters who were clearly her grandchildren, and of her husband in front of a boat.

"Thanks, we love them both." She led Mary to the wicker sofa. "Please have a seat while I get us something to drink. I have tea or sparkling water?"

"Oh no, thank you. I'm fine." Mary walked over to a large portrait of a monarch butterfly on the wall. "This is lovely."

"Thank you. I commissioned Madeline to paint it for me."

"Wow," Mary said, genuinely impressed. "She is quite a talent."

"You're right about that. I'm proud to display her work. Speaking of the book club..." Frances walked over to the hallway and retrieved a large box, big enough to hold a clothes dryer. It had been decorated with gold embossed wrapping paper. "I wanted to get your opinion on the donation box for the book drive. It's big, I know." She smiled at Mary. "I guess you could call me an optimist."

"It will hold plenty of books," Mary said, nodding her approval. "And I'm sure I can find a good spot for it during my grand opening. We want it front and center so we get a lot of donations."

"Thank you again for helping us with this project." Frances gestured for Mary to sit and took a seat in the chair next to Mary. "I really hope it can make a difference."

Mary believed she was sincere, and more than that, she genuinely liked the woman. But she still needed to know the truth.

"You're welcome. I'm just happy my grand opening didn't have to be postponed after the break-in at my shop. I have to admit, I'm still a little rattled by it."

"Of course you are," Frances said, her gaze not wavering from Mary's face. "Anyone would be."

Mary smoothed one hand over the silky fabric of the seat cushion. "I just wish I could think of a reason they took that photograph of my uncle, but I haven't had much success, I'm afraid." She sensed the slightest tension in her hostess. "Can you think of anything?"

Frances didn't say anything for a long moment. "Not a good reason, no. Weren't there some vandals out that night?"

"Yes, and they painted some windows at the Gallery and the county clerk's office, but the attack on my shop seemed more targeted." She looked steadily into Frances's eyes. "That made me curious enough to look into it further."

A knowing smile curved Frances's mouth. "Well, Mary, then you've come to the right place. I must say that you're one of the politest interrogators I've ever met." Despite her calm demeanor, the use of the word *interrogators* showed how rattled she really was.

"Oh, Frances. I'm not trying to interrogate you," Mary said gently. "I'm just trying to figure out the truth and I'm really hoping you can help me."

Frances took in a deep breath. "The truth is that I'm the woman in the photo, although I believe you already know that."

"Frances, please know that I'm not accusing you of any-thing. I just want to understand—"

"My deep, dark secret," she interjected with a wry smile. Then the smile faded. "You may not know—or perhaps you do—that Frances is my middle name, not my first name. I spent a very short time in Ivy Bay, less than a year. Then as countless people have done before me, I decided I needed a complete makeover. So after I moved away, Stella Tuttle became Frances Tuttle, then Frances Curran. Believe me, I'm a completely different person now than I was back then. My husband doesn't even know who I really was."

Mary could hear the intensity in Frances's voice. Her metamorphosis from Stella Tuttle to Frances Curran clearly had meant a lot to her. Enough to commit a crime to keep it a secret?

"Stella attracted bad men and bad luck into her life," Frances continued, speaking of herself in the third person. "When I changed my name to Frances, I reversed course. I made a new life and have repented from my old one." She nodded toward the donation box on the floor. "And now it's time to give back."

"Was my uncle George one of those bad men?" Mary asked softly, almost afraid to hear the answer.

"No," Frances said without hesitation. "And we were not involved, despite what some people thought at the time."

Mary released a breath she didn't know she'd been holding. "So you and Uncle George didn't have an—"

"No, honey. We weren't having an affair," Frances affirmed, a strange inflection in her voice, "but I wouldn't call either of us innocent."

Mary's heart rate rose. Finally, she was getting to the heart of the mystery. "Frances, please tell me the story," she said, not even trying to mask the earnestness in her voice. "I need to understand why you broke into my shop."

Frances's voice had a mix of sadness and chilly resolve. "Oh, I didn't break into your shop, Mary. And I'd rather not discuss it anymore." Mary's heart sank as Frances continued. "Bravo to you for connecting me to the photograph, but I simply won't explain anything else. It's not your business, I'm afraid, and as I said, I've left it all in the past. I'd very much like it to remain there."

Mary was flummoxed. "I... But..." She couldn't even formulate a sentence before Frances had escorted her out the door.

TWENTY-THREE

———◆◆◆———

S he said what?"

Mary looked at her sister, seeing the same bewilderment in her eyes that she'd felt when Frances had said it. "Her exact words were: 'We weren't having an affair, but I wouldn't call either of us innocent.'"

They sat at the kitchen table eating BLT sandwiches and potato salad for dinner. Betty had prepared the meal while Mary was visiting Frances.

"But what does that mean?" Betty asked, setting down her sandwich. "Does it mean they weren't having an affair, but they flirted with each other? Or what?"

"She wouldn't elaborate." Mary tried to work up an appetite, but she was still too unsettled by her meeting with Frances. "She was composed and polite, but she refused to explain anything else. And she denied breaking in to the shop." Mary picked up a stray piece of bacon that had fallen off the sandwich. She eyed it for a moment in thought before taking a small bite. "At least we have good reason to believe Uncle George didn't have an affair."

Betty speared a chunk of potato salad with her fork. "I guess that's true." Then she smiled up at her sister. "We should be happy, shouldn't we?"

"Yes," Mary said emphatically. "And we should also take what Frances said with a grain of salt. She's a smart lady. Instead of saying that she wouldn't call Uncle George innocent, she included herself as well, so we can't say she's trying to cast any sort of blame on him."

Confusion filled Betty's blue eyes. "But blame for what?"

"That's what I don't know yet. Why else would she try to hide her past with Uncle George? And she may have denied breaking in, but I'm not sure I believe her. What does she gain by confessing to me, after all?"

"Good point. So what do you do now?"

"I'm going to keep following the clues." Mary rubbed a hand over her face. "That's Mystery Solving 101 in almost every detective book I've ever read. But I feel like I'm running out of clues to follow."

"Why don't you take the night off, Mar?" Betty suggested tenderly. "You've been so busy between getting the shop ready to open and tracking this mystery. I think you should take a break, at least for one evening."

The idea appealed to Mary. "Maybe you're right. I can make ice cream for Tess to sample and possibly figure out what to do with that picture frame." She looked up at her sister. "Did I tell you I decided to hang the other photograph of the back of the building in place of the stolen one?"

"No, but I love the idea. There's just something rustic and natural about that photograph, with the wild grasses and greenery. Something very Cape Cod."

Mary agreed; it was a piece of artwork as much as a piece of her shop's history. Now that she had a plan for the evening, her appetite was coming back. She'd take a break to clear her head and start fresh on the mystery again tomorrow.

———

Later that evening, Mary stood in front of the stove, slowly circling the wooden spoon around the pot. This was the critical phase of her ice-cream recipe. She wanted to caramelize the bananas without letting them scorch.

"That smells absolutely divine." Betty walked into the kitchen and set a home decor magazine on the table. "When will it be ready?"

Mary laughed. "Not for quite a while yet, so you might want to grab a snack if you're hungry."

Betty reached for one of the three bananas on the kitchen counter.

"Not those, Bets," Mary said. "I need to puree them for the ice-cream base. You can have some of the fresh raspberries I found at the market. They're in the fridge, along with some extra whipping cream."

"That sounds even better than a banana. Can I make you some too?"

"No, thanks. I had some earlier. And don't let Gus see that cream, or he'll never leave you alone. He'd lap up the entire bowl, if I let him."

Betty looked around the room. "Where is Gus?"

"The last time I saw him he was in the living room, looking out the window. He loves to watch the sailboats on the water."

Mary turned the burner down as the mixture in the pot started to bubble. She was making one of her favorite recipes, caramelized banana walnut ice cream. A little sea salt to the recipe added a nice balance to the caramel, but it was important to get the proportions just right.

"I think you underestimate your ice cream talent," Betty said, as if reading Mary's mind. She set the raspberries and cream on the kitchen table. At that moment, Gus appeared in the kitchen and made a beeline for the bowl of cream. "Oh no, you don't." She held it out of his reach.

Mary laughed. "It's okay. You can give him a little. If we don't, he'll be under our feet the rest of the night."

Betty poured a small amount of the thick cream into his food bowl. Gus bounded over to it and began lapping it up.

"I don't blame him." Betty licked a spot of cream off her finger. "It is delicious. Fattening, but delicious."

When Gus finishing licking the bowl clean, he padded out of the kitchen and up the stairs.

Mary carefully lifted the pot of caramelized bananas off the burner and set them on a trivet to let them cool. Then she turned to the mixing bowl, ready to make the base.

"Oh, I almost forgot," Betty said. "Jean invited us over for brunch tomorrow morning. Do you have time to go?"

"I'll make time," Mary said, thrilled with the invitation. "I hope that means she's feeling a little better."

"I think it does," Betty said as she dished the raspberries into a small bowl and added a dollop of cream. "She sounded a lot better on the phone and has some books and things she said we might want."

"I'd love to have something that belonged to Uncle George and Aunt Phyllis," Mary said with a wistful smile. "Just for a keepsake."

While the bananas were cooling, Mary decided this would be a perfect time to deal with the frame. She hurried up the stairs to her bedroom, only to find Gus on top of her dresser again. He was lying directly on top of the picture.

"Pardon me, little man," she said, lifting him off and placing him on the floor. "I'm afraid you're going to have to find another place to relax."

She carried the picture downstairs and placed it on the kitchen table. Then she bent over to examine it. The crack in the oak frame was near the top right corner and seemed a little worse now than before. She tested it with her fingers to feel how deep the crack was.

As much as she hated to remove the frame, it was probably the best chance she had to try one more time at a solid repair job. If it didn't work this time, then she'd take it to a professional.

Betty stood at the kitchen sink, rinsing out her bowl.

Mary picked up the frame and turned it over, setting the bottom edge on top of the table. She used a paring knife to slowly slice a crease in the top corner of the paper backing, not wanting to further damage the cracked frame by just tearing it off.

As she began to carefully peel the brown paper away from the frame, a shower of one-hundred-dollar bills began to rain down on the table.

TWENTY-FOUR

Mary stood frozen in place, stunned by the sight in front of her. Where had all that money come from? And how long had it been in the frame? As the shock began to wear off, she realized she knew the answer. It had been there since 1957. The printed seal on the brown paper backing had told her so.

Betty turned at the sink and then blanched at the sight in front of her. "What on earth is going on? Where did all that money come from?"

"It was inside the picture frame." Her voice was barely a whisper.

Betty walked over to the table and spread out the bills to count them. Then she slowly looked up at her sister, disbelief shining in her blue eyes. "There's two thousand dollars here, Mar."

The implications of this were starting to sink in. "I'd say we just found another motive for stealing that other picture. If there's money hidden in this frame, there might have been money in the other one as well."

"But why? Why would someone hide money in a picture frame?" Betty asked, still staring at the money.

Mary thought about the question, realizing it wasn't an easy one to answer. "I don't think we can know why until we figure out who put it there."

Betty turned to her, an inquisitive gleam in her eyes. "I think you just found another clue."

Follow the clues.

That's what Mary needed to do, but she was afraid this clue led her right back to Jean and D.J. Especially since D.J. had been standing at the back door within a few feet of this picture when the security alarm had gone off. She also thought about Frances. Had Frances known there was money in the frame? If so, why had she chosen now, after all these years, to steal it? She and her husband moved back a year ago, and perhaps she hadn't realized the photo was still around. But surely she didn't need two thousand dollars. Frances and her husband were clearly in comfortable financial standing. Mary supposed that both the money and the relief of taking the photo out of circulation certainly could have been motive enough for Frances, but she'd expressly denied breaking in. Mary didn't have much reason to believe Frances, yet something about the denial rang true.

Mary thought again about Jean. Maybe Uncle George had told Jean about the money in the frames but had lost track of them. He seemed to be the most likely one to have hidden money there, since she'd found them in his old building and they showed photos of his shop.

But why hide the money in the first place? Unless... She remembered Frances's cryptic comment about neither she nor George being innocent. Was this hidden money what she'd meant by that remark? Had they engaged in some kind of criminal activity together?

"You're awfully quiet," Betty said with a bemused smile. "I can almost see the wheels turning in your head."

"They're turning all right." Mary knew she had to get back to her ice cream if she wanted it to turn out well. "Here are two of the questions I just thought of. What do we do with this money, and who does it really belong to?"

Betty sat down at the table, patting the bills into a neat pile. "Well, I suppose legally it would belong to you since the pictures were found in your shop and you own it."

"You're probably right, Bets, but I don't think I want it," Mary said. "Especially since we don't know where it came from."

She walked over to the table and picked up the stack of one-hundred-dollar bills. They were perfectly crisp after being sealed up for over fifty years.

"Maybe we could use the money to buy books for the book drive," Betty suggested.

Mary had the same thought. Then something else occurred to her. "What if Uncle George had simply put money in the frames for his future?" *Money that he'd legally earned,* she thought. "That should go to Jean."

Betty nodded. "You're right, of course."

"And maybe Jean even knows how it got there. But why wouldn't she just ask for the money? I would have gladly given it to her, and she must know that."

The more she thought about it, the less it all made sense. She certainly had some questions for Jean and D.J. The brunch tomorrow would be the perfect time to ask them.

The next morning, Mary dropped off a pint of ice cream for Tess at Bailey's and headed over to the bookshop to check in with Kip. She'd tossed and turned all night, unable to sleep with all the thoughts running through her head after finding that money in the frame. She put the two thousand dollars safely in her locked fire-safe box back at the house, not wanting to carry it around with her.

Kip was putting the finishing touches on the children's nook. "What do you think?"

Mary clasped her hands together, thrilled with his work. "It's even better than I imagined. Thank you so much for getting it done on time. I can't believe what a difference a week makes."

Kip started packing up his tools. "And the stairs are done too, so we're all set."

"Perfect! Why don't you give me an invoice, and then I'll write you a check."

"Um, okay," he said, looking rather uncertain and not moving to write up an invoice. Mary assumed he was uncomfortable asking for money and would send an invoice in the mail. She tried to break the tension. "Do you have big plans for the weekend?"

He perked up instantly. "Well, I just got hired for a job to build a deck, which should take up most of my weekend. Heather is coming today and will stay with her grandparents." Kip paused as if he had forgotten something, but then he shook it off and continued on. "Heather plans to clean out my garage while she's here. She thinks we can get some money at the flea market for some of my tools and stuff."

"Attagirl," Mary said with a wink and a pat on his back. "I can't wait to meet her," she said.

He grinned as he glanced out the window. "Actually, you can meet her right now. She just pulled up."

A few moments later, Kip made the introductions. "This is Heather," he said proudly, "my fiancée."

Mary could see why Kip was smitten. Heather was a very pretty young woman with auburn hair, brown eyes, and a light sprinkle of freckles over her face. For some reason, she looked familiar.

The two of them shook hands. "Congratulations on your engagement," Mary told her.

"Thank you," Heather said softly. "And congratulations on your grand opening. This looks like a fun place to buy books."

"That's just the look I was going for," Mary said. "Fun and relaxing. A getaway, of sorts."

Heather smiled. "Oh, that's the name of my grandpa's boat, *The Getaway*." Heather and Kip were holding hands, and Kip was looking at her. It was cute, Mary thought, how attuned he was to her.

Then something clicked. *The Getaway.* Hadn't she seen that before?

"You're the Currans' granddaughter!" A memory of seeing Heather's senior picture on Frances Currans' fireplace mantel flashed in Mary's mind. She briefly wondered if Heather knew anything about her grandmother's past but then realized that Frances had said her husband didn't even know.

"I am," Heather said, smiling. "They spoil me quite a bit, but I love it." Then she slipped her arm in the crook of Kip's elbow. "Kip spoils me too. He's the greatest guy ever. Kind of a pack rat, but a great guy."

Kip looked up and grinned, a shadow of discomfort on his face. Mary wondered if Kip was even more modest than she had at first thought. "Oh, I have plenty of faults," he said with a shy chuckle. "Anyway, Heather, like I told you, Mrs. Fisher's grand opening is coming soon."

"Oh, you must be so excited!" Heather said.

"I am," Mary said, that giddy feeling washing over her once more. Her shop was almost ready, and her grand opening was drawing nearer every day. Her dream was getting so close to coming true, and she could hardly wait.

———

Later that morning, Mary and Betty drove to Uncle George's house to have brunch with Jean.

When they reached the double doors, Mary rang the bell, feeling more nervous than expected. She had no idea how Jean or D.J. would react to the news about the two thousand dollars.

Only a few moments passed before the door swung open and they saw Jean standing on the other side. "Hello!" she greeted them. She reached out to give them each a big hug. "I'm so glad you're here. Please come in."

Mary and Betty walked inside. For a moment, Mary wondered if they'd come to the right house. Nothing was the same as she remembered. The main entry hall, which had once featured a marble statue and a gilded candelabra on a glass side table was now empty. As they followed Jean into the formal living room, Mary almost gasped out loud.

Most of the furniture was gone.

Aunt Phyllis had collected vintage nineteenth-century Victorian furniture, but only one lone settee remained. Even the Persian rug in front of the fireplace was missing. It was as if the place had been looted.

Mary could see the outline of perfect squares and rectangles on the walls, marking where pictures had hung for decades.

Betty looked over at her, her eyes filled with dismay. Then she turned to Jean. "It looks so different without all your folks' furniture."

Jean swallowed hard. "I know. But it's not gone. I've put most of it in storage. The rest I'll either give to you girls or get rid of it." Then her face brightened. "And D.J. is going to sell some of it on a Web site he created."

"Where is D.J.?" Mary asked, peering down the long hall.

"Oh, he apologized for not being here. But one of his computer-programmer friends from Boston is in town to see his relatives for the weekend, and they decided to have breakfast at the Black & White Diner. Apparently, breakfast with friends is more appealing than breakfast with relatives, but, you know...boys will be boys," Jean said with a sigh of resignation.

"It's okay," Betty said. "We've all been there." Mary nodded in agreement but was surprised that D.J. had double booked. She hoped he hadn't been avoiding her.

Mary kept looking around her, trying to reconcile this almost barren place with the home she'd once known and loved. She knew Jean had come here to clean out her parents' house, but she was planning to stay for a month. It seemed odd that she was in such a rush to be rid of it all.

"I just put the breakfast casserole into the oven, so I'll go fetch us something to drink." Jean headed for the doorway. "Be right back."

When they were alone, Betty turned to her. "This makes me sad."

"I know," Mary said softly, not wanting Jean to overhear. "But we still have memories here. It seems everything changes no matter how much we want them to stay the same." She thought of a Bible verse that had comforted her when she'd been getting her own house ready to put on the market: "There is a time for everything, and a season for every activity under the heavens" (Ecclesiastes 3:1).

Betty smiled at her. "Perfect verse, as always."

Jean walked back into the living room holding an armful of bottled iced teas. "I brought several different flavors, so you can choose one you like." She set them on one of the few remaining tables in the room. "Please help yourselves."

"Thanks, Jean," Betty said. "Mary and I were just talking about how much we loved this place when we were little girls."

"I loved growing up here," Jean said, her voice trembling a little. "I was never bored, which is probably a strange thing to say for an only child."

Mary knew if she waited for an opening, one might never come, so she took a deep breath and said, "There's something we wanted to tell you about; something we found last night."

Jean arched a brow. "That sounds intriguing. What did you find?"

Mary licked her dry lips. "There was two thousand dollars hidden in that old photograph I found in the cellar. The one that wasn't stolen during the break-in."

Jean stared at her as if she spoke a foreign language. "What?"

"That photograph of the back of your dad's auction house," Mary clarified. "There was two thousand dollars inside of it."

Jean's brow furrowed. "Well, that's strange."

"It was quite a shock for us," Betty told her. "It was all in one-hundred-dollar bills too."

Mary watched her cousin, but she couldn't tell anything by her expression. "Do you have any idea how it got there?"

Jean turned to her. "I assume Dad put it there. He was always sticking money in odd places. I've found five hundred dollars so far just by cleaning up around here."

Mary preferred that explanation to the alternative—that he'd hidden it for some nefarious reason. "Maybe that's it."

"Of course," Jean said, growing perkier. "He never did trust banks, you know. I remember him and your dad arguing about that more than once."

Now that she thought about it, Mary did too. "Then I guess the money belongs to you. I'm sure your dad would want you to have it."

"Let's talk about that another day," Jean said, walking over to the door that led into Uncle George's study. "We still have some time before brunch is ready, if you'd like to take a look at some of the things that I think Dad would like you to have."

Betty and Mary glanced at each other, both surprised by Jean's easy dismissal of the money. It either meant she didn't care or she wanted to act like she didn't care. Mary could usually read her cousin like a book, but she hadn't been too good at it these last couple of weeks.

As Mary walked into the study, she inhaled the faint scent of cigar smoke and felt a pang of remorse that her uncle would never be in this room or this house again. She turned her attention to the cardboard boxes that lined the west wall of the room, some two or three deep. But considering the size of the house, there really wasn't much here at all.

Mary grew concerned. "Are you sure you're ready to part with these things, Jean? They say a person shouldn't make any major decisions after a recent loss of a loved one."

"I'm sure," Jean said, her voice hushed but firm.

Betty looked at their cousin. "Where would you like us to start?"

Jean hesitated and then pointed to the left side of the room. "I put the books and some old maps over there. On the right are the dishes mom used to collect and a few of the silver pieces that I don't want. Of course, there are other items mixed in with those boxes, so you can just start sorting through them and see what you find." She moved back toward the door. "Now if you'll excuse me, I'll be back in a few minutes."

Mary and Betty looked at each other, neither one of them moving toward the boxes.

Betty took a slow turn around the study, and Mary leaned down to open a box nearest to her, where she discovered an extensive collection of classic westerns by Louis L'Amour and Zane Grey.

She lifted out those books to see what lay underneath. There was one more book there, slightly wedged under the bottom flap of the box. Mary pulled it out, noting the barely visible letter fragments that remained of the title, and the brown leather cover was creased with age and the volume felt surprisingly light in her hands. The title had worn off the cover long ago, and the binding creaked as she opened it.

There was nothing inside.

A large hole had been carved out in the center of the pages. There were a few intact pages at the front and back of the book, so it looked normal when it was closed. But this volume was obviously used for a purpose other than reading.

"This is strange," Mary said, turning to her sister.

Betty walked over to join her. "What is it?"

"This book." An odd sensation settled over Mary as she flipped it back open to show her sister.

Betty ran her fingers over the smooth, cut edges that had left a crater three inches deep in the center of the book. "What in the world? Why would someone do this to a book?"

Mary thought about the stolen photograph—the one with Stella Tuttle aka Frances Curran holding a book behind her back. She flipped to the inside front cover of the book and looked down at the bottom corner. The paper had been torn there, so there were no initials.

Mary heard footsteps coming toward them and hastily closed the book. Her mind was spinning as some of the clues started coming together.

"Did you find anything you like?" Jean asked.

Mary folded the top flaps of the box together. "I'd like to have this book, if that's okay." She had no idea if Jean knew about the hollow book or not, but if she did, Jean probably would have shown it.

"And I'd like this pewter doorstop," Betty said, keeping the tone casual.

Jean nodded as she placed her hands on her hips, showing no signs of discomfort over the items they had chosen. "Okay, now I just need to figure out what to do with the rest of this stuff."

"Why don't you take it to the flea market and see if someone will put it on consignment for you? They do that all the time."

Jean looked intrigued. "That's a wonderful idea. I'll do it tomorrow. Do either of you want to go with me?"

"I wish I could," Betty said, "but I have a checkup with my rheumatologist in Boston tomorrow, so I'll be gone most of the day."

"I'll go with you," Mary volunteered. "I got such great deals on the last books I found there that I want to see if I can find some more."

"When do you want to go?" Jean asked her. "Morning or afternoon?"

"Morning would probably work best for me. Shall I pick you up at ten?"

"Sounds good." Jean smiled. "And that breakfast casserole smells ready, so let's go eat."

As Mary followed Jean and her sister into the dining room, she thought about the hollow book. The empty space inside was just big enough to hold a nice chunk of cash. In fact, that two thousand dollars she'd found in the picture frame would be an almost perfect fit.

TWENTY-FIVE

———◆◆———

Mary and Betty drove home from brunch in comfortable silence. The meal had been pleasant despite Mary's reservations. She'd put it all aside for the time, and they'd further reminisced about their childhood and told stories of their own children.

Betty broke the silence when they were almost home. "I'm confused, Mar. Why didn't you tell Jean about that hollow book you found in that box?"

Mary hesitated, hoping her reason didn't sound too selfish. "I know I probably should have," she admitted, "but I think that might be the same book that Frances Curran is holding in the photograph. I didn't bring the enlarged copy with me, so I couldn't compare them there." She looked at her sister. "Do you think I was wrong?"

Betty didn't say anything for a long moment. "No, I don't think so. Neither one of us can deny that Jean has been acting very strangely. I know she's going through some difficult personal issues, but that doesn't really explain some of the things that have gone on since she got here."

"That's what has me so worried," Mary admitted. "Something's not quite right, but I can't put my finger on it. I don't know if this book can help me figure it out or if that's just wishful thinking, but I have to try."

"We can always give it back to her later," Betty gently reminded her. "She might not know anything more about it than we do."

Mary stared out the passenger window at the beautiful scenery passing by her. She loved Ivy Bay, with its blue skies and billowy clouds. Yet, she couldn't help but worry that there were black clouds ahead.

She turned to her sister. "I have to be honest—I think it's possible Jean is the one who broke into my shop. I don't want it to be her, but there are just too many odd things she's done that we keep trying to explain away. And that hidden money would be a strong motivation."

"I've been thinking the same thing," Betty admitted. "Although I think it would be more likely for D.J. to break in than Jean." She bit her lip. "I hate even thinking such a thing, much less saying it."

"So do I. The reality is that there are only three people, at this point, who had a possible motive to steal that photo: Frances, Jean, or D.J. Unless there's someone else out there who isn't on my radar."

Betty glanced over at her. "If it is Jean or D.J., would you rather not know? Rather not solve the mystery?"

Mary didn't even hesitate. "I love my cousins, but Gram always reminded us that the truth would set us free. I think I know better than ever what she meant by that. If I never discover who broke in to my shop, then I'll always live with the suspicion that Jean or D.J. might have done it. But if I learn that one of them *was* responsible, then I can move on to understanding and acceptance and forgiveness." She looked at her sister. "I guess that's my long-winded way of saying that I have to keep going, no matter who the culprit turns out to be."

When they arrived at the house, the first thing Mary did was check on Gus, who was sleeping peacefully on her bed. Then she opened her closet door and retrieved the handheld magnifying glass she kept in her knitting basket.

She carried everything downstairs, including the enlarged photo that showed the book in more detail.

Betty sat at the kitchen table, having already changed into a powder-blue summer dress that looked crisp and cool. The hollow book was on the table next to her. "So?"

"I'm almost afraid to look." Mary set the enlarged photograph on the table between them and then peered through the magnifying glass.

A long moment passed. Betty asked, "What do you see?"

"I think I see a few letters in the title, but most of it is hidden by her skirt."

"What are the letters?" Betty got up to grab a notepad and pencil from the counter and rejoined Mary at the table.

"There are two rows of letters. The top row is I-R-E. The bottom row is I-D-E."

Betty wrote them both down, tore the top sheet off and slid it in Mary's direction. "Any guesses on what those mean?"

She shook her head, her gaze moving to the notepad on the table. She noticed the slight indentations on the top sheet where the pencil had pressed into the paper above it. That gave her an idea. She reached for the notepad and tore off a fresh sheet from the middle of the pad.

"Can I borrow that pencil?" she asked her sister.

"Sure," Betty said, looking intrigued.

Mary placed the paper over the bits of letters that remained of the title on the hollow book. Then she gently began to rub the smooth side of the pencil lead against the paper, providing just enough pressure for the letters on the book to start to form underneath.

"It's actually working," Betty said in amazement.

Mary smiled. "It's a trick I've read in several mystery novels. Even Alfred Hitchcock used it in the movie *North by Northwest*."

Mary kept shading the paper until the letters were all filled in. A few weren't fully formed, but there were more than enough there to make out the title.

"It's *Candide*," she said. "The I-D-E were the last three letters of the title."

"So the I-R-E must be the last three letters of the author Voltaire," Betty concluded.

Mary nodded. She opened the book. She looked again at the place where the paper was torn, only this time she noticed a tiny, faded sketch about an inch above the tear. She put the magnifying glass to the sketch. It was a butterfly.

She held up the hollow book. "There's no question: This piece of classic literature with a gaping, money-sized hole in the middle belonged to the future professor, Stella Frances Tuttle."

It was long after midnight, but Mary was still awake in her room. She'd spent the rest of her day in the bookshop, polishing shelves and pondering her latest discovery. Now she sat down at her desk and pulled a clean sheet of paper from her drawer. Then she drew lines down the paper to form three columns.

In the first column, she wrote UNCLE GEORGE. In the second column, she wrote STELLA/FRANCES. And in the third column, she wrote FRED VARGO.

Then she began to write down what she knew about each one of them that might pertain to the case.

UNCLE GEORGE
Father and husband
Owned the auction house from 1954–1960
Lived in Ivy Bay all his life except for year and a half in Virginia
Liked get-rich schemes
Appeared in the stolen photograph
Knew Stella Frances Tuttle Curran
Probably knew Fred Vargo
Had $2,000 hidden in one—if not both—of his picture frames

STELLA/FRANCES
Lived in Ivy Bay with godmother in 1957
Engaged to Fred Vargo in 1957
Lived in Hanover
Knew Uncle George
Married Albert Curran in 1959
Retired literature professor at Dartmouth

Appeared in the stolen photo
Holding a hollow book by Voltaire in photo
Grandmother to Heather Wade

FRED VARGO
Engaged to Stella Tuttle
Part-time car mechanic
Flashy with money
Ladies' man
Implicated in stealing cars
Spent time in jail
Testified against a car dealer for shorter jail time

There were probably more things she could add, but she was starting to grow sleepy. She studied the chart for a long time, hoping to see some kind of connection. It was funny how her uncle had been involved in so many schemes that had failed, yet his house had been filled with fine furnishings and paintings for as long as she'd known him. She supposed he got some of them through his auction house, one of his businesses that may not have made him rich but certainly took care of him.

She sat back in her chair and sighed, feeling like she was making this all too difficult. Her Gram had always said the simplest explanation was usually the right one. Mary had seen that axiom proven true time and time again in mystery novels and in real life.

So maybe she needed to go back and answer a simple question. Like, why would you hide money in a hollow book?

Mary picked up the Voltaire book, opening it to see the cavity inside. This particular book, by an eighteenth-century

French novelist, wouldn't provoke the interest of too many people.

She looked at her chart again, and a new thought occurred to her. Maybe Fred wasn't the only one who had committed a crime. Frances's comment that she and Uncle George weren't entirely innocent may have had nothing to do with romance, but instead, with the law.

———

"Good morning, Mary," Victoria said as she unlocked the door of the library the next day. Today she wore a pair of zebra-striped cat's-eye glasses with her white linen pantsuit. "You're here bright and early."

"I'm a woman on a mission," she said, following Victoria inside. "I just have a little research to do and I'm hoping you have the *Richmond Times-Dispatch* online."

"We sure do." Victoria flipped on the three rows of overhead lights. "Is this a secret mission or can you share it?"

"Secret," she said, with an apologetic smile. Part of her hoped it would be a futile mission as well. But every instinct told her she was on the right track.

"Well, let me know if you need anything."

"Thanks." Mary waited until Victoria booted up the computers. Then sat down and accessed the *Richmond Times-Dispatch*. When it popped up on the screen, she clicked the archives link.

Mary stared at the search box, giving herself one last chance to back out. Then she typed George Nelson into the box and hit the Go button. The waiting was the worst part as the computer was in thinking mode.

Then a link appeared, and Mary's heart sank. Massachusetts Man Convicted of Money Laundering.

She took a moment to let the reality sink in, even though she'd expected to find something like this. Then she read the short article.

George Nelson, of Ivy Bay, Massachusetts, was convicted today on two charges of possession of stolen goods and money laundering. Nelson's partner, Fred Vargo, had made a plea deal with Virginia prosecutors in exchange for his testimony against Nelson. For two years, the two men had obtained stolen goods, then sold them through Nelson's auction house in Ivy Bay, splitting the proceeds. Nelson gave the court a public apology and is awaiting sentencing.

Mary fell back in her chair, realizing that Jean had probably kept this family secret for over fifty years. Now she understood why Jean had been sent to stay with her grandparents one summer when Betty and Mary were also there. It was the same summer as Uncle George's trial, and Aunt Phyllis had probably gone down to support him. Selling his auction house might have been to pay his legal bills or just to rid himself of the place where he'd be tempted back into crime. Mary knew, from his words and deeds, that her uncle had found redemption.

She believed Frances had been involved too, although the name of Stella Tuttle didn't appear anywhere in the story.

She had intimated as much with that "innocent" remark, and there was also the fact that she was holding the hollow book in the photo. A book that had no doubt passed between Stella and Uncle George.

Mary had been so afraid of finding out something bad about her uncle, but now that it had happened, she realized it didn't change her love for him. In her eyes, he'd always be the sweet, gentle man who loved his family.

She was about to pick up Jean for their shopping trip and was torn between telling Jean what she knew or keeping it a secret. She eventually chose the latter, on the very slim chance that Jean might not know her father's criminal history.

Unfortunately, this still didn't confirm who had broken into her shop.

"Are you sure you want to give all that stuff away?" Mary said as she turned her car onto Route 6A, which would take her and Jean to the flea market.

"I'm sure," Jean said, staring out the window. "I'm tired of dealing with it all."

Mary could understand the sentiment, but she was surprised at the hint of bitterness in Jean's voice. Jean had adored her parents and treasured their times together. But it was possible the problems with her husband just made everything else seem overwhelming. Then another thought occurred to her. Receiving those e-mailed pictures from Mary had sent Jean into a panic. There, in black and white, had been her father with his partner in crime. She'd come to Ivy Bay soon after. Maybe cleaning out her house so fast and spending twenty minutes in the cellar of Mary's bookshop was Jean's way of making sure that no more evidence of her father's criminal past was found. She still wasn't sure if D.J. was involved or was simply a hapless former college student. Something told her that Jean wouldn't tell anyone about her father—even her own son.

When they arrived at the flea market, Mary found a good spot in the parking lot, then turned off the ignition.

In a flash, Jean was already outside and rounding the back bumper.

"How can I help?" Mary asked her.

"Oh, you don't have to do a thing, dear," Jean replied. "Since we're parked so close, I think I'll just bring interested vendors over to the car instead of dragging those boxes around. So if you could just leave me your keys, that would be great."

"Of course." Mary handed over her car keys. "Do you want me to wait for you?"

"There's no need to do that," Jean said. "You go ahead and start shopping. I'll take care of these boxes and join you after a bit."

"Good luck." Mary slung her bag over her shoulder and headed into the flea market. Today, she was just browsing, but keeping an eye open for any good mystery books that might come her way.

As she walked down the sandy aisles of the open-air flea market, she was impressed by how many new items had appeared since last week. She was intrigued by some bundled spices that she could use for her ice cream and the tableful of cat toys that Gus might enjoy.

Mary walked slowly along the aisle, taking in everything on one side before turning and doing it all over again on the other side. She'd only walked past a few tables when she saw some books in a pile at a corner booth. There were quite a few mysteries among them, including some for preteens and young adults.

The table was full of all kinds of different items, making it difficult to sort out the books. She moved some vintage clothes catalogs to a different spot on the table, and her eyes fell on something familiar.

It was a picture frame, just like the one that had been stolen. The picture was missing, as was the glass.

Mary pulled it from beneath some other picture frames and turned it over, telling herself it couldn't be the same one. But a familiar round ink stamp with "Bratt Frame Shop 1957" told a different story.

Mary waved down the vendor. "Excuse me?"

"Yes," he said, walking over to greet her. He was a young man with a dark goatee and bright blue eyes.

"Can you tell me where you got this picture frame?"

"It's a consignment piece," he said. "I don't give out names, but the initials are on the price label, if that helps you."

Mary looked at the initials. HW. They didn't register at first, but then she realized what they stood for. And, just like that, everything fell into place. Just as she had hoped, Mary now knew it hadn't been Jean or D.J. who had broken into her bookshop. She knew who it had been, and she had a good theory as to why. Now she just had to decide what to do about it.

TWENTY-SIX

◆◆◆

Mary walked into her bookshop on Monday morning, ready to close the book on the mystery of the stolen photograph. She sat down and booted up her computer.

After finding that frame at the flea market, she'd spent most of yesterday in prayer, first at church, and then on the beach in the afternoon. Betty and Henry had both lent her a listening ear and given her their full support.

But this still wouldn't be easy.

Kip walked through the front door, toolbox in hand. "Good morning, Mrs. Fisher. Good morning, Gus. It's another gorgeous day outside."

Mary had hardly noticed the weather, too caught up in what she was about to do. "Hey, Kip. I need to tell you something."

He stopped and looked up at Mary. "What's going on?"

She looked at him squarely. "I know you're the person who broke into my shop and stole that photograph."

Shock flashed in his eyes. "Mrs. Fisher, you can't be serio—"

She held up one hand to stop his denials. "I *know*, Kip."

Fear and uncertainty had replaced his contagious smile. He raked one hand through his hair, as if torn about something.

And Mary knew what it was. A criminal act from over fifty years ago had led to this.

The door to her shop opened again. Footsteps, firm and confident, moved toward them. Kip turned to see Frances Curran behind him.

"What's...going on?"

"It's okay, Kip," Frances told him. "You don't have to try and protect me anymore. It's time we both came clean. We owe that to Mary and to the people who care about us."

Mary had e-mailed Frances last evening—she knew Frances checked e-mail because Betty told her that all their book club correspondence was via e-mail. Mary hadn't received a reply and was surprised—and happy—to see her here this morning.

Kip looked between the two women, his confidence shaken. "I don't understand what's going on."

"It's my fault, you see," Frances said, looking knowingly at Mary. "I was so afraid of someone identifying me as the girl I used to be, that I forgot who I have become." She lowered her voice. "I panicked when the book club toured your shop and I saw that photograph. I think Madeline, as an artist, noticed a resemblance, but she didn't say anything. But it was enough to scare me. I called Kip and asked him to get rid of the picture. And he did it for me—for the grandmother of his fiancée."

"But why did you make such a mess of the store if you only wanted the picture?" Mary asked.

"I'm afraid that was my fault too," Stella said. "I suggested he make it look like a more serious break-in to throw the police off the trail."

Kip hung his head. "I'm so sorry, Mary. I don't know what to say."

"And I think that was a problem for both of you," Mary said softly, disappointed in Kip but also understanding that sometimes young people do really dumb things. "Neither one of you could confess without implicating the other."

"And then we were both stuck." Frances turned to Mary, her voice quavering. "I felt so bad each time I saw you, but I didn't want to get Kip in trouble with you or with Heather, who still doesn't know what happened." Frances drew in a shaky breath. "My husband doesn't know either, about the break-in or about Stella Tuttle. But he will by the time the day is over."

"She couldn't have been all bad," Mary said, trying to break some of the tension. Kip had turned white as a sheet when Frances had mentioned Heather's name.

He turned to Mary. "If neither one of us confessed, then how did you know?"

"Because I found the missing picture frame at the flea market on Saturday. It had been consigned there and had the initials HW on it. I knew that your fiancée Heather Wade had cleaned out your garage. She must have found the empty picture frame there and decided to sell it, not knowing where it had come from."

A smile quivered on Frances's mouth. "My godmother had posted my wedding picture in the Ivy Bay newspaper. I was a young bride then and so afraid that the life I'd built for myself by stealing from others would collapse. I should have realized then that I was on sinking sand. Now the truth will come out, and I'll have to live with the consequences."

Mary didn't want to pry too much, but there were still a hole or two that she wanted to fill. "You must have made quite a bit of money in the money-laundering scheme."

Frances nodded soberly. "I earned enough money to pay for a Dartmouth education. When Fred and I were dating, I learned that he was fencing stolen goods through the auction house. When I found out how lucrative it was, I wanted in too. My godmother was a brilliant woman, but she never had the means to do something important with her life. I didn't want that to happen to me."

Mary glanced over at Kip, who wasn't saying much. Part of her felt sorry for him. He'd probably thought he was doing something chivalrous for his fiancée's grandmother, but the price had been too high. "And you used the Voltaire book to transfer money back and forth between Fred and Uncle George and yourself."

Frances heaved a long sigh. "That was Fred's idea and he ruined one of my favorite books. It was also his idea to take the photo of us when George started feeling guilty about the whole thing. The photo of the back of the store was just for 'symmetry,' he had said. He wanted leverage over us."

Mary finally had the last puzzle piece solved. "And Fred put money in the picture frame as further evidence of George's involvement."

Frances bowed her head slightly. "Yes. I had hoped you wouldn't learn about that."

"And you offered the money in the frame to Kip, as payment?"

Frances nodded somberly, and Kip jumped in. "I still have the money, Mrs. Fisher. I… It's five hundred dollars. I put it away to start a nest egg. We have so little money, you know, and I...I just wanted a head start. I'll give it back, though. Every penny." Anguish and guilt clouded his eyes. "I'm so sorry, Mrs. Fisher. I don't know how to make this up to you. I'll go to the police, of course, and tell Heather. And of course, I won't charge you for any of the work I've done on your shop. That's why I didn't invoice you. I would have felt awful taking your money, even if I hadn't been found out. I hope you can forgive me, Mrs. Fisher."

Mary had already forgiven him, but she could see that Kip was going to have a hard time forgiving himself. "We'll work something out, but I don't think we need to get the police involved."

His mouth gaped. "But...I did it. I broke in. I have that money."

"And I believe in second chances," Mary told him. "I just hope you make yours count." She looked at Frances, then back at Kip. "As Heather's grandmother knows, we're holding a book drive at the shop this week for disaster aid. Kip, I'd like you to donate the money." She knew that she should have spoken with Jean about the money first, but Jean clearly didn't particularly care about the hidden money, and she especially wouldn't want it knowing the dark history behind it. She felt confident to make this choice for her cousin: Jean would want to give the money away as much as Mary did.

Tears filled Kip's eyes, and he gave a determined nod. "I'll do that, Mrs. Fisher."

Mary sent out a silent prayer for them, knowing in the deepest part of her heart that she had done the right thing.

TWENTY-SEVEN

◆◇◆

Mary was surprised to find Betty waiting for her outside the bookshop when she returned from lunch later that day.

"Hey, there," Betty said. "I am so anxious to hear how everything went this morning."

"Even better than I expected," Mary told her. "Kip is truly remorseful, and we've worked out a way for him to repay me."

"I'm so glad." Betty took hold of Mary's shoulders. "And now you can just focus on your big grand opening! Can I have a sneak preview?"

"Come on in."

Gus peeked over the edge of her carrying case as Mary unlocked the door and walked inside.

Betty followed her and then emitted a loud gasp. "Oh, Mary. That nook is wonderful." She walked over to one of the short bookcases, running one hand across the smooth white top. "And look at the garden gate!"

Mary watched with amusement as her sister pushed the gate open, walked inside the nook and pushed it out again to leave.

"The gate even has that cute little twang," Betty said, "like the sound that Grandpa and Gram's screen door used to make."

"I'd love it if you'd paint flowers on it for me," Mary told her. "You've got the artistic touch in the family."

"I'll be happy to do it." Betty flashed an eager smile. "I've also brought you something. I wanted to give it to you before your grand opening tomorrow."

Mary didn't see any gifts that Betty had brought in with her or even a purse that might have a gift in it. "What is it?"

"Wait right here," Betty told her, heading for the back room.

Now Mary was even more confused. Then she heard the sound of the back door open and the low tenor of a man's voice. A moment later, she saw Evan backing slowly into the room, hauling something big and heavy.

Betty moved toward her. "Remember that bathtub I bought at the flea market?" She grinned.

"The old bathtub?" Mary asked warily as Evan and another man carried the tub into the room. Only, as they got closer, she could see that this tub might be old, but it sure wasn't gray or rusty anymore.

The vintage claw-foot tub was now painted a bright white on the outside and lined with a plush blue carpet on the inside. It looked clean and fun and adorable.

"Like it?" Betty asked, barely able to contain herself. "When I saw it, I knew right away that it would be perfect for the children's nook. I've made some pillows to throw in it that will match the rest of your decor. Can't you just see a little one lounging in it, surrounded in comfy pillows, reading the latest Ron Roy *Capital* mystery?"

Mary turned to her, still in awe. "How do you do it? How do you turn something that most people think belongs in a junk pile into...this gorgeous thing?"

Betty beamed. "So you like it?"

"No, I absolutely *love* it!" Mary walked over to give her sister a hug.

Evan paused when he reached the children's nook. "Do you want it inside, Aunt Mary?"

"Yes, please," Mary replied. Then she watched them set it down in the middle of the nook. She couldn't imagine a better spot for it; it was as if the space had been made for such a centerpiece.

"I think this is one of the best gifts I've ever received," Mary said honestly. "Thank you so much, Bets."

"You're welcome." Betty beamed with pride.

"There's just one more thing the nook needs to make it complete." Mary moved toward the back room to retrieve the rocker and carry it into the main part of the bookshop.

"Do you want me to get that for you?" Evan offered.

"No, thanks. I've got it."

"Okay, then, we're going to take off," Evan said, as he and his helper walked toward the door.

"Thanks, guys," Betty called after them.

Mary carried the rocker into the nook and set it down in the corner. "There. Now it's complete."

Betty stepped up beside her. "It feels like Gram is here with us, doesn't it?"

Mary nodded, too overcome with emotion to speak. She'd wanted a bookshop of her own for so long, and it was even better than she'd imagined.

Later that afternoon, Mary opened the door to her shop and was met by a teenage boy carrying a big bouquet of burgundy calla lilies that obscured his face.

"Are those for me?" Mary asked.

The boy peeked around the bouquet far enough to read the card attached to the flowers. "If you're Mary Fisher, they're for you."

"I am Mary Fisher."

He set the vase of flowers on the counter and looked around the shop. "Do you have any comic books for sale?"

"No, but I'll be selling comic novels."

He scrunched up his face. "Are those like comic books, but longer?"

She smiled. "Something like that. I could show you some now, if you have time."

"Sorry," he said, heading toward the door, "I've got more deliveries to make. Maybe some other time."

Mary watched him leave and then reached for the card that was tucked into the flowers. She opened the envelope and began to read the short message. *Thinking of you on your big day, Mom, and wishing we could be there. Hope all your dreams come true. Love you forever, Jack and Elizabeth.*

Mary smiled as tears blurred her vision. It was such a sweet, thoughtful thing to do. She immediately reached for her phone and dialed her daughter's number.

"Hello?"

Mary loved the sound of her daughter's voice. "Hey, it's me."

"Hi, Mom. Did you get the flowers?"

"They just arrived." Mary looked over at the ruby-red blooms. "The calla lilies are gorgeous."

"Good. I told the florist in Ivy Bay exactly what I wanted, but you never know what you're going to get if you don't pick it out yourself."

"How are you?" Mary settled into her chair. She wished she could talk to her children every day, but she knew they led busy lives, so she treasured every moment that she could spend with them, either in person or on the telephone.

"We're all fine here. Chad is keeping busy at work and he's coaching Emma's softball team. Your granddaughter is turning into a real slugger."

"That's wonderful. How about Luke? Is he playing baseball again this year?"

"No, he chose to play soccer instead and he's having a blast. I hope you can come up for some of their games. We'd love to have you stay with us."

Mary hoped so too. She kept telling herself that she'd have time to do a little traveling after she got her shop up and running, but she'd need someone to cover for her if she was gone for more than a few hours. "I'll do my best. I'd love to see them play."

"How are you doing?" Lizzie asked. "And how are Aunt Betty and Gus?"

Mary began to tell her about everything that had been happening in their lives and, in doing so, realized how very busy she'd been these last few weeks. And just how swept up she'd been in her adventure.

"So does Ivy Bay feel like home to you?" Lizzie asked, after expressing much amusement and curiosity over Mary's story.

"It's always felt like home to me," Mary told her. "Ever since I was a little girl. I'm meeting new people and reuniting with old friends. I feel very blessed."

"I'm so glad to hear it. We sure do miss you, Mom," Lizzie said softly. "But at least you're not too far away. I just wish I could make it to your grand opening tomorrow."

"I know, darling. But it's okay. The shop's going to be here for a while," Mary said confidently.

"You better believe it!" Lizzie laughed. "Well, Mom. I'd better let you go. These rascals are going to run me ragged!" Mary smiled. She could hear two shouting children in the background. It didn't seem like that long ago that Lizzie and Jack had been the ones ruling her roost.

"Thanks again for the flowers. I'll let you know how the grand opening turns out."

"I'll be praying for you," Lizzie said, "just like I do every day."

"I love you, honey. Tell Chad and the kids I said hello and give them all a big hug for me."

"I will. Bye, Mom."

"Bye." Mary ended the call and then phoned Jack. Her call went to his voice mail, and she left him a short message, thanking him for the beautiful flowers.

After Mary hung up the phone, she placed the calla lilies on the counter and then looked around her bookshop, which would be open for customers tomorrow. "We're doing it, John," she whispered. "We're really doing it."

TWENTY-EIGHT

———◆◆◆———

Henry walked into the bookshop later that afternoon as Mary carried a pile of her custom-ordered shopping bags to the front counter.

"Put those down and come with me," he ordered, a mischievous twinkle in his eyes. "There's someone who wants to talk to you."

A few minutes later, they had walked into the ice-cream shop and joined Tess Bailey at one of the tables near the back, while her daughters, Jamie and Paige, served a cluster of customers at the front counter.

Tess spooned a bite of ice cream from a pint, which Mary immediately recognized as the one she had delivered to Tess last Friday.

"What did you say the name of this ice cream was again?" Tess asked her, as she scooped the ice cream into a dish.

"Caramelized Banana Walnut. I caramelized both the bananas and the nuts and added some cinnamon and nutmeg to give it a nice comfort-food feeling. But how did Henry—"

"I *am* a regular patron at the ice-cream shop, if you haven't already figured it out yet. I noticed Tess was enjoying her ice cream and I told her I'd have what she was having," he said, as if his explanation was obvious.

"And when Henry told me he was headed to your bookshop next, I asked him to retrieve you," she said, and Henry gave a chivalrous nod. "This ice cream is amazing." Tess took another bite, chewing a little more slowly. "The flavors are so complex. What's this one? Is it...salt?"

"Sea salt," Mary said, blushing.

"Oh, I just love the salty crunch. It's a perfect balance with the sweetness of the caramel."

Mary was impressed with Tess's palate. "Well, I'm so glad you like it."

"Like it?" Tess licked the back of her spoon. "I want to put it on our menu."

Henry smiled. "Now that is a compliment."

Mary just gaped.

"I mean it." Tess scraped the bottom of her dish for the very last bite, then set it aside. "I'd like to feature your caramelized banana walnut ice cream in my store this month. And then another flavor of yours the following month. And so on. You'll have a special place in the case. 'Mary's Flavor of the Month.'"

Mary's cheeks grew warm. "I don't know what to say. I'm so flattered...."

"Please say yes," Tess implored her.

"Hypothetically speaking," Mary began, smiling, "suppose I did say yes. How exactly would this all work?"

"Well, you'd give us the recipe," Tess began, "along with any special instructions, and we'd make one batch. We'd have you taste test it before we ever put it on the menu, just to make sure we had it right."

"So you wouldn't need me to make any of it?"

"Not unless you wanted to."

Mary liked that answer. She had so much on her plate she worried about being tied down to making large batches of ice cream on a regular basis. But this plan sounded just fine to her. It'd give her a reason to keep experimenting. "You know what, Tess? That sounds lovely."

Tess smiled. "So do we have a deal?"

Mary took a deep breath. "Deal."

The day of the grand opening dawned warm and clear in Ivy Bay. While locals and some early tourists headed to the beach with their picnic baskets, pleasure boats at the marina began to board passengers to take them out on the sparkling waters of Cape Cod Bay.

And Mary Fisher prepared herself to officially open Mary's Mystery Bookshop for the first time. She stood at the front door, ready to open it to the people who had already started forming a line outside. But she paused long enough to whisper a prayer. "Lord, thank You for this day and the many blessings You have given me. I've dreamed of this for so long and ask for Your guidance as I begin this new journey in my life. All glory is Yours. Amen."

Then at 10:00 ᴀᴍ she flipped the Open/Shut sign and opened for business.

One of the first people to walk inside was Pastor Miles. "Hello, Pastor. I didn't know you were a mystery fan."

"Oh, I can't get enough of them." He looked around the shop. "So it's a good thing you have a lot of books. I can see I'll be spending some time here."

"I hope you will," she said sincerely. She glanced over at the snack table, watching the steady line of people passing by it. Mary had catered sandwiches from the Tea Shoppe. "Well, you are welcome to look around. If you find anything you like, I will be happy to ring it up for you."

"I think I'll do that," Pastor Miles said, moving toward the bookcase closest to them. "I see a few titles I've been wanting to read."

Mary turned around to see Tabitha Krause, her mother's childhood best friend, enter the shop, with a petite younger woman behind her. Mary moved toward Tabitha, whose white hair was swept back in a loose and feminine bun.

"Mrs. Krause, how lovely to see you. It's been such a long time." Then Mary offered her hand to the younger woman.

"I'm Dawn," the woman said. "Tabitha's caretaker."

"Nice to meet you, Dawn," Mary said and looked back at Tabitha. Memories flooded through her of the time she'd spent with her mother and Tabitha over her summers in Ivy Bay. Tabitha reached out to give Mary a hug and then pulled back and held her shoulders.

"I'm proud of you, Mary." Her crow's-feet folded with her smile. "What a beautiful job you've done too." Mary grew misty-eyed. She imagined this was how her mother would have reacted.

"Thank you, Tabitha. It's so nice to see you. I'll come by your house and visit you soon. Okay?"

"I'd love that," Tabitha said, and Dawn began to guide her through the crowded room."

A short time later, she lovingly punched the buttons on her cash register as the first book sold. After handing the brown bag with a Mary's Mystery Bookshop sticker centered on it to the customer, she took a deep breath and looked around the store. The room was abuzz with Ivy Bay citizens and tourists. In *her* bookshop. She could hardly believe it— her dream had come true. She took it all in, amazed by God's goodness.

The shop enjoyed a steady stream of customers, including Mason Willoughby, Virginia Livingston and Bea Winslow. Mary also saw Susan Crosby from the bakery and Johanna Montgomery, a reporter for the Ivy Bay Bugle, as well as Chief McArthur.

"Good on ya, kid," he had said when he first arrived. "The place looks good as new."

Mary grinned proudly at him but didn't say anything about Kip. Chief McArthur had already closed the case, and now Mary had too.

She also noticed that the donation box for the disaster-aid book drive was already half full, and that didn't include the five hundred dollars Kip had found in the picture frame. He had left it in an envelope slipped under the door to her shop, presumably overnight. In it was a note expressing remorse, gratefulness, and optimism.

Around lunchtime, more people were gathering at the snack table, including D.J., who waved to Mary with a plate stacked high with treats from Sweet Susan's. Mary smiled back, proud to have him at the event.

She saw Jean standing between a pair of bookshelves and thumbing through a mystery by P. D. James. Mary and Betty had decided not to say anything to Jean about Uncle George's criminal record while she was dealing with so much else right now. Maybe they never would. Mary had prayed that the

Lord would give her wisdom, when and if the time was ever right.

"Find anything you like?" Mary asked her.

Jean looked up from the book. "Well, I've been reading this book for the last fifteen minutes or so. I guess that's a good sign that I'm going to take it home with me."

"How are you doing?"

A smile softened her face. "Much better than before. It's funny, isn't it?" Jean said wistfully. "How people don't really change."

"What do you mean?"

"When I was growing up, I used to hide in the house whenever I got scared or annoyed or angry. I'm sure part of the reason was because my mom was so protective of me. That summer she spent in Virginia with my dad was the first time I'd been expected to learn to take care of myself." She smiled. "Gram never put up with any nonsense. If she'd seen me these past couple of weeks, she would have set me straight."

"You've been going through quite a bit," Mary said gently. "Gram would have understood."

"I hope that's true. But I'm done with shutting myself in that house. I want to enjoy myself while I'm here."

"Now that's what I like to hear."

"I'm going to let you get back to your guests," Jean said, "and I'll get back to my book. But first promise me that you and Betty can come over for dinner this week."

"We'll be there," Mary promised as she saw her neighbor Sherry approaching her.

"Congratulations." Sherry handed her a potted fern with a blue ribbon on it.

Mary took the plant from her. "Thank you so much." She set it on the reading table. "I'm so glad you stopped by."

"I wouldn't miss it." Sherry looked around the shop. "It looks like you've got a great turnout so far. It's fun watching you enjoy the limelight for a while."

When Mary turned around, she saw Henry watching her.

"The limelight looks good on you," he teased.

Mary walked over to him, her cheeks growing warm. "When did you get here?"

"A few minutes ago. I wasn't sure there was room for one more, but I managed to squeeze my way in."

She looked around the bookshop. "I think it's going well, don't you?"

"It sure is. How does it feel to be open for business?"

Mary watched a couple of children sitting in the bathtub with books open on their laps while the adults mingled among the shelves. Laughter and easy chatter filled the air. "It feels like I'm right where I'm supposed to be."

ABOUT THE AUTHOR

Kristin Eckhardt is the author of more than thirty-five books, including fourteen for Guideposts. She's won two national awards for her writing, and her first book was made into a TV movie. She and her husband have three children and live in central Nebraska. Kristin enjoys baking, reading and spending time with her family.

A CONVERSATION WITH KRISTIN ECKHARDT

—◆—

Q: *What draws you to Mary's Bookshop as a writer?*

A: Mary's Bookshop is a wonderful series because it's set in one of my favorite places in the world—a bookshop. I've always loved bookshops and libraries, because they're filled with such a wide variety of characters and settings and wonderful adventures. I worked in a library as a teenager and couldn't resist reading between the stacks as I returned books to the shelves. I've loved books since I was a child and still remember all of my old favorites. Mary's Bookshop is a wonderful opportunity to share my love of books with readers.

Q: *Which character in the series do you most relate to?*

A: Mary Fisher really speaks to me in this series. As I mentioned, like Mary, I've recently moved to a new home, so I know the challenges of starting over someplace new. We both also have an abiding faith that guides and sustains us. She's very close to her family and enjoys having fun. I especially like Mary's relationship with her sister. My sister is my best friend, so I understand that special bond that Mary and Betty share. I feel very blessed to bring Mary and her family and friends into the homes of readers. I hope you enjoy reading their stories as much as I enjoy writing them.

Q: *If you could open a bookshop anywhere, where would it be? And what kind of bookshop would it be?*

A: If I owned a bookshop, it would be located somewhere warm, perhaps in the southwest United States. Phoenix, Arizona, is the home of my sister and one of my favorite cities, so that would be near the top of my list. My bookshop would carry both fiction and nonfiction books, with a very large children's section. Since my favorite genre is mystery books, I'd have fun stocking the shelves with all of my favorite mystery authors. I'd also invite book clubs to meet at my shop for fun and lively discussions.

Q: *What is your favorite mystery book/author?*

A: My favorite author is Agatha Christie. She creates such wonderful sleuths, from Miss Marple to Hercule Poirot to Tommy and Tuppence. Her stories are full of charm and she has such an engaging writing style. I especially enjoy her book *Then There Were None*, a classic tale of secrets and suspicion. There is nothing I like better than nestling in a cozy chair with a cup of hot tea and an Agatha Christie novel!

Q: *Mary loves to make new ice-cream flavors and enjoys reading mystery novels. What are some of your hobbies?*

A: I love to collect vintage cookbooks. I have cookbooks and recipes that belonged to my grandmothers, and I enjoy reading the small notes that they wrote beside the recipes. I plan to create a cookbook of family recipes for my children so they can be passed down to future generations.

I also, of course, enjoy reading both fiction and non-fiction books. I love to find new authors and immerse myself in their stories—the more books, the better! When I travel, I like to listen to audiobooks and sometimes find myself driving around the block a few times when I've reached my destination just to hear more of the story!

Q: *Tell us about your family.*

A: One of the greatest blessings in my life is my family. My husband and three children are the center of my life and we always have fun together. I am close to my parents and my sister and brother and their families. We all love to read and enjoy talking about books and movies. Best of all, I come from a family of wonderful storytellers, so we always have something to talk about!

CARAMELIZED BANANA WALNUT ICE CREAM

━━━◆◆━━━

Here's Mary's recipe for her signature ice cream at Bailey's Ice Cream Shop!

> 4 ripe bananas, sliced
> ¼ cup brown sugar
> 1 teaspoon cinnamon
> 1 tablespoon butter, melted
> ⅓ cup walnuts, chopped
> 2 tablespoons brown sugar
> ⅛ teaspoon coarse salt
> 1 teaspoon oil
> 2 cups heavy cream
> 1 cup whole milk
> ½ cup sugar
> ¼ teaspoon salt
> 2 teaspoons pure vanilla extract

Preheat oven to four hundred degrees. In a medium bowl, place sliced bananas, quarter cup brown sugar and cinnamon. Toss to coat. Line a nine-by-thirteen-inch baking dish with aluminum foil and place bananas in it in a single layer. Pour melted butter over the top. Bake in preheated oven for thirty minutes, stirring occasionally, until caramelized. Set aside to cool.

In a small skillet, place the walnuts, two tablespoons of brown sugar, coarse salt and oil. Cook over medium-high heat. Cook until the sugar caramelizes the nuts, about four to six minutes, stirring occasionally to separate the nuts. Transfer to a baking sheet covered with waxed paper to cool. Chop into small pieces, if necessary, and set aside.

Meanwhile, combine the heavy cream, milk, sugar, salt and vanilla, whisking until sugar is dissolved. Place this mixture into the refrigerator to chill.

Once the bananas have cooled completely, puree them in a blender or food processor until smooth. Then whisk the bananas into the milk mixture until well blended. Stir in the cooled walnuts. Refrigerate several hours or overnight until chilled.

Churn mixture in ice-cream maker according to the manufacturer's directions. Then place in an airtight container and freeze several hours to set.

FROM THE GUIDEPOSTS
ARCHIVES

———◆◆◆———

"The Spirit of the Lord spoke through me; his word was on my tongue." —II Samuel 23:2 (NIV)

When Ellie, a new co-worker at the bookstore, told me that she used to be a counselor before she got laid off because of budget cuts, I patted her hand in sympathy. "This retail job must be a real comedown for you," I commented. If I'd expected her to agree with me, I was in for a surprise.

"Oh no," she said. "I come in contact with more hurting people in a day here than I did in my old job in a week."

"How on earth do you know that?" I asked. Most of the customers I met seemed confident and pulled together.

"Why, just yesterday," she said, "a lady came in looking for a book on divorce."

I remembered the woman vividly. She'd looked annoyed, I thought, so I'd passed her on to Ellie.

"Well, anyone looking for a book on divorce or grieving is obviously looking for help," I admitted, "but you make it sound like everyone can use help."

"I think that many of them can," Ellie said. "Do you remember that tall man who wanted a book on finances?"

I did remember him. He'd seemed so snappish that I'd kept right on shelving books while I let Ellie help him.

"He was facing bankruptcy," she said quietly. At my astonished look she said, "As I walk them to the right shelf, I try to say a kind word and then I listen carefully. And I ask God to help me say the right thing."

So I tried it. A man wanted a book on "neighbor law," and when he poured out his frustration about the child with a drum set who'd moved in above him, I briefly poured out my sympathy...and left both of us with a smile on our faces, for a change.

God, help me to help someone with a kind word or an understanding ear today. —Linda Neukrug

SECRETS *of* MARY'S BOOKSHOP
Rewriting History
by VERA DODGE

———◆◆◆———

Mary stood in the doorway of her bookshop, gazing at the street corner in the twilight. From behind her in the shop came the hum of dozens of voices, punctuated occasionally by peals of laughter and the unmistakable ring of the old-fashioned cash register. Mary had discovered the till, with its heavy drawer and gorgeous brass scrollwork, in an antique store just weeks before she opened the shop. The clunky register might not have been the most practical purchase in the world, but it reminded her of the days she'd spent as a girl in Ivy Bay, decades ago, and the old-fashioned feel and slow pace of life that had drawn her back to town to open the bookshop after she lost John. As soon as she'd seen the old register, she'd marched up to the counter at the antique store and slapped her brand-new business credit card down without hesitation. Then the next day, she sent back the fancy new electronic register she'd already purchased. Of course, she wasn't living in the past as far as business was concerned—she did have an up-to-date computerized system to keep track of accounts and ordering.

And right now, for the first time, somebody else was running the cash register: Rebecca Mason, Mary's very first employee. Or perhaps, Mary thought with a wry smile, Rebecca's seven-year-old daughter Ashley had taken over management of the old cash register.

When Mary first opened the shop, the idea of spending all her days among the books had seemed like a dream come true. But she quickly discovered that, despite her love for the shop, it just wasn't practical for her to try to run it all by herself. The ad she ran in the local paper had brought a flurry of applications, but Rebecca's had stood out among the rest. Rebecca had worked in bookstores in college, was an avid reader, and was a writer as well. She had even attached a page of her publications to her résumé, listing all the little magazines and contests she'd placed in. Mary had been ready to hire her on the spot, but when she called Rebecca for an interview, Rebecca had asked immediately whether Mary would mind if she brought her daughter with her.

"She's seven," Rebecca had told her. "During the school year, she'll be in class during the days, but for the summer months, while her dad is out on the fishing boat, she's with me. She's just great. I think you'll love her."

Mary hadn't been so sure about that. And she hadn't been so sure about the professionalism of a woman asking to bring her child along with her to a business interview. In fact, Mary had started to rifle through the other applications on her desk while she was still on the phone with Rebecca, wondering if someone else might be a better fit. When she ended the call, she told herself that even if the little girl managed to behave herself at the interview, she'd have to be clear with Rebecca that she'd need to find some other place for Ashley during the days, so that Rebecca could concentrate on her work at the shop.

But as soon as Ashley swept into the shop, in a pale blue gingham shirt under a pair of sturdy overalls and her ash-blonde hair in a pair of pigtails, Mary had been undone. And for all her girlish charm, Ashley had comported herself very much like a young lady. She read quietly in the corner while Mary and her mother talked, and then she gave Mary a quite serious review on the strengths and weaknesses of Mary's children's section. And Rebecca herself had done a wonderful job in the interview. She was smart but didn't show off, was confident but not brassy, and had a warmth and quick enthusiasm that Mary knew would be perfect with customers in the shop. Half an hour after Rebecca arrived, Mary had offered her the job, and the interview had changed to a training session. Ashley had padded over to join them, and she caught onto Mary's directions for operating the old cash register before her mother, who was used to the computerized versions she'd used at the bookstore where she'd worked in the past.

"Wait," Rebecca had said after Mary's first explanation. "Do I press this button?" The one she chose was on the opposite side of the real drawer release, but before Mary could correct her, Ashley jumped in.

"No, Mom!" she said and reached unerringly for the right button. At the touch of her small finger, the drawer sprang open, and she regarded Mary and Rebecca with a beatific smile. "See?" she said.

"I don't know," Rebecca had joked. "Maybe you should give the job to her."

Mary had laughed and never did give the speech she'd planned, about how Rebecca should leave Ashley home. For the last several days, since Rebecca started, Ashley and Rebecca had both been a welcome presence in the shop. Rebecca had quickly picked up on Mary's systems for organizing and ordering stock, and she had done a great job connecting with customers and suggesting titles that Mary wasn't even familiar with. And Ashley spent most of her time curled up in the rocking chair in the children's section, reading Nancy Drew and Encyclopedia Brown titles.

"She's such a good reader," Mary had told Rebecca.

Rebecca had sighed. "I know," she said. "I can barely get her to do anything else."

The three of them had established a comfortable rhythm in the shop. Mary had even left Rebecca alone in the shop yesterday afternoon for the first time, while she ran some of the much-needed errands she'd been neglecting since the store opened. But tonight was the big test, not just for Rebecca, but for Mary herself.

Mary glanced down at the cell phone in her hand. There were no new messages or texts. The last call she'd received from Addison Hartley's publicist was to let her know that the famous mystery writer was only a few minutes away.

The publicist's name was Janine Briarwood, and she always spoke in a clipped rush, as if she were trying to spit out the last set of orders before the ship she was on sank. Mary had given her the number at the bookshop half a dozen times, but she persisted in calling Mary's personal phone and calling it at any hour of the day or night. "If you wouldn't mind just meeting us outside," she'd said this time. "We just like to have someone escort us in. Otherwise, you never know what might happen."

Mary's lips had curled into a smile at this. She wondered what sort of danger, exactly, Janine thought the crowd of book lovers waiting inside might pose to Addison Hartley in a safe little town like Ivy Bay, other than a repetitive-motion injury from demanding too many autographs. But she'd gone outside to wait anyway. Addison Hartley wasn't somebody Mary was in a position to refuse. He'd topped the mystery best-seller lists for the better part of two decades, and his books weren't just pulp titles that people cycled through and then tossed away. Each one of them built on the previous, creating a wide, vivid world with seemingly endless detail and backstory. His readers were devoted and passionate, and the Internet was full of message boards where people compared notes on the world he'd created, identifying gaps, guessing at what he might do next—even working up recipes based on meals he'd mentioned in his stories. The president had been photographed last year on Air Force One while reading one of Addison Hartley's books.

He was one of Mary's favorite authors too. In fact, he'd been on the top of the wish list Mary had scrawled for author events when she began to dream about opening the shop. She didn't think he'd really come, but she was dreaming at the time, so why not dream big? And then, after the shop opened and she came across the list again, she thought, why not? She sent an e-mail off to his publicist, inviting Hartley to an author event at the shop, promising that the whole town of Ivy Bay would turn out for it—which they pretty much had.

She hadn't been able to believe her good fortune when Janine wrote back with a handful of potential dates. And she still couldn't really believe that he was about to drive up any minute.

"Should I look for anything in particular?" Mary had asked Janine when they spoke a few minutes ago.

"It's nothing special," Janine had told her. "Just a standard limo."

Mary shook her head. It seemed that Addison Hartley lived in a completely different world than she did. Janine's request for an escort might seem over the top to Mary, but Mary had no idea what he'd had to deal with in the past. She'd never had a crowd of people fighting to meet her or get her autograph. And as far as she knew, nothing she had ever written had been read by the president.

Still, when the limo finally turned onto her street, she had to suppress a smile. Parts of Cape Cod were undeniably high-end, with lavish mansions crowded along the coast and fancy cars clogging the streets. But Ivy Bay had always been a more laid-back community. It was a true fishing village and was out of the way enough that it hadn't been completely overrun by tourists, although more and more of them were drawn these days by Ivy Bay's unspoiled charm. The sight of the limousine nosing its way between Ivy Bay's neat but humble downtown storefronts was just so out of place that she couldn't help but laugh. At the same time, a thrill ran through her. The limousine among the wind-ravaged Cape buildings, the twilight all around, and the fact that Addison Hartley was about to walk into Mary's very own bookstore all had an air of unreality. Still, the little scene on the street continued to play out. The limousine rolled smoothly past the other stores before coming to a stop outside the bookshop.

Mary gave a little wave to let them know they were in the right place and smiled, her eyes darting over the tinted glass of the limousine, looking for any human face that might smile back. The limousine purred at the curb, but no one got out.

Mary's smile faded. She folded her arms, not sure what to do next. Should she wait for them to come to her? They didn't expect her to go down and knock on a window, did they?

As she was wondering, one of the doors of the limousine finally swung open, and a thin, birdlike woman in a black suit got out. Her face was young, but her suit was severe, and her straight black hair was cut in a blunt wedge that fell just to her jaw. She strode across the sidewalk to Mary, stuck her hand out, and gave her a brilliant smile. "I'm Janine," the woman said. "You must be Mary."

Mary smiled and pressed Janine's hand in return. "Welcome to Ivy Bay," she said. "We are just so honored that Mr. Hartley—"

As quickly as it had appeared, Janine's smile vanished, replaced by an expression of intense urgency. "Now, are we all ready in there?" she asked.

Mary tried to give a nod that would give Janine confidence. "I think so," she said. "I think Mr. Hartley will be very pleased. This is one of the biggest turnouts we've ever had at the store."

Mary gave a proud little glance into the store as she said this. The crowd completely engulfed the two comfortable chairs in the reading area in the back of the shop. Mary and Rebecca had brought up chairs from the basement to hold the overflow, but even those were taken now, and many people were standing at the back and even between the shelves. It was a mixed crowd too, because Addison Hartley's fan base was so broad: older men and women Mary knew from church; high school students; a few young couples including the Courts, who owned Meeting House Grocers; and Susan Crosby of Sweet Susan's Bakery. She also saw Leroy Steckler, a man who had known Mary's great uncle George, as well as Tabitha Krause, Mary's mother's childhood best friend. Mary wasn't surprised to see the elderly woman there; when Mary had recently visited the woman's Ivy Bay home, she noticed a Hartley hardcover on the coffee table. And, of course, there was Betty, her sister, who had arrived an hour early to make sure she got her seat in the front row.

Janine frowned in what might have been confusion. "But," she said, "you haven't been open very long, have you? I checked the business history. It's only been a short while."

"Well, yes," Mary said, descending into confusion in her own turn. "But we have had a few events, and—"

"Nothing like this, I'm sure," Janine interrupted her.

"Well, no," Mary had to agree.

"When we bring Mr. Hartley in," Janine said, "we want to start the event immediately. No mingling with fans beforehand. They're welcome to ask questions during the Q and A and have their books signed afterward, but once the line dies down, we'll be leaving. You may need to make some apologies for us. You understand."

Mary nodded, but she was nodding at Janine's back. Janine had turned to the limo again and was opening the back door. A moment later, Addison Hartley himself stepped out onto the sidewalk.

Mary's face broke into a smile. He was a little bit older and a little bit pudgier, but the familiar face that had graced the back of so many of her favorite books was unmistakable. "Mr. Hartley," she said, "we are just so delighted to have you here in Ivy Bay."

As Addison Hartley shook her hand, she noticed another difference between him and his author photo. In the author photos, he always looked straight into the camera, his eyes so piercing, even from the page, that she felt he might be searching out one of her own secrets. But in person, he could barely seem to meet her gaze.

"Please," he said, glancing away, "call me Addison."

He looked into the glowing windows of the shop at the people milling about inside, with something of a haunted expression. But Janine touched his elbow, and he squared his shoulders.

"Everyone's so excited to meet you," Mary said. "Nobody's talked about anything else in the shop for weeks. Or in the town either, really."

"Well," Addison Hartley said, still looking through the shopwindows, "shall we?"

Mary swung the door of the shop open and gestured for him to enter, but he insisted she go first. When she walked into the store, followed by Addison Hartley, with Janine on his heels, the voices rose suddenly in surprise and exclamation and then hushed as the little procession reached the small podium where Mary had set up a microphone and a glass of water for Addison.

She stopped beside it. "Are you ready?" she asked, her voice low. "I'll just introduce you, and then you'll be up."

Addison nodded.

Mary stepped to the microphone and cleared her throat. She glanced over the crowd, taking in the faces of a few old friends and new customers. Her sister Betty gave her a wink from the front row, where she was seated next to her sister-in-law Eleanor. "I'm so glad to see so many of you here tonight," Mary said. "And I'd like to ask you to join me in giving a very special Ivy Bay welcome to Mr. Addison Hartley."

The room broke into applause, and there was even a whoop of enthusiasm from the back.

"Mr. Hartley hardly needs my introduction," Mary said. "Many of you may know him better than you know me."

Laughter rippled through the room.

"He's been on the *New York Times* best-seller list fifteen times since his debut novel *Stones Speak* twenty years ago. He's won Edgar Book, Agatha, and Hammett Awards. But the highest praise I can actually give to him as a bookstore owner is the response his books get from my customers. Some authors write books that people just read to pass the time. But Addison Hartley creates a world where people want to live. His readers love his books. They still remember stories he wrote many years ago, and they can't wait for the next one to come out. To me, that matters more than any best-seller list or award. Ladies and gentlemen, Addison Hartley."

Mary circled back behind the counter as Addison stepped up to the podium. From his basket below the counter, her cat Gus looked up at her balefully, as if asking why exactly she had let all these strangers into their perfectly nice, quiet little store. She bent down and scratched his head. Pretty soon they'd all be gone, and he'd be able to roam the stacks and shelves the way he usually did, curling up on an Agatha Christie omnibus or sprawling out on a stack of the newest arrivals.

To her surprise, Addison Hartley didn't make any of the opening comments that she'd often seen authors give at other events she'd attended, explaining the background of the story or the research he'd done while writing it. Instead, he just cracked open a copy of his latest book and began to read.

Once he started reading, though, nobody seemed to notice the lack of introduction. The story was immediately absorbing: a mystery set in a small coastal town, with lots of touchstones to draw in an audience like Ivy Bay's. Everyone in the shop listened raptly, until he stopped reading about ten minutes later. Then the hands began to go up around the room. Addison chose one and pointed.

When the other hands went down around the room, Mary could see it was Rebecca who had the question. "I'm a writer," Rebecca said, blushing. "And I'm just wondering if you can tell me where you get your ideas? You've written so many books over the years. Where do all the ideas come from?"

Addison Hartley seemed to dodge Rebecca's gaze, Mary noticed, just the way he'd dodged her own. Mary looked at him with sympathy. It seemed like almost every reading opened with this question. She could understand why he might be tired of answering it. "Well," he said, looking up at the ceiling, as if for some kind of help. "I guess you're never really sure where the next idea might come from. You're just glad when it does." Then he added, "But it can be hard."

Around the room, heads nodded.

"Well, you make it look easy," Rebecca said.

He nodded at a middle-aged man in a green-and-blue plaid shirt. The man smiled somewhat nervously. "I'm always impressed with the research that goes into your books," he said. "Can you tell us a bit about that process?"

Addison raised his eyebrows. "Research is just as important as pure imagination to me," he said. "You've heard the sayings, 'You can't make this stuff up' or 'Truth is stranger than fiction.' I find it to be true. A lot of the things that seem strange in my books are actually drawn from real life."

The man in the plaid shirt nodded. "Thank you," he said.

Like everyone else, Mary glanced away from the man in the plaid shirt and looked around again as hands began to go up around him. But then a woman, who stood beside Rebecca near the back, caught her eye. There was nothing flashy about her—she was about Mary's age, with short, well-styled graying-blonde hair, and she wore a conservative collared shirt with white polka dots on navy. She was intensely familiar. Mary had the sense that she'd known her and known her well. But Mary couldn't remember where. Was it college? One of the libraries she'd worked at? Or even further back, from her high school days in Boston?

Then the crowd broke into laughter over Addison's next answer, and the woman smiled as well. As she did, forty years fell away in an instant, and Mary knew exactly who she was: Claire Wilkes, her summertime best friend from Ivy Bay. She'd had no reason to expect Claire to be there—Claire's family had moved away years ago, and by then, she and Mary weren't on speaking terms. But when Mary saw Claire's familiar face now, all the old affection from previous years rushed back to her. She'd always felt bad about how things had ended between them. But before that, Claire had shared years of girlish secrets with Mary, and she and Mary had spent some golden times together. Maybe Claire's appearance now was a chance to patch things up and make them right, after all these years.

Addison Hartley and Claire Wilkes on the same night. Lord, You certainly know how to surprise a woman.

She glanced at Betty, to see if her sister had caught sight of Claire. Betty would be just as surprised to see her as Mary was. But Betty was totally absorbed in Addison Hartley's next answer.

Mary looked back at her old friend. As she watched, Rebecca leaned over and whispered something to Claire. Claire nodded and said something in return. Mary slipped out from behind the counter and began to make her way through the crowd toward them. As she did, Claire glanced up. When the pair locked eyes, Mary smiled and gave a small wave, but Claire immediately turned her head. Then, trying to stay unobtrusive, Mary ducked behind a shelf, still making her way through the crowd.

But when she emerged, Claire was gone.

Mary scanned the crowd, but Claire was nowhere to be found. Then her eye caught a slight motion at the door as it swung shut, and a shadow passed by the window in the night outside. Had Claire left before the book signing was even over? With the woman gone, Mary's certainty fled. What were the chances that Claire would come to her bookstore after all these years? Especially on a night like tonight. Could she just have been mistaken in the excitement of the event? Had it really been Claire?

Mary had been waiting for weeks to meet Addison Hartley, but she could barely pay attention to any of his question-and-answer session. Memories of Claire, the Ivy Bay of her youth, John, and everything that had gone on between all of them swirled in her mind. After about a dozen questions, Addison glanced at Janine, and she took the microphone, thanked everyone, and then began to hustle the crowd into a line of autograph seekers. The bookstore erupted into a happy buzz.

"Rebecca," Mary said, finding her in the crowd. "The woman you were talking to. Where did she go?"

"Who?" Rebecca said, puzzled.

"You were standing beside her, during the Q and A," Mary insisted.

Rebecca's brow furrowed.

"Her name is Claire," Mary told her. "Claire Wilkes." Was Claire's name still Wilkes? Mary wondered. Had it even been Claire whom she'd seen?

Rebecca spent a moment in thought. Then she shook her head decisively. "No," she said. "I don't think I met a Claire."

"Are you sure?" Mary pressed.

Rebecca shook her head, somewhat helplessly. "I've met so many people tonight," she began, glancing toward the counter. "Oh my gosh!" she said. "Look at that!"

Mary followed her gaze. Behind the counter, seated on the high stool, Ashley was calmly taking a pair of bills from the first customer in a long line that had formed there.

"I'd better—" Rebecca began.

"Go," Mary finished.

She made her own way to the signing table, where Janine was briskly opening books, placing them before Addison, then shuffling the fans off so the next one could take their place. She nodded at Mary with what might have been an expression of approval. Mary gave her a tentative smile.

True to her word, when the last book was signed, Addison got to his feet and Janine bustled him out the door. Mary followed them out onto the street.

"I can't thank you enough," she said. "I hope you enjoyed the event. We're just so grateful you took the time to visit with us."

Addison Hartley shook her extended hand without meeting her eyes at all and disappeared into the limousine.

"Great event," Janine said briskly, switching her brilliant smile on, then back off again before she followed him into the car.

The big black car pulled away from the curb and disappeared into the night, and the famous author was gone, leaving Mary alone on the street as the customers began to trickle out of her store.

But despite all the excitement leading up to the event, it wasn't the famous author who stayed on Mary's mind. Instead, she looked around the darkened street wondering about her old friend. Had that really been Claire? Where had she been all these years? What did she think about what had happened between them so long ago? And where had she gone?

A Note from the Editors

We hope you enjoy Secrets of Mary's Bookshop, created by Guideposts Books and Inspirational Media. In all of our books, magazines and outreach efforts, we aim to deliver inspiration and encouragement, help you grow in your faith, and celebrate God's love in every aspect of your daily life.

Thank you for making a difference with your purchase of this book, which helps fund our many outreach programs to the military, prisons, hospitals, nursing homes and schools. To learn more, visit GuidepostsFoundation.org.

We also maintain many useful and uplifting online resources. Visit Guideposts.org to read true stories of hope and inspiration, access OurPrayer network, sign up for free newsletters, join our Facebook community, and follow our stimulating blogs.

To order your favorite Guideposts publications, go to ShopGuideposts.org, call (800) 932-2145 or write to Guideposts, PO Box 5815, Harlan, Iowa 51593.